D0090499

More Praise for *Eat What You Kill*

"A fast-paced, well-written story about a twisted young man, born poor, who idolizes Ayn Rand and the pursuit of money . . . You will most assuredly be hooked from the beginning to the very last page."

—*James Sheehan, author of* The Mayor of Lexington Avenue

"A dark story that is impossible to put down . . . It's like a spinning car collision on an icy overpass, but with plenty of surprises along the way. And if there's a gruesome sequel, I will want to read it."

—*Michael Sears, author of* Black Fridays

"A slick, stark, efficient thriller that knows its way around Wall Street, like what would happen if Bud Fox took a graduate course in murder by numbers." —*Stephen Romano, author of* Resurrection Express

"*Eat What You Kill* is the most anticipated debut novel of the year. Scofield has penned a New York story for the ages."

—*Matthew D. McCall, author of* The Next Great Bull Market

"Wall Street certainly eats what it kills in this fascinating, mind-twisting debut novel. Scofield knocks it out of the park and has us hanging on the edge of our seats wanting more of the kill."

—*Suzanne Corso, author of* Brooklyn Story

EAT
WHAT YOU
KILL

Ted Scofield

St. Martin's Press ⚐ **New York**

EAT WHAT YOU KILL. Copyright © 2014 by Ted Scofield. All rights reserved. Printed in the United States of America. For information, address St. Martin's Press, 175 Fifth Avenue, New York, N.Y. 10010.

www.stmartins.com

Designed by Omar Chapa

Library of Congress Cataloging-in-Publication Data is available upon request.

ISBN 978-1-250-02182-3 (hardcover)
ISBN 978-1-250-02181-6 (e-book)

St. Martin's Press books may be purchased for educational, business, or promotional use. For information on bulk purchases, please contact Macmillan Corporate and Premium Sales Department at 1-800-221-7945, extension 5442, or write specialmarkets@macmillan.com.

First Edition: April 2014

10 9 8 7 6 5 4 3 2 1

To Christi, Mom, and Dad

EAT
WHAT YOU
KILL

PART I

Americans were the first to understand that wealth has to be created.
The words "to make money" hold the essence of human morality.

—AYN RAND, *ATLAS SHRUGGED*

CHAPTER
ONE

Evan Stoess could choke back the bile that soured his throat. His soul was a different story.

He stood in the shadow of a Dutch elm tree, the strong summer sun behind him over Central Park. Sweating in his dark suit, he watched the front entrance of 940 Fifth Avenue. He shifted from foot to foot, impatiently focused on the ornate building and its money-soaked green canopy. He waited; he watched.

Evan's ritual often lasted more than an hour, and sometimes his quarry never appeared. Later in the season, when the ocean warmed and the city slowed, the happy family frequently departed earlier in the week. But New York City's summer had been elusive, and this, the second Friday of June, welcomed its first seasonal weekend. Evan was certain of success and more than willing to wait.

"Un-*fucking*-believable," he whispered to a pigeon as a silver Bentley convertible rolled up to the canopy. The winged rodent ignored him, a typical response from all creatures in Evan's opinion. At five feet ten inches tall, one hundred sixty-five pounds, Evan's medium build, sandy brown hair and brown eyes were, in a word, *average*. He'd learned early in life that his everyman looks would neither open nor close any doors, so he developed other means of attracting attention.

The Bentley wore a temporary license tag, but it betrayed nothing. The gleaming machine reeked of newness. Evan swore he could smell the leather. He loosened his tie and silently cursed the rat with wings.

A white-gloved attendant jumped out of the Bentley just as the doors of 940 Fifth opened. Evan's restless shifting ceased as he slipped imperceptibly into the shadow of the elm, comfortably adjusting to the undulating stones familiar beneath his feet. He took a deep breath, every muscle relaxed, the palette changed before his eyes, the surreal scene unfolded. He relished and feared this moment.

First out the door were two radiant children, perfect in their Norman Rockwell–like innocence. The little girl was six; her blue seersucker sundress, headband, and sandals matched and she carried a pink Cheeky Chats backpack. She bounded out the door as a six-year-old should, but before reaching the sidewalk, regained her composure, turned gracefully with a flip of her long blond hair, and looked for her little brother.

"Tyler, hurry! The beach!" Evan could hear her say.

Tyler was a few months short of three years. He half ran, half stumbled toward Ashley and the waiting Bentley. Wisps of his blond hair stood straight up as he smiled at his sister. Tyler appeared in a pair of ubiquitous Ralph Lauren ads the past spring, and he dressed the part today—pressed and pleated khaki shorts, a white button-down shirt and dark blue sweater vest. *Did Polo really make loafers that small?* Evan wondered. The co-op's porter stood between the children and the busy avenue, arms extended in both a welcoming and protective stance. Evan held his breath.

Holding hands loosely, the couple emerged. To Evan's eyes they floated more than walked. Frame by frame Evan followed them. All sound silenced, the city stopped, as Geoffrey and Victoria Buchanan prepared to leave for the Hamptons.

The synchronized scene progressed as it always did and, Evan hoped, always *would*. Once the parents had reached the sidewalk and secured the children, the porter who fetched the car from the garage opened the trunk and waited for the doorman who carried the family's luggage. Another doorman followed Geoffrey and Victoria with two car seats. With remarkable efficiency he secured the seats, and the children in them, while the trunk filled with the weekend's necessities—toys, food and drink from Eli's, two sets of golf clubs and, in a handsome case, for shooting skeet with his uncle, Geoffrey's great-grandfather's handmade Purdey over and under shotgun. Summer wardrobes waited at the beach.

Amidst the seamless action, Victoria and Geoffrey moved effortlessly, as if in slow motion. As always, Evan was mesmerized. He watched Victoria slip in the driver's side and hop the center console to avoid avenue traffic as Geoffrey shook hands with the ranking doorman and nodded at the others. *They genuinely like him. They respect him,* he said to himself. The men waved as the Bentley pulled away from the curb and turned east on Seventy-fourth Street. Ashley also waved, her cherubic expression surely visible from space.

Evan tensed as the magic evaporated, and he promised never to forget the memorable sighting. Inspired by what he had witnessed, he hated himself and *vowed* to get this life, the life he *deserved*. He stepped from the shadow to the curb and spit into the street.

Rain or shine, he always walked around Central Park's reservoir before returning to his shitty walk-up apartment near the East River. It was part of the Ritual.

He always fumed. Bitter. Angry. Obsessed. Sometimes, he cried.

CHAPTER

TWO

Victoria Calumet Buchanan. Everything Evan knew about her, he learned in *Town & Country*. And Page Six.

Not Geoffrey Thomas Buchanan. Evan kept a dossier on him that would impress a G-man.

Born in Manhattan forty-five years ago and Dalton "prepared," Geoffrey had lived an aristocrat's life, spending holidays and summers at homes in Cap d'Antibes, East Hampton, and Bermuda. After graduating from Princeton, he put his biology degree to work at a major pharmaceutical company before returning to Harvard Business School. After HBS, he started and sold two biotech companies, retired, and spent nearly five years traveling the globe, summering in Lake Como, where he bought a villa next to George Clooney's. In the evenings they played twenty-one on George's basketball court. The "quiet" life did not suit him, however, and he returned to work, not because he had to, but because he enjoyed *the challenge*. Now Buchanan served as Chairman and CEO of PharmaPur, Inc., a pharmaceutical company that went public a few years ago. He was also an avid sportsman, popular philanthropist, and gilded member of New York's elite.

A confirmed bachelor until eight years ago, Geoffrey met Victoria Calumet at a Bridgehampton polo match. *The New York Times*'s wedding feature gushed, "It was love at first sight." *No shit,* Evan thought when he read it. For his part, Evan was quite sure Victoria was the personification of the tired cliché "God's gift to man." Just thirty-four years old, only five years Evan's senior, Victoria had recently been described in a tabloid as "Cameron Diaz's twin but with a *Playboy* centerfold's rack." *Not even close.* Geoffrey and Victoria honeymooned for a month at the Oberoi, an exclusive resort in Mauritius. A genuflecting *T&C* profile piece featured half a dozen photos. Evan made a mental note to visit the Oberoi before he died.

Victoria was Southern perfect by birth, Atlanta, and Vanderbilt educated in art history. After earning her master's degree, she moved to Manhattan to work for Larry Gagosian in his most prominent Chelsea art gallery. Her parents collected Koons and were Buckhead royalty, of course, but she was smart and talented and, by all accounts, not at all caught up in the *Social Diary* scene. She certainly didn't obsess about getting Ashley into the "right" Upper East Side nursery school, but Ashley was accepted anyway, *sans* kickback.

Even Page Six acknowledged that Geoffrey and Victoria were as happy as they were rich.

The whole fucking thing left Evan enviously apoplectic.

CHAPTER

THREE

"Pack your bags, brainiac. You're going to Kentucky."

Andrew Leary was a likable fellow. He had been Evan's boss for three years, since Evan graduated from business school. Evan would have preferred a different term of endearment, but *brainiac* would do.

"Medipharm?"

"Medipharm."

"Both of us?" Evan asked.

"No sir, you're flyin' solo. Chloë's great-uncle died and I've got to do the funeral in Scottsdale. Couldn't swing a cameo—she wants me there for the whole production." Andrew rolled his eyes.

"But . . ."

"Hey, you dug up this opportunity, found this thing. Fly down there and write the report. If you give the word, we'll pick up coverage and take a 13D position."

Evan's eyes widened and his stomach churned.

"And don't forget to order new business cards." Andrew paused, for dramatic effect. "Congratulations, brainiac, you've been promoted."

After three years of scut work as an assistant analyst in the research department of Equity Capital Management, better known as ECM, Evan was finally a junior analyst covering his own companies. Well, *company*. But there would be more. There *had* to be more—or, Evan feared, he'd never make the big bucks, never really matter, never feel secure, never *belong*.

ECM. A midtown investment bank, a small firm commonly categorized as a "bucket shop." Evan often wondered where this term originated, but he never asked. He thought perhaps from the quality of the companies that bucket shops typically did work for—buckets of shit—with an occasional diamond in the trough. "It's our job to polish the turd," Andrew would say.

ECM managed to be a somewhat profitable bucket shop, primarily for Marshall Owen, its founder and majority owner. Mr. Owen had gained a level of notoriety twenty years earlier when he won a famous Supreme Court case, *U.S. v. Owen,* a ruling still taught in law schools. Today he was comfortably, apologetically, *rich*, the type of man whose baseless guilt compelled him to introduce seven-figure guests to his housekeeper. But Evan aspired to much more. Evan wanted to be, *needed* to be, *filthy, guiltless rich*. It was Rand 101: Men who apologize for being rich will not remain rich for long.

Mr. Owen compensated his producers very well, and that is what attracted Evan to an eat-what-you-kill firm generally off the radar screen for most B-school grads. *"Risk versus reward,"* Evan told Career Services. *"Fuck reputation and prestige. I'll take a small salary with big bonus potential. Just show me the money."*

Andrew Leary's father was Mr. Owen's childhood friend so, logically, Andrew was the head of ECM's twelve-person research department. He drove an E550 to work every day and lived in Westchester County with hot Chloë, a golden retriever named Reagan, and two undisciplined and therefore overmedicated munchkins. Evan didn't know his kids' names.

Andrew rarely hired people for his department; he didn't have to. By New York standards, the hours and workload were reasonable, and the pay for performers on par with larger firms where naïvely grateful slaves slept in their offices. Before Evan arrived, no one had quit Andrew's group in more than five years.

But one person did manage to die three years ago, not in a tragic kiln accident as Evan imagined, but from leukemia or some other horrible disease. *Not at all funny.*

Nepotism was the rule, but Evan secured an interview by blackmailing ECM's philandering human resources manager. He had to follow Mr. Jean Deburau after work for only three nights before discovering his unattractive but easily impressed indiscretion. A phone call to the poor sot elicited an exhilarating surge of adrenaline, followed by a placid period of euphoria. If Evan had a therapist, it would have made perfect sense.

The interview in the Four Seasons Grill Room went well. Andrew and Evan graduated from the same prep school, Ridgewood Academy, fifteen years apart, but only Evan knew that was the totality of what they had in common. Fortunately, it was enough. Evan remembered:

"Are you hungry?" Andrew asked over a bowl of lobster bisque. "We don't hire the Bear's motley rabble of P.S.D.'s, but I do need *hungry*. Can you eat what you kill?"

Evan nodded. "Absolutely. I wouldn't have it any other way."

"Good. Marshall wants to close the trading floor since those two professors fucked everything up. Spreads have gone to shit and we're not making dick. Do you know what that means?"

"Yes, sir," Evan recited, "spreads have narrowed to odd-eighths and smaller since a NASDAQ study revealed collusive behavior among market makers, and now decimalization threatens . . ."

"No no no, brainiac." Andrew was smiling.

"It means banking and research have to pick up the slack. Marshall needs a winter place in Stowe, I need a fresh Benz, and my wife Chloë has her eye on that new hundred-grand supercharged Range Rover. Get it?"

"Got it."

"Good. You're hired."

After an obviously contemplative moment, Andrew continued. "You're different. Not typical Ridgewood Academy. I can't explain it."

I can, Evan wanted to say. *My mother lives in a trailer that cost less than one semester at Ridgewood with my drunk-ass unemployed useless stepfather and crack whore half-sisters. My presence in the gilded halls of Ridgewood was at once a gift and a curse. I learned how to escape the hellhole of having nothing, of being nothing. I learned that making money was the most important thing in life, that nothing else mattered. I was taught to be an Atlas, to hold the world up with my wealth. But unlike the silver spoons, I suffered for my faith. If the Ridgewood jocks weren't beating me for being poor, the trailer trash were for thinking rich. I am the very essence of the Bear's P.S.D's:* Poor. Smart. *With a deep, deep* Desire *to get rich. I am, to my very core,* Eat What You Kill.

"Thank you, sir."

A week later, he was working at ECM in Andrew's department, small salary but substantial bonus potential. He shared a cute young administrative assistant with two other guys. Her name was not Fawn Leibowitz.

Today, banking and research *had* taken up the slack, and Andrew joked about the *latest* Wall Street scandal.

"Research and banking sharing information about customers? Duh-huh . . . no shit. What the hell do they think we do? *Lose money?*"

CHAPTER

FOUR

Evan stumbled across Medipharm Corporation while thumbing through a copy of the *Journal of the American Medical Association* that he randomly snagged from a recycling stack on the curb near his apartment. *Thank you, Tess McGill. You never know where the next great idea will come from.*

As an assistant analyst, Evan crunched numbers and reviewed SEC bullshit. He wasn't expected to pursue new business, but when he noticed the words "promising new drug" in a footnote, a little research was in order.

Medipharm had been a private company until six months ago when it merged with an inactive public shell. Hidden in Kentucky at the University of Louisville's respected biomedical incubator, Medipharm was overlooked. If ECM picked up coverage, it would be the first. Evan saw an opportunity to make a market in an unknown pharmaceutical company. He would write a research report touting Medipharm and recommending that people buy its stock. ECM's investment bankers would advise the company on transactions and when to offer and sell new stock. And ECM's traders would buy and sell Medipharm's stock for themselves and customers, collecting a commission with every trade. So many opportunities, and, for Evan, an opportunity to make millions.

•   •   •

"*Where* are you flying off to?"

Evan didn't have any friends, any *real* friends, but his neighbor Fleur came pretty close. They sat on the stoop of their five-story walk-up, enjoying the last fifteen minutes of the evening's summer sunshine.

"Kentucky. Louisville. The place with the Derby."

"Why again, Eee-van?" Evan loved Fleur's Kiwi accent.

"To check out the company, kick the proverbial tires, and meet with the CEO." Evan anticipated the next question and continued with barely a pause.

"Medipharm. It's a young pharmaceutical company, developing a new drug to treat Alzheimer's disease."

"That's excellent. My great-aunt died from Alzheimer's five years ago. I hope your company can help find a cure."

Evan said "Indeed, I do too" and looked to the sky. Against the blue screen he saw himself strolling out of 940 Fifth to a waiting Bentley, hand in hand with a radiant, faceless beauty.

CHAPTER
FIVE

When his taxi's pine-and-Marlboro-scented driver told him that movies were filmed in Louisville because it looked like New York City, Evan wasn't surprised. The Ohio River hugged the city's edge like the East, and River Road sure as hell resembled that stretch of the FDR Drive in the Seventies where it goes under the bone-broke-me-fix hospital.

"*Stripes* with Bill Murray and the other *Ghostbusters* guy was shot right along here," the cabbie added.

Evan recalled the classic scene. "Please, no cough syrup or action photos, okay?"

"Huh?"

"Never mind."

The man momentarily looked at Evan in his rearview mirror like Evan's hair was ablaze, then he flashed his tobacco-stained teeth.

"You know your hotel is featured in *The Great Gatsby*." *Back to our regularly scheduled programming.*

"*Featured?* Really." The cabbie mistook the sarcasm for genuine enthusiasm.

"Heck yeah. *Great Gatsby*. Fitzpatrick."

"Fitz*gerald*. And this must be South Egg."

That look again. Evan instinctively touched his hair. Not on fire.

•   •   •

Evan could picture Gatsby's Daisy and Jordan in the Seelbach Hotel, with its dignified Southern elegance quietly maintained by tall, thin black gentlemen in white jackets. His room had antique furniture and a canopied bed that made him vaguely uncomfortable—like he had to sleep on his back all night. Dead still, arms crossed over his chest. Like a corpse in a coffin. Or, as Hemingway once described a sleeping F. Scott, like a little dead crusader sculpted on his tomb as a monument to himself.

Evan wandered down to the lobby, fragrant with stargazers, around six o'clock and asked the concierge for a dinner suggestion. Nothing too formal or stuffy. Walking distance. Preferably palatable to a New Yorker.

As he walked east on Main Street, he noticed the resemblance to New York, but it stopped with the architecture. The many people leaving their offices and heading home were, well, *different*. Evan considered analyzing how and why, but then thought better of it and decided to just enjoy the stroll.

Proof on Main, connected to the very cool 21c Museum Hotel, served a better-than-average burger and fries. *Somewhere between JG Melon and the clandestine Burger Joint in Le Parker Meridien on Fifty-seventh*, Evan concluded as he sat alone at the end of the bar, reading Medipharm's latest quarterly report.

A guy about his age sat on the stool next to him and ordered a Miller Lite. His pants said Dockers and his banana yellow golf shirt said Humana.

One sip. "How you doin'?"

Evan looked up from the 10-Q, somewhat shocked. *Oh yeah, the South.* In New York it would take at least a beer or two to get to this point, and preferably an opposing set of genitalia. "You enjoyin' the day?" Or at least a minute or two.

"Sure." Pause to contemplate next move. "And you?" *Shit. Big mistake.*

"Oh, not too shabby. Work today was a first rate bitch an' if my old lady knew I was here she'd have a shitfit but I hear there's a wreck on 71 and I'm in no kinda mood for that today if you know what I mean even if the kids have soccer practice are you married?"

Evan looked at him in complete awe. Did his jaw actually *drop*?

"'Cause my mother-in-law had bunion surgery this mornin' and Sheila is supposed to drive her home this evenin' but that can't happen if I'm sittin' on 71 so I might as well be sittin' here waitin' fer her to clear." Deep breath. "I'm Jerry Shoemaker like the jockey. You in town for business? I see the report you've got there. The devil finds work for idle hands, huh?"

Evan flashed a mental picture of his mother, standing at the kitchen sink, her assigned station in the double-wide and in life, barking orders at him and his half sisters. "My mother used to say that, *the devil finds work for idle hands.*"

"I think every mom does," Jerry replied with a satisfied nod. "But it's the idols in your heart you really got to watch. They'll getcha, eat you alive. Every time."

After a painfully scintillating back-and-forth about New York, feet, Medipharm, the sorry state of health care reform in America, bike-sharing programs, marriage, moving Derby to prime time, the new college basketball coach, the origin of a mysterious dish called a hot brown, and something awful named "spaghetti junction," Jerry finished his Lite and ordered another.

"Where are your folks from?"

Evan winced. "Long story."

"Just ordered another beer. Mine are both from E-town about forty-five minutes south of here but moved to J-town years 'n' years ago. Sheila's are natives, went to Atherton High School class of '57."

"Okay. Good to know."

Jerry smiled and took an approving gulp of his fresh beer. Then he looked at Evan and waited for more.

Why? Why does he want to know? Evan considered asking him, but again thought better of analyzing the indigenous species. *What the fuck? Could be cathartic.*

"My mother, stepfather, and two half sisters live in South Paterson, New Jersey. George adopted me so I have their last name."

Jerry raised his eyebrows and gently lowered his chin, a subtle invitation.

"Stoess. Evan Stoess. George says 'Stoess, rhymes with mess,' the prick."

"Ohmigosh, we have a Stoess Hardware store nearby, been 'round forever . . ."

"You don't say." *Take a hint, Jerry.*

"Sorry. I'll shut up."

Evan continued. "They still live in the same shitty trailer park I grew up in. Freakin' nasty. George, my worthless stepfather, is a filthy motherfucker, pardon my French, and he's always hated my ass. He treats my mother like shit and knowing him he's probably banging my half sisters, the sick bastard."

Jerry looked shocked, his eyes wide. "Wow. You *definitely* are from New York. What's he do, this George?"

"He's a cliché. Drinks heavily. Watches *Divorce Court*. Been unemployed for something like seven years. My mother says he's holding out for a management position." Evan laughed at his skillful *Vacation* reference. "But I'm not about to be Clark Griswold and offer up my wallet full of cash."

Jerry smiled. "Well, you've certainly done well for yourself, despite it all."

"Thanks, but I'm a special case."

"How so?"

"I managed to attend the best private school in New Jersey, for twelve long years. They called us 'lifers,' those of us there from first grade through graduation."

"Scholarship?"

"More like court order. But not exactly."

"*Really.*" Jerry Shoemaker was interested.

"Actually, more like *atonement*. My real father . . ."

Suddenly Jerry's cell phone, hanging from his belt, sounded a neutered Air Supply tune.

Much like Jerry, Evan guessed.

"Shoot! That's Sheila. Hold on a sec."

Jerry stepped away from the bar for fifteen seconds of apologetic conversation.

"Gotta run. Nice meetin' you. Good luck."

"Thanks. You too."

Watching Jerry walk away, Evan's thoughts drifted to the soul-sucking trailer park where he grew up. Perhaps to satisfy the call for catharsis, a horribly painful memory surfaced, one of the most humiliating moments in a life littered with humiliation.

When Evan was in fifth grade at Ridgewood Academy, unbeknownst to him his mother applied for an "adopt-a-family" holiday program with a local charity.

On the day before Thanksgiving, shortly after Evan returned home from Ridgewood looking forward to a long weekend, the Stoess family trailer had visitors. Evan recalled watching out the nicotine yellow window as two cars invaded the Pleasant Grove Community, a Jaguar and a BMW, and four well-dressed women emerged bearing Thanksgiving groceries and Christmas decorations.

As the women approached the front door, Evan saw their faces and recoiled in horror. Ridgewood mothers were delivering his Butterball and tinsel. He ran to his bedroom and slammed the door just as his mom welcomed the group.

"Thank you, thank you. Please come inside."

"Well . . . our pleasure, Ms. Stoess! Our pleasure."

Like Brangelina visiting starving children in a war-ravaged nation, the pearl-laden ladies put on brave faces as they entered the fetid abode and unsuccessfully tried to mask their pity.

Evan recognized one of the women as the mother of a sixth-grader and regular volunteer at the Ridgewood bookstore. Another he recognized from a school assembly; she was a state senator. A third he had seen many times at bake sales. Hidden in his dark bedroom, Evan held his breath and pleaded for them to leave.

"Only my son is here at the moment," he heard his mom say through the thin door. "Evan, come here please," she said in an unusually pleasant voice.

Evan panicked. "Mom . . . Mom . . . I'm busy," he stammered.

"We have visitors. Come on out, please." Sing-song.

"Mom, I'm doing my homework!"

"NOW!" she yelled and then shamefully turned to the visitors. "Boys."

One Ridgewood mother cringed. Another fiddled with her pearls.

Evan opened the door. Following the exchange, all eyes were in his direction.

The bake sale mom was closest. "Well, hello . . . young . . . man," she said with an expression that changed from fake happiness to startled surprise. She recognized Evan. Evan could see that the other ladies did too. He looked down at his bare feet, ashamed, humiliated and broken, and whispered, "Hello."

After a moment of awkward silence that seemed to last a lifetime, the bookstore mom said suddenly, "We really must be going." Bake sale mom, looking directly at Evan with confused pity and amazement, said, "Yes, we *must* wish you a happy holiday and be on our merry way." Evan could sense *their* surprised shame, and it heightened *his* humiliation. Seconds later, the adopt-a-family volunteers were gone. Evan's mother spoke as the pity caravan beat a hasty retreat, presumably to the nearest gated community.

"That's odd. They left in an awful hurry."

"Rich people are different from you and me, Mom. Really, *very* different. I know. *I know.*"

CHAPTER

SIX

Despite his best efforts, Evan slept on his back the entire night. He cursed himself in the shower.

The Seelbach's doorman suggested a taxi, but Evan chose to walk the half mile or so to the Louisville Medical Center. For mid-June, the weather was unseasonably mild and the Kentucky sun sat high in the sky despite the early hour.

Evan walked toward a relatively tall building that suspiciously resembled a huge stick of roll-on deodorant, stopped at a Starbucks, then turned south on First Street until he reached the medical center's biomedical incubator.

Steve Wilson, the executive director, greeted Evan at the new double glass doors.

"Evan Stoess, I presume. Right on time."

"Dr. LeMaire?" Steve didn't look like a prominent research physician and freshly minted CEO of a public company.

"Oh no." He chuckled. After a quick introduction, he added, "But I'll take you to Dr. LeMaire."

They walked what seemed like serpentine miles through the massive facility, most of which, Evan noted, smelled of the intoxicating aroma of fresh paint and new carpet. After yet another quick series of turns, Evan asked, "Should I drop bread crumbs?"

"All of the buildings are connected, with about two dozen companies under incubation. I'll get you back when you're ready to go."

Evan knew he was being manipulated, and it worked. He was impressed. Shiny new laboratories. Myriad bespectacled scientist-types. Steve's mellifluous chamber of commerce commentary. That buzz-inducing aroma.

And Dr. Mitchell Isaac LeMaire.

Evan had read Dr. LeMaire's bio in the usual filings and press releases, but he was not prepared for the man himself.

Well over six feet tall, Evan observed, with a square jaw, broad shoulders, perfect television smile—the good doctor could easily have been one of those male fitness models staring him down from so many corner newsstands. *"And I say that with an unblemished record of staunch heterosexuality."* He laughed at the classic Costanza quote as he shook hands with Dr. LeMaire.

"Welcome to Medipharm, Mr. Stoess. Glad to see you're in a good mood this morning."

"Thanks, Dr. LeMaire. Please call me Evan."

"Will do. Call me Mitch."

For the next two hours Mitch and Evan engaged in the business-meeting equivalent of a kumbaya group hug, discussing topics ranging from Medipharm's new drug to the divine inspiration of *Seinfeld*. Following a superb power lunch at Vincenzo's, Evan all but assured Mitch that ECM would raise Medipharm's profile with a strong "buy" recommendation. Mitch would be hearing from ECM's investment bankers as well.

Evan returned to the Seelbach for his requested late checkout. A taxi wouldn't do it, not today. Evan called the concierge and requested a limo for his trip to the airport. *Was a stretch Escalade warranted? Probably not.*

On the flight back to LaGuardia, Evan reviewed his notes and mentally envisioned his glowing research report on Medipharm and Dr. Mitchell Isaac LeMaire. Given access to enough capital, Mitch could improve and save the lives of millions of people. A true Cinderella story, and Evan held the glass slipper. *Finally, this is how* my *story begins*, he thought. *Goddammit, this is* it.

Mitch was forty-six years old, married with three young children. He jogged just about every day in a park, he told Evan, designed by the same guys who did Central Park. Six weeks earlier he completed the annual Derby Festival miniMarathon, thirteen miles. He practiced neurology in Boston for eight years before moving to Kentucky to pursue his entrepreneurial dream, lured by Louisville's reputation for biomedical research and its "Bucks for Brains" program. With a broad smile, Mitch called it the "Please-Ignore-*Deliverance*" program.

Mitch's brain was valued at two million bucks, plus a Valhalla Golf Club membership, and Medipharm was born eighteen months ago to "develop and market life-saving drugs of the future." Specifically, while in practice Mitch conceptualized a powerful drug combination that he believed would delay or actually forestall Alzheimer's disease, if detected early.

Disappointed with Aricept and other drugs created to slow Alzheimer's progress, Mitch pulled together years of research that linked the disease to cholesterol. Most notably, he studied research in the *The Archives of Neurology* showing that patients on cholesterol-lowering statins experienced a seventy percent reduction in the prevalence of Alzheimer's. Amazed, Mitch found other published studies implying that anti-inflammatories and blood pressure medications might contribute to the treatment and prevention of the disease.

Statins. Anti-inflammatories. Anti-hypertensives. Armed with this knowledge, the indefatigable Dr. LeMaire moved his family to the Bluegrass State and within a year had synthesized his dream product and anticipated cash cow.

Code-named AtornaplodineOne, or "Ator," Mitch's creation was *primarily* a unique combination of three prescription medications: the popular statin atorvastatin calcium, the non-steroidal anti-inflammatory naproxen sodium, and amlodipine, the channel-blocker used to treat high blood pressure. The combination alone was not rocket science, and it wasn't effective. It was Mitch's unconventional use of excipients—the inactive substances that regulated assimilation, stability, and disintegration of the drug combination—that made Ator a "wonder drug." After he had finalized the blend of excipients, Mitch was confident AtornaplodineOne would both prevent and treat Alzheimer's. "With the demographically inevitable graying of America, the market for Medipharm's revolutionary new drug is virtually limitless . . ." Evan mentally composed for his research report. *And so is its potential to put millions in my pocket.*

To facilitate Ator's development, six months ago the company's venture capitalists merged Medipharm with a public shell company, changed the shell's name, and executed a reverse split. Medipharm now traded over-the-counter for $1.10 per share. The goals for the "reverse" merger were attention and cash. Medipharm needed a boatload of money to fund research and development, not to mention the testing and FDA approval process. Limited tests on university patients were "extremely promising," but the drug was still months, or longer, from hitting the market.

Although Mitch received some support from the university, Medipharm was basically a one-man show until a cash infusion could support the hiring of additional researchers and the funding of stage-two clinical trials. "But don't worry," Mitch joked. "I gave up cliff diving and competitive bungee jumping when my first child was born."

As far as anyone knew, Medipharm had only one direct competitor, K&R, a German pharmaceutical company developing a very different drug that treated the same problem. Advanced human trials were under way in France, but Mitch was not concerned, assuring Evan, "Even if they've found something, which I doubt, there's room for two."

On a Delta mini-jet over Ohio, Evan smiled at the memory. *"Room for two." Shit. Here's hoping a few frogs don't make it.*

Late that night, back in Louisville, Mitch went home to his wife, already asleep in bed. He brushed back her hair and gently kissed her forehead. She stirred.

"We're going to be rich."

"We already are."

CHAPTER
SEVEN

A voice mail, text message, and two missed calls told Evan that Andrew Leary was anxious for an update, but he would have to wait. The call of the Ritual could not be ignored.

In the taxi crossing the Triborough Bridge, as he passed the ominously majestic nuthouse, Evan thought about the monthly Ridgewood Academy Alumni newsletter, which, he believed, should be delivered to *his* door with a barf bag. Reading the alumni update, seeing the rich a-holes get married, spawn little rich a-holes and, then, worst of all, get *richer*, left him envious, delirious, and nauseated. Usually the very thought of it had this effect, but not today. No. Today he recalled Gore Vidal's famous aphorism: "Whenever a friend succeeds, a little something in me dies."

Nothing could be more true, Evan admitted. He knew a *big* something would die in the Ridgewood assholes when they learned of *his* success. He would report his Wall Street promotion and the deals he was closing. His "children" wore green and earned interest, and his tormenters would be shocked. *Good. Fuck them.* His taxi banked left onto the Drive, and Evan snapped back to reality. The alumni update could wait. The Ritual called.

•　　•　　•

Evan jumped out of the cab a couple of blocks north of his destination and walked to the shadow of his Dutch elm tree.

Worried that he was too late and had missed the show, he stood there with his Canal Street "Executive Roller Bag" leaning against the trunk. Its presence annoyed him. *Pathetic piece of shit.* Evan hated cheap luggage.

His ECM-issued BlackBerry vibrated.

"Andrew. Hey. Yeah, I'm just leaving Louisville. Major delay here. Very positive meeting. Serious banking possibilities. We'll talk in the morning, okay? Great." Click.

If Evan was the boss, he'd certainly know his minion's flight number so he could punch it up on the Web and catch the idiot in a lie, but Andrew trusted people. *Sucker.*

At six thirty, without much deliberation for a change, he decided he'd missed them; he should have known. The weather was perfect and Geoffrey had decided to beat the traffic. On most Fridays, as punishment, he would have sentenced himself to a lap around the reservoir. Sometimes, after a particularly memorable sighting, the same lap was a much-deserved reward. He couldn't explain this phenomenon, only that the park was his sanctuary where he could perform complicated mental machinations. The cinder track around the reservoir evoked thoughts and emotions bigger and better than Evan thought himself capable.

Today was different. He walked home. Evan didn't fume; he didn't fantasize. Instead, he thought about Medipharm; he thought about *work*. He tried to conjure up deep thoughts, but they wouldn't emerge. He missed them.

Normally, the idea of thinking about work bullshit after a missed opportunity would anger Evan, but not today. *Why?* The answer struck him as he glanced up at the El Dorado's twin towers. *Money. Success. The twin pillars of life. Medipharm. The path to both.* Content that he wasn't losing it, Evan relaxed, took a deep breath of air heavily scented with roasting Nuts 4 Nuts, and enjoyed the circular stroll.

CHAPTER

EIGHT

The next morning Evan woke up before his ancient Sony cube alarm clock began to feebly emit hits from the eighties, nineties, and today. *Wanting* to get out of bed and go to the office was a welcome novelty, and when Andrew arrived at 8:00 A.M., he was in his cubicle reviewing his notes.

"Give me five minutes, brainiac."

Evan gave him six and then made his pitch.

"We should come out with a strong *buy* and very aggressive price target, take a large equity position in both Medipharm and Logitex, the distribution/marketing partner, and get Mark down to Louisville to talk about a secondary equity offering and whatever else he can come up with to generate banking fees. Oh, and they also need some PR."

"You think this is the real deal?"

"I do." Evan projected calm confidence, but he could feel rivulets of sweat running down his back, saturating his waistband beneath his suit jacket.

Andrew leaned back in his chair, scratched his chin as if it had stubble, and looked hard at Evan.

"I hate dealing with the FDA. Risky. Takes forever."

"Dr. LeMaire knows half the people on the advisory committee, and the Agency just about always follows its recommendations."

"Just about always?"

"Yes. Seriously."

"Evan, listen to me."

Evan listened. Andrew only called him "Evan" when he was drop-dead serious.

"I talked to Marshall yesterday and he's getting anxious. You know this market sucks and our trading margins are in the shitter. Marshall and I want something big this quarter, something we can all get behind and make some real cash. We need *bank,* Evan, and frankly, this opportunity, Medi-pharm, is perfect. *We* really *need* it. For two reasons. Are you listening?"

"Yes, I'm listening," Evan replied, but every time Andrew said *we,* he shuddered.

At Ridgewood Evan was forced to read every book and treatise authored by Ayn Rand. At New York University on academic scholarship, he *volunteered,* taking every elective in which the *Atlas Shrugged* author was taught. He eidetically memorized multiple passages, could still recite them chapter and verse, and he knew that *we* was a word of weakness, misery and shame. *We* was a coward's word, undeserving and impotent. Only *I* mattered.

Andrew continued. "First, we think it has legitimate potential. We found it before anyone else and we love the story, particularly the clean shell and this Dr. LeMaire.

"Second, and listen closely. It's your first call. You're young and new to the street and, if it blows up, it's on you. *Capiche*?"

Loud and clear. "If it flies, you're saying *we* all win, but if it falls apart, *I* am back to scouring Edgar and crunching numbers."

"That's right. You killed it, you skinned it, you'll eat it. A chance to be a hero or a goat. It's that simple. So what do you want to do?"

Evan pictured the Ridgewood alumni newsletter. "Evan Stoess resides in Manhattan where he was recently promoted to equity analyst at his prominent investment bank . . ."

"You'll have my report in forty-eight hours."

"Okay." Andrew looked relieved. Evan wondered if the pressure to make *bank* was even more than he was letting on. Andrew and Marshall lived lavish lifestyles and had no intention of scaling back.

Andrew stood up. "Let's do it. We'll get the traders on Medipharm and Logitex, and Mark can be on a plane tomorrow."

"Holy shit, this is for real?" Evan shocked himself with a question he intended to think and not speak.

"Oh yeah. Dress rehearsal is over. Welcome to our world, where you either win or lose. Welcome to *the big time*."

Two weeks later, Evan began to understand The Big Time.

In a quick fortnight, ECM released Evan's wildly optimistic research report; an "unaffiliated" affiliate took a huge equity position in both Medipharm and Logitex; and Mark closed a lucrative banking deal involving both a secondary equity offering and outrageous advisory fees. Mitch LeMaire visited New York; Marshall loved him.

Inspired by Blodgett's infamous Amazon prediction, Evan's twelve-month price target for Medipharm was $15 per share. Medipharm's stock, already up to $1.50 due to the affiliate purchasing, moved to $2.00 as a few small-cap speculators took notice.

ECM was buried neck-deep in Medipharm, and Evan was holding the shovel. Around his midtown office, for the first time, he was *somebody*. Truth in advertising, Andrew made him the point man. His call. His responsibility.

Coworkers Evan had seen every day for three years but never spoken to now routinely stopped by his desk. A decent-looking chick from the compliance department asked what he was doing for lunch. An hour later, they were at Just Salad eating overpriced weeds. She giggled when Evan observed, "Kale is iceberg lettuce that won't shut up about what it read in *The New Yorker*."

Evan was euphoric and considered calling his father with the news. But he decided to wait. He had never spoken to his real father, but when he finally did, the topic had to be worthy of the occasion. He would wait for the stock deal to close.

Unfortunately, after the initial flurry of activity, not much happened. Evan created spreadsheets showing how much money he'd make if Medipharm climbed to five, ten, and fifteen dollars per share. In his dreams he read of his riches in the Ridgewood newsletter, and he embraced the jealous reaction of his former classmates. Remarkably, envisioning his own success was better than his usual practice of worshipping at the altar of schadenfreude.

Then, on the last Monday of June, lightning struck, and The Big Time kicked Evan in the ass.

CHAPTER
NINE

"Life's a bitch and then you marry one."

That's what the smug asshole said to Evan as the elevator door closed just before Evan could jump in and ride up to ECM. He slapped the door with his hand and heard the schmuck laugh on the other side. *I'll get him*, Evan promised himself. And he would. Important people who publish research reports always do.

Around noon, Andrew stuck his head over Evan's partition. From Evan's perspective he looked like a groundhog emerging from a hole.

"Kinda quiet, huh?"

"Yep." Evan punched up Medipharm on his computer. Only 2,200 shares traded. At $2.10. Very quiet. He picked up his telephone receiver and guided it toward Andrew. "Blue horseshoe loves Medipharm?"

"Don't you *wish*. If only it was that easy in the real world."

Andrew wandered off and just as Evan heard Andrew's office door close, Evan's computer beeped. Somebody somewhere wanted ten thousand shares of Medipharm. A second bid for five thousand shares. A third for twenty thousand more. *What the fuck?* Evan rang Andrew's extension.

"I already had lunch, Evan."

"Uhh . . . Andrew, you'd better call the traders and check out Medi. Somethin's up."

Steadily, sellers emerged and the stock ran up to $2.75. Then the limit orders kicked in and, as insiders' supply hit the market, trades got done and the price jumped to $5.00 by the day's close. Evan was in Andrew's office swapping theories when Marshall Owen burst in, elated.

"Gentlemen, we just made a king's ransom filling orders, not to mention the gain on our own position. What's the word on the street?"

Andrew replied on behalf of both of them.

"Nothing yet. We're waiting."

They didn't wait long. At five o'clock the explanation came across the wire.

As it turned out, K&R, Medipharm's German competitor, killed a whole bunch of frogs. Or almost. As reported in the soon-to-be-released *British Journal of Medicine* and picked up by every major news organization, K&R's drug caused severe liver damage "in an unacceptably high number of test subjects" and clinical trials were summarily cancelled. Only one company in the world had a competing drug in the works, Medipharm Corporation, and its formula didn't implicate the liver, or any other organ system for that matter.

Obviously, somebody found out before the news officially broke. ECM's traders thought the buyers were in Europe, out of reach of the SEC. Didn't matter. Now that the news was out, Tuesday would be monumental.

The next morning, fuel was thrown on the fire. Juliette Auberge, an Oscar-winning and universally beloved actress, announced she had been diagnosed with early-stage Alzheimer's, voiced her profound disappointment with the K&R development, and called for the fast-track approval of Medipharm's alternative "cure."

All hell broke loose. The media flocked to Louisville to interview Mitchell Isaac LeMaire. In New York, Wall Street offered up only one Medipharm analyst to the hungry commentators. Evan's phone started ringing, and it did not stop.

Medipharm's stock exploded, tripling before Tuesday's close, $15 per share. Evan's prescient prediction rocked ECM and the Street. On an otherwise slow summer news day, the media was all over it. He revised his *I'm rich* spreadsheet while talking on the phone to reporters. The swollen streams of zeroes and commas were intoxicating. Hashtags demanded wider columns.

When the markets closed Evan found himself in a chauffeured black sedan with Marshall Owen, heading south to the CNBC studio for an appearance on *Closing Bell*. His day had become a Salvador Dalí painting. Marshall was beyond ecstatic—he seemed to gesticulate wildly yet in slow motion and he called Evan *son*, but to Evan it was all melting clocks. Marshall's voice sounded just like the vacant adults in Charlie Brown cartoons. The narcotic effect of imminent celebrity paralyzed Evan's ears but, oddly, if he concentrated, he could read Marshall's lips. *Bizarre.*

Marshall was giving him a securities law primer, telling him what he could and could not say about ECM's "semi-legal" relationship with Medipharm.

Evan knew most of this scrivener nonsense already and decided not to concentrate. *Your first call. You killed it, you skinned it, you'll eat it. Hero or goat. Welcome to our world.*

When the Lincoln's door swung open and the street noise slapped him in the face, reality returned abruptly, too fast, too loud, *too much.*

"You're late. You're on in five minutes. No time for makeup."

The pimply production assistant wore a cumbersome headset and carried a clipboard. He sported an oversized skull thumb ring and a vintage tie clip. He looked like a complete idiot. When he reached for Evan to hurry him out of the car, Evan growled.

"Do not fucking touch me."

The over-inked PA retreated. "Whoa. Easy, big guy."

The scene slowed to normal speed and Evan felt relief that Marshall had not heard his momentary transgression.

"Sorry man. Little stressed."

"No worries," the PA sniffed with a faux Chelsea lisp. "Let's go."

CHAPTER

TEN

The studio lights were blinding and white-hot as only studio lights can be, but Evan was in the zone and didn't even notice.

"Welcome back to *Closing Bell*. Before the break we took an extended look at Medipharm Corporation, whose stock tripled today. In the studio with us now is Evan Stoess, an analyst with Equity Capital Management who follows today's big story, Medipharm. Welcome, Evan."

"Thank you, Ben. Great to be here. It's been an exciting couple of days for an exciting company. Medipharm's wonder drug is poised to revolutionize the treatment of Alzheimer's disease, and I am thrilled to be facilitating its research and success." *Damn. I am so good.*

"Very well. Until yesterday, nobody had heard of Louisville-based Medipharm. What attracted you?"

"An excellent management team and sound research fundamentals, Ben. I've been looking for opportunities in this space for months, and, as they say in Kentucky, Ben, you don't bet on the horse, you bet on the jockey, and Dr. LeMaire is an extraordinary research scientist with an impeccable history of innovation. After exhaustive research on a number of promising possibilities, I chose Medipharm . . ."

"Excuse me. Your firm, ECM, doesn't exactly have a track record in this market segment. Some might suggest it was just dumb luck."

Evan wasn't fazed. He knew Ben's d-bag M.O.

"I was bullish on Medipharm long before the unfortunate K&R announcement and Hollywood interest, and in fact ECM inked a secondary equity deal weeks ago to fund Medipharm's continued development and research initiatives. Call it what you like, Ben, but I share Medipharm's vision, as does ECM."

Evan turned to look directly into the camera.

"Together we will save lives."

Ben couldn't hide his amusement with Evan's impressive schtick; the result was heavy sarcasm.

"Isn't that beautiful, ladies and gentlemen? Wall Street altruism at its finest. I'm sure we'll be hearing more from Evan Stoess and Medipharm. Thank you for being here."

Evan's mind flashed. He wanted to scream. *Altruism? Give me a fuckin' break, Ben. If anyone should know Rand, you should: Altruism is incompatible with freedom, with capitalism and with individual rights. You cannot combine the pursuit of happiness with the moral status of a sacrificial animal. If any civilization is to survive, it is the morality of altruism that men must reject.*

But instead he said, "Thank *you*, Ben. Always a pleasure."

"And now we'll turn to Harper Steel at the international desk for a look at what's ahead."

Ben's demeanor perceptively changed as he turned from the camera towards Evan.

"Impressive. You handled it well."

"Handled *you* well, you mean?" Evan shot back. He wanted to add, in Phil Hartman's Frank Sinatra voice, *I've got chunks of guys like you in my stool, Ben*. But he did not.

"We'll see."

Behind the white lights, Evan could sense Marshall applauding and backslapping the crew. Evan turned away from Ben, stood, and walked off the set toward his happy boss. He didn't hear Ben's parting comment.

"We'll see, kid. Don't get cocky."

•   •   •

Back in the Lincoln, Evan wondered who might have seen his stellar performance on national television. *"Whenever a friend succeeds, a little something in me dies."* Which Ridgewood assholes were sitting in their corner offices, slack-jawed with shock and envy? Had his father seen his performance? The very thought of it frustrated him, so he put an abrupt end to the contemplation and turned to Marshall, who had just snapped shut his old-school cell phone.

"What's next, Mr. Owen?"

"You were brilliant, son. Absolutely brilliant. Let's head back to the office for an update, then it's surf and turf at Old Homestead. Sound good?"

"Yes sir."

"Sit back and enjoy the ride."

Five hours later, Evan sat on his sofa, numb and satiated. Surf, turf, single malt. Between the hours of ten and midnight he saw his CNBC interview replayed twice; he couldn't believe his eyes. A few minutes before eleven o'clock, Fleur knocked on his door, presumably to watch *Seinfeld*. She didn't own a TV. Evan didn't answer. Not in the mood.

The certified check, sitting on the scarred Ikea coffee table he rescued from a York Avenue gutter, said $50,000. A "retention bonus," Andrew remarked as he handed Evan the envelope.

"And there's plenty more where that came from. Your slice of the banking fees alone should be five times that, plus we'll get you some equity in the secondary you can flip."

Evan remembered Marshall saying, as he sipped his first taste of Lagavulin, "You'll remember that bonus when the big boys start calling you, yes you will!"

Despite the Islay-assisted food coma, Evan struggled to sleep. The check was still on his coffee table. *What would Geoffrey Buchanan do with a $50,000 check? Probably wipe his ass with it.* He smiled and his thoughts turned to Wednesday's itinerary—an early sit-down with *The Wall Street Journal*, Mitch's noon arrival for interviews and an important meeting with institutional investors, then, with any luck, another TV appearance after the market's close.

The stock market would close, and doors would open. An alien at Ridgewood and a pariah in the trailer park, Evan had always been alone, on the outside looking in. The rich kids hated him for being poor and the poor kids hated him for thinking rich. All he wanted was to belong, some-where, *anywhere*, but all doors had been closed to him. But today, finally, the key was within his reach. The key to money and success and relevance. The key to *the inside*. He fell asleep, whispering the dream, *belong*.

CHAPTER

ELEVEN

Despite rising earlier than usual and hustling to his office, Evan arrived ten minutes late for his interview with *The Wall Street Journal*. An urgent matter intervened. He spotted smug elevator asshole in his building's lobby, talking with a guy waiting at the reception desk for a security pass.

He stepped behind a marble column to survey the scene. Smug asshole shook hands with the fellow and dashed into a closing elevator. Evan emerged and quickly approached the waiting stranger.

"Damn, just missed him."

"Huh?" The guy looked surprised.

"Was that Phil Hayden you were just talking to? He looked just like an old friend from Rochester. Haven't seen him in years." Evan was invitingly earnest.

"Oh. No. That was Alex Pearson."

"Uncanny resemblance. Does he work in the building? I swear he could be Phil's twin."

"Yeah, he's an associate with King & Case, the huge law firm."

"Ahh, okay. Sorry to bother you. Have a good one."

"Yeah. You, too."

Evan stepped aside, pretended to answer his cell phone, and waited for the guy to move on. Then he turned and left the building.

Okay, Alex Pearson, you stupid smug fuck. Time to pay.

Evan walked to the lobby of the office building next door and its antique row of private pay phones. He took a seat in a remarkably comfortable little booth and found King & Case in the white pages. He dialed *67 and then the main number.

"King & Case. How may I direct your call?"

Evan smiled and cleared his throat.

"Your human resources director, please."

"One moment and I'll connect you to Ms. Davis." The hold music was Sinatra. *I'll do it my way,* Evan hummed along with the tune.

"This is Evelyn Davis."

"Good morning, Ms. Davis. My name is Erwin Handleman and I'm the HR manager here at Provident. Are you King Case's HR director?"

"I am. How may I help you?"

"I'm reviewing an application for employment. One of your associates has applied for an in-house position at my company."

"Really? Which one?"

"A . . . Mister . . . Alex . . . Pearson."

"*Really?* Does he know you're calling me?"

"We do it randomly, but he initialed a disclosure statement indicating we could contact his current employer when he completed the employment application packet."

"Okay." Evelyn Davis was taking notes now.

"I apologize for the inconvenience. This will only take a moment. I trust he does *work* for King & Case. He is the *chair* of your associates committee?"

"Uh, no, he is not. We don't have a formal associates committee."

"Really?" Evan paused, loudly turning a few pages of the phone book. "Checking bullets now . . . Did he lead the effort to revamp your firm's ethics guidelines?"

"Not that I'm aware of. That's handled by the senior partners."

"Well that's ironic, isn't it? Did he originate over seven hundred thousand dollars in new business last year?"

"Absolutely not. Even senior associates rarely originate in our corporate group."

"Ms. Davis, I have a real problem here. Before calling you, I checked Mr. Pearson's education background and previous employment and let's just say they were . . . well . . . *embellished*. He indicated he's applied for several other in-house positions. Have you received other calls?"

"Yours is the first."

"Well, I think I've heard enough. Thank you for your time."

"*Thank you*, Mr. . . ."

"Handleman."

"And you're with Provident—"

"That's right. Thanks again." Click.

Twenty minutes later, Alex Pearson received a call from King & Case's managing partner. When Smug Asshole left his office, his computer and files were promptly removed. His passwords, iPhone, and Amex were cancelled. The managing partner escorted him from the building. *"You know the rule, Alex. Zero tolerance."*

The rest of Evan's day was also a huge success—interviews, meetings, Medipharm's stock up to $18.00— but nothing approached the rush, the adrenaline surge, the pure thrill he experienced ruining the life of one Alex Pearson. Like the Ridgewood pricks and trailer park trash, Pearson deserved it. No. He *earned* it.

CHAPTER

TWELVE

"Nick & Toni's tonight, Evan?"

"Sure, Lydia." Evan didn't speak from experience, but he had heard of it, so it must be a scene worthy of his presence. He was spending the weekend at Marshall and Lydia Owen's house in East Hampton and, dammit, it was *awesome*.

The evening before, after the Jitney dropped him off in front of the Palm Restaurant, he had taken a dilapidated taxi to Geoffrey and Victoria Buchanan's Further Lane estate. The gated driveway prevented a view of the far-off home, but he asked the driver to wait as he peered down the long drive, hoping to see *something*. He felt like Axel Foley staking out Victor Maitland's Beverly Hills manse. *Actually, I really am* on vacation, he joked to himself. The cabbie cleared his throat for the third time and Marshall and Lydia were expecting him, so he called off the quest and headed to his host's house north of the village, not far from Gardiner's Bay.

"People will tell you that south of the highway is the place to be, but we prefer the solitude of the Northwest Woods," Marshall had said unconvincingly the day before.

Ten days had passed since he buried Alex Pearson, and life had only gotten better. When Evan returned to work the Monday after all hell broke loose, he had been moved from his cubicle to an office with a decent view facing west to Rockefeller Center. Some wiseass had taped BUD FOX on his door. Evan left it there. *Fuck yes Bud Fox. If he hadn't been such a pussy and betrayed Gordon Gekko, he would have been set for life.* Evan assured himself, *I won't make that mistake.* A check for $25,000 waited on his new desk, perfect timing considering the half dozen calls he'd received from headhunters representing "*reputable, first-tier* investment banks." After a dozen major media appearances, Evan was a hot commodity, and Marshall knew it.

Over the previous weekend he had spent about half of the first fifty-thousand-dollar bonus, the most precious and vindicating experience of his new life: From Barney's, three new Tom Ford suits and a bad-ass solid black Bell & Ross Ceramic Phantom; from Ralph Lauren's palace, also on Madison Avenue, a Hamptons wardrobe; and, from Hammacher Schlemmer on Fifty-seventh Street, a bunch of awesome crap he didn't really need, but had to have. "A gift of over $5,000" would get his name in the Ridgewood alumni newsletter *and* annual report; he mailed a check for $5,001.

He heard from his mom and George the day a brief clip appeared on the local news. Certainly they didn't watch financial news channels and as far as Evan knew they had never picked up a real newspaper—both would interfere with Honey Boo Boo viewing on TLC. They called his home number. Rand taught Evan to be immune to the whiny extortions of worthless relatives, so he screened it. *Thank God for caller ID.*

He had hoped to summon the strength to contact his father and, hours before leaving for East Hampton, considered calling him. He wondered how his father would respond to a forgotten child he had never met. Over the years Evan had convinced himself that, unlike George, his real father *would* care, his real father *would* encourage, his real father *would* love. But he couldn't help but wonder. The wonder became fear, the fear became despair, and the despair paralyzed him. Evan caught the Jitney on East Eighty-sixth Street. The fancy bus had free wi-fi and a faux hardwood floor. It smelled like money.

Now he sat on a Jonathan Adler sofa with Lydia Owen in her Hamptons great room overlooking a heated pool. Evan could see Andrew swimming laps while hot Chloë reclined in a cushioned lounge chair, enjoying her time away from their children.

Lydia, an elegant and beautiful lady, was a grandmother three times over, but Evan was attracted to her nonetheless. *A GMILF, perhaps?* She moved with a graceful ease, always a smile on her face, reminiscent of a happy senior citizen cyclist in a Centrum Silver commercial. And she exuded an effortless confidence that Evan envied.

"Perfect. My niece will be here shortly from the city and can join us at Nick & Toni's. Evan . . . she is just your type."

Evan thought he was everybody's type, and nobody's. People told him he resembled a brooding Edward Norton, both in body and face, and that made sense to him. *Could be worse,* he concluded.

During his twelve long years at Ridgewood, his narrow frame was accentuated by the ill-fitting blazers, shirts and slacks his mom bought at discount and thrift shops. George forced her to buy Evan's uniform attire in sizes too big so they had "room to grow." Evan would protest, but George was a mean drunk, particularly when money was involved.

The Ridgewood assholes nicknamed Evan "Kmart." He hated them for it but would smile and take it. If he didn't protest, the assholes lost interest and moved on. *A pilgrim in an unholy land,* he thought now.

On one occasion, a young, Ivy League English teacher named Mr. Winnifield sarcastically suggested that Evan upgrade his sole blue blazer before the glue gave out and it fell to the ground in patchwork pieces. Winnifield got a good laugh from the crowd. Evan laughed too. That evening Evan typed an anonymous letter to Winnifield's petite, tennis-playing wife, the teacher's raison d'être based on the number of photographs of her on his home room desk and bookshelf.

> *Dear Mrs. Winnifield,*
> *It is with great regret and a troubled heart that I write this letter to you.*
>
> *Last week I discovered that my wife is having an affair with your husband, Kevin Winnifield. I confronted my wife and she*

did not deny it, but swore it was over. For both our sakes I pray she is telling the truth.

Apparently they met through Ridgewood Academy, although my wife only volunteers occasionally. She says your husband is a master of deceit and very careful—he has had previous affairs and would never be caught. After much deliberation, I decided you deserve to know the truth. We both deserve to know the truth.

Good luck and God bless you,

Anonymous

Mr. Winnifield didn't make many jokes after that; in fact, he morphed into a short-tempered, neurotic dick.

"*How are you* today?" Evan would ask with troubled concern.

"Fine, Evan. *Fine.*"

"That's good to hear. And how is your lovely bride?"

By the end of the spring semester, the framed pictures were gone and rumors circulated that Mr. Winnifield's wife had left him and he had found comfort in a bottle of Jack Daniel's. He didn't return to Ridgewood in the fall. When Evan heard the triumphant news, he celebrated with a single fist-pump.

"Pardon me, Lydia."

"Just your type," Lydia repeated. "Pretty, thin . . ."

"Good heavens, Lydia, I'm sure Evan doesn't require any assistance with the ladies." Marshall had returned, carrying a silver tray with a pitcher of gin and tonics and three exquisite crystal tumblers.

"Why Marshall! Will we be getting tipsy this lovely afternoon?"

"I say, why not? We'll keep Andrew in the pool and have him drive his new G63 to Nick and Toni's tonight. Bonnie has reserved a first-rate table for us, I'm sure. How's that sound?"

Marshall handed Evan a stiff gin and tonic. Marshall didn't know Bonnie Munshin, had only seen her work the room at the restaurant and read about her in the *Times,* but he impressed himself with the skillful reference. Lydia was also pleased. She took a healthy sip of her drink.

"Sounds ideal, Marshall. Simply ideal."

They comfortably sat in silence, gazing out the picture window at the pool and woods behind, allowing the alcohol to do its job. The bucolic scene and Andrew's rhythmic strokes were hypnotic. As the Christofle IV dripped its liquid relaxation into Evan's veins, he lost his past, lost his identity, and willfully entered the hollow dream. When he noticed his reflection in the bay window, he whispered, "I did it. This is where I belong."

CHAPTER

THIRTEEN

Evan broke the silence. "What's her name, your niece?" He silently added, *If you say Darien Taylor I'll shit twice and howl at the moon.*

"Marin," Lydia replied. "Marshall's brother's eldest daughter."

The content threesome had just finished G&T round two.

"And she lives in the city?"

"Oh yes, Upper East Side, a lovely prewar junior four between Fifth and Madison. Doorman building."

"Of course."

"She just recently broke with her boyfriend Chad. He graduated from Stanford Law and decided to go with one of those upstart Silicon Valley firms. Marin couldn't bear the thought of leaving the city and moving to the *Left Coast*, as she calls it. Plus, she had tired of the long-distance romance."

Marshall grunted. Evan wasn't sure why.

"She's a positively *splendid* human being. She's an accessories design executive at Louis Vuitton and recently cochaired the Junior Gala at the Guggenheim!" Lydia's voice rose an octave with excitement as she spoke. "Just a splendid—"

As if on cue, the crunch of car tires sounded on the gravel driveway. Marin Owen had arrived.

Lydia jumped up and acrobatically maneuvered between the end table and the Jackson Press. She noticed Evan's surprised expression.

"SoulCycle," she said over her shoulder with a wink and a smile.

"Precious angel, you made it!"

"Hello Auntie Lydia. Sorry I'm late. I stopped at the Barn for Stacey's four o'clock."

Evan could hear the voices behind him. The sound of family made him visibly shudder, like a damp January chill running down his spine.

The door closed and a heavy bag dropped on the hardwood floor.

"Evan, come meet Marin."

"Aunt Lydia! You didn't tell me you had company." She did her best to mask her irritation, but she failed.

"Oh please darling, you're an angel."

Evan stood and had to briefly steady himself. In his mind's eye he pictured the hefty Minnie Driver in the movie *Circle of Friends*. He turned toward the front door.

Holy shit. Tie me to the bedpost. Tie. Me. To. The. Bed. Post. The Eve 6 song played in his head.

Evan's eyes watered, his retinas burned. Marin Owen was white-hot. Literally. Her white-blond hair was pulled back in a tight ponytail. Her tan skin glistened with post-exertion sweat. Her flawless face was truly angelic, no makeup and none required. Perfect eyes. Perfect nose. Perfect lips. *Women would kill for her eyebrows.*

As he took a tentative step forward, Evan let his eyes wander down her body. *Kill me now*, he absentmindedly mouthed. Marin had a remarkable set of full buoyant breasts that didn't match her athletic frame. She wore clinging white workout pants, thin cotton with an almost terry-cloth look. She had dangerously rolled down the waistband well below her hips. Evan could see at least six inches of prime real estate below her belly button. Her white panties were visible beneath the thin material, seductively contrasting with her tan skin.

On top she wore only a white sports bra, cut low and seemingly barely able to contain her. The air-conditioning had hardened her nipples and

Evan could see their tantalizing pink outline under the white spandex. *Please. For the love of all things holy. Kill me now.*

The entirety of the vision was more than he could bear. He feared he would hyperventilate, drool uncontrollably, and pass out. Seriously.

Evan forced himself to look at Marin's Debi Mazar blue *eyes* as he crossed the room.

"Marin, may I present Evan Stoess? He's a rising star at Marshall's company. Evan, Marin Owen."

"Please pardon my appearance," Marin said as she extended her hand. "I wasn't expecting guests."

"No problem," Evan replied as he accepted her firm handshake. Like her aunt, Marin conveyed a sense of secure confidence Evan immediately associated with wealth and social privilege. Despite the fact that her ample assets were far and away the most impressive and powerful presence in the room, she showed nary a hint of shyness nor embarrassment.

They maintained eye contact for an extra second and Evan's heart exploded in his chest. She couldn't be real. She couldn't be *here,* in his boss's Hamptons entry hall. It just wasn't possible.

Lydia spoke.

"After that spin, you probably want to shower. You're upstairs in your usual orchid bedroom. We'll have a fresh batch of drinks waiting when you come down. Dinner isn't until eight, so plenty of time. *Say hello, Marshall.*"

"Hello Marin," Marshall yelled from his chair in the window.

"Hello Uncle Marshall," Marin replied, touching Evan's shoulder as she leaned around him to see her uncle across the room. "I'll be down in a few minutes."

"Okay darling."

Evan reached for her Monogramouflage Louis Vuitton weekend bag but Marin grabbed it before he could get there.

"Don't worry, I can manage." She smiled at Evan and bounded up the stairs, the heavy bag tightening her toned triceps muscle. Evan and Lydia watched her climb the staircase, Evan admiring what he could now see were tiny white thong panties. When she disappeared around the corner, he looked at Lydia.

"SoulCycle," she remarked.

CHAPTER
FOURTEEN

Evan sat on a designer sofa in East Hampton sipping deliciously dry Bombay Sapphire gin from Christofle crystal. The supple leather was a beautiful, rich pearl color. He recalled the last time he sat on a pearl-colored cushion, faded, ripped and stained. He and his mother were in a grimy New Jersey emergency room. Faye Stoess pressed a soiled dish towel to her bleeding forehead.

"Sorry to see you again, Ms. Stoess," the doctor said. Evan was eight years old. Their neighbor, Kitty Gee Crenshaw, sat by his side.

"Oh, I'm so clumsy. I slipped and hit my head on the kitchen counter."

"Ms. Stoess—"

"Doctor, I *fell*. I'll try to be more careful."

Visibly concerned, he replied "Well, if you 'fall' again, I'll have to report it to the police. Do you understand?"

Kitty Gee cringed. Evan nodded his head.

"That won't be necessary," Faye replied as the MD turned his attention to a new arrival.

Faye turned to her neighbor. "Thanks for coming, Kitty Gee. It'll be awhile before they get back to me. Would you mind driving Evan home? George should be out by now."

"Sure, Faye, no problem. What did you do this time?"

Faye sighed, tired and broken. "I told him I'm pregnant."

•   •   •

Back at Pleasant Grove, Evan peered through the screen door.

A drunk George Stoess paced clumsily in their double-wide, mumbling to himself.

"Goddamned bitch got knocked up. How the fuck am I supposed to pay for that shit? Bitch thinks money grows on trees. Not *my* money. I told her . . . I told her . . . but she won't ever fuckin' listen to me . . . god*dammit* . . . bitch . . . got what she deserved . . ."

George finally collapsed in a *Brady Bunch*-era La-Z-Boy, a thin and thready stream of urine circumventing his swollen prostate and staining his sweatpants and the chair's putrid cushion. He passed out and dropped his Schlitz tall boy on the shag. Evan quietly opened the screen door and snuck past George. He slept under his bed that night. When he left the next morning for school, George hadn't moved. Little Evan hoped he was dead.

It was one hundred and twenty steps from the double-wide to Evan's bus stop. Ridgewood's private bus service picked him up first and dropped him off last.

Boarding the bus with the bone-colored dawn, mornings weren't a problem. Pleasant Grove's resident SNAPs were not early risers. But in the afternoon, if his bus was five minutes late and the public school kids were already home, the one hundred and twenty steps were a terrifying gauntlet, an inglorious Via Dolorosa.

Gus Mally was the worst. His dad was the mayor of Pleasant Grove and therefore the chief warden. On good days, Gus would get in Evan's face and scream at him. *"Who the fuck do you think you are? You think you're better than us 'cause you wear a faggot-ass tie to school? You suck, Richie. You ain't nothin' and my daddy says your momma's a whore!"*

Richie. At Ridgewood, Evan was Kmart. At home, he was Richie. Even George adopted the moniker.

On bad days, Gus and the other kids threw rocks at Evan. Not pebbles, *rocks*. Evan learned early not to run. If he ran, they smelled blood and would chase him down. So, shielding his face with his Trapper Keeper, Richie walked. One hundred and twenty steps.

FIFTEEN

Evan had never walked a red carpet, never attended an event *with* a red carpet, but he imagined walking into Nick & Toni's on a perfect summer Saturday came pretty close.

He had a difficult time containing his excitement. The urge to pump his fists and cheer nearly got the best of him. Despite the three stiff drinks, his mind was crystal clear. It was like the first CNBC interview—he was in the zone.

Hot Chloë insisted that Marshall sit in the passenger seat of Andrew's new Benz, so Evan found himself wedged comfortably between her and Marin for the ten-minute ride south to the village restaurant. Andrew activated Pandora and Evan hummed along with the tune. *Got you where I want you.*

Marin smelled like fresh flowers and wore a white sundress and sandals. Extraordinary. For a second, while rounding a sharp curve, Evan's elbow touched her left breast, and his pulse doubled. *Sweeeet.* He felt like a horny seventeen-year-old. Horny and smitten.

The freakin' *parking lot* was an adrenaline rush. Several Ferraris didn't attract a second look, but a coven of unfulfilled man-boys in linen pants with freshly Bumbled coifs swarmed a new Lamborghini Egoista. Andrew's

G 63 AMG found rest in the rear of the lot, between a vintage Jaguar E-Type and a glowing BMW i8.

As the six of them crossed the parking lot to the elegant French-door entrance, Marin took Evan's arm. A wave of unexpected calmness enveloped him. Anticipating only nausea, Evan relaxed, fell in step with Marin behind Marshall and Lydia, and approached the red carpet.

Those unfortunate untouchables without reservations watched the group glide through the entryway, past Bonnie's podium and bar area, and into the front dining room as if they were royalty. Evan loved it, a parade of envious stares and, he was sure, whispers.

Nearing their table, a middle-aged gentleman returning to his seat in Siberia did a double take.

"I know you!" he exclaimed to Evan, pointing. "You're Evan Stoess, the Alzheimer's drug guy from CNBC!"

"That I am. I hope you're buying Medipharm."

"Damn straight. It's paying for my dinner tonight. You enjoy your meal, okay?"

Evan nodded and began to feel his sense of wonder evaporate. Perhaps it wasn't a mistake? Perhaps he belonged here, with these people. He'd earned it, hadn't he?

As they were seated, the group could sense the many eyes on them of the people who had heard the brief exchange. An attractive young lady, late teens or early twenties, hopped up from the adjacent table and eagerly approached Evan.

"Mr. Stoess, I'm Sofia Lalas. I'm an intern at Morgan and watch CNBC all day. I'd love to work for you after I graduate."

Evan fished a business card out of his front pocket and offered it to her with a smile.

"ECM is a great firm to work for, the best. I'll look forward to hearing from you. Good luck with school."

Sofia Lalas beamed, held the card with two hands like it was a priceless objet d'art, and returned to her seat.

"Quite the celebrity," Lydia said proudly to the entire table with raised eyebrows. "How exciting."

Later in the evening, when Marshall ordered the table's fourth bottle of Opus One, Bonnie herself made a brief appearance. When she departed to check on Lorne Michaels and Jimmy Fallon at the coveted table number twenty, Lydia threw up her hands, proud and purposeful, and declared it "the best night ever." Had he gotten laid, Evan concluded the next morning, she would have been right.

Instead, it was *nearly* the best night ever. Evan had his "A" game going. Witty and fluent, he charmed the crowd as he retreated to Ridgewood, but for the first time not as Kmart. He was Evan Stoess. He could talk to these people. He was indeed one of them.

Evan thought Marin was impressed, and as they left the crowded restaurant she took his hand and led the way. They paid quick homage to the canine mosaic, nodded respectfully to Kelly Ripa and Mark Consuelos, and congratulated Bonnie and Carolyn on the delectable antelope. Outside, even at the late hour, anticipatory diners continued to mill about, pleading eyes darting to and fro, like sheep waiting to be sheared. Evan savored the moment, larger than life, and vowed never to forget it.

Back at the house, approaching midnight, the happily sauced group sat around the lighted pool. Lydia made Irish coffees for the ladies; Marshall poured "real" single malts for the boys while bitterly cursing someone or something named "Yamazaki."

"When are you going back?" Marin asked Evan, almost in a whisper.

"I was thinking about the four o'clock Jitney, if that's okay with you, Lydia?"

"Why certainly Evan. Stay as long as you like."

"If you can stay until Monday morning," Marin interjected, "you're welcome to ride back with me. You'll be in the office by noon, I promise." She raised her finely threaded white-blond eyebrows and looked toward Marshall.

"Fine with me. Andrew, do we need Evan in the office first thing on Monday?"

"I think we can survive without him."

"Splendid," Lydia announced, and then, for no apparent reason, added, "Before long Evan will have his own house in the Hamptons."

With that, Marin rested her head on Evan's shoulder.

When Evan's eyes opened the next morning, his first thought was Marin. She had retired with the ladies while the gentlemen finished their Lagavulin. Despite the many libations, his head was clear and he was ready for action.

He quickly showered and shaved, Listerined and flossed, and pulled on a pair of navy blue linen shorts and a crisp white button-down Polo shirt. Standing in front of the mirror, he debated how many buttons to leave open. He went with two.

Downstairs hot Chloë prepared egg white omelettes while the other "adults" perused the Sunday *Times*. Lydia sensed Evan's unspoken question.

"Marin went to an early Physique 57 class in Bridgehampton. She'll be back soon. Come sit. Eat."

Unfortunately, Evan's dream of seeing Marin Owen in a bikini went unfulfilled. Sunday in East Hampton turned out cloudy with steady rain. The group drove out to Montauk for lobster rolls at Navy Beach, toured about for an hour or so, then returned to the house. Andrew and hot Chloë left for the suburbs before dinner. The remaining foursome went to Rowdy Hall for mussels and ribs.

Despite the weather, Evan was satisfied with the day. He and Marin seemed to get along pretty well; she shared that she was conceived in Marin County, hence her unusual name. The alcohol-inspired spell from the previous evening was gone, but he thought he'd advanced the ball. As they approached their table at the pub-like restaurant in the heart of East Hampton village, the weekend palpably winding down, Evan wondered when or if he'd see Marin again.

"Where are you next weekend?" Lydia asked Marin as iced teas arrived.

"I'm not sure, Auntie Lydia."

"Evan?"

"Hmm . . . let me think . . . I'm not sure either," Evan lied.

"Well, here's a thought," Lydia began. "Marshall and I will be upstate visiting Louise and Paul. Marshall, could Marin have the house for the weekend, perhaps invite Evan out again and a few other friends? How wonderful would that be?" Lydia winked and sported a cheerful matchmaker's grin.

Evan choked on his drink. *Holy shit, Lydia!* he wanted to say. *Are you freakin' kidding me?* The ensuing second of silence was maliciously painful. *Well, at least rejection will be quick. No need to waste time.*

"That would be wonderful, Auntie Lydia. Thank you. Uncle Marshall?"

"Sure. Fine with me."

Blood returned to Evan's brain and Handel's Hallelujah Chorus played in his head. He considered a quick Tiger Woods fist-pump but decided not to tip his hand. *A Festivus for the rest of us!* He said to himself. But then he forced himself to calmly reply.

"Should work for me. Yeah, sure, count me in."

"Splendid," Lydia said, turning to Marin and placing her hand on Marin's arm. "Shall we make dinner reservations? Call Jean-Luc? Or Sunset Beach? I read in *Dan's* about Saint Tropez Saturdays. Would you like to host a barbeque? Marshall could put up the badminton net."

Marshall grunted and, while his wife and niece discussed all-important dinner reservations and party plans, turned his attention to Evan.

"Well, you clearly have Lydia's seal of approval. We're closing the first Medipharm deal this week, the PIPE?"

Evan sat up straight to reply.

"Yes sir. The closing is scheduled for Friday. The firm will do quite well. The institutions jumped on the deal and Mark and Andrew negotiated eight and a half percent."

"Eight and a half. That's right. Fantastic. Remind me how much Mark and Andrew promised you."

"Two hundred thousand at the close," Evan responded tentatively.

"Fair enough." Motioning to Marin, Marshall added, "You'll need every penny."

Evan turned his gaze to her.

Ah, lustrous Marin, my Ginevra. But poor boys shouldn't think of marrying rich girls. Poor boys are always on the outside, looking in. Fitzgerald knew it, and lived it, but he had nothing on me.

CHAPTER
SIXTEEN

Fleur's jaw dropped and her eyes bugged when she heard the number.

"Two hundred *thousand*? You're kidding."

"Nope," Evan replied with an insouciant arrogance lost on Fleur. "I'll have the money on Friday. *Money*, Fleur. Money I *earned*. 'Run for your life from any man who tells you that money is evil,'" Evan quoted from memory. "That statement is the leper's bell of an approaching looter."

"Okay, right, I'll remember that," Fleur said with a funny look on her face. "The shit you say sometimes. But now it's party time, neighbor. Buy me a television?"

"Eat what you kill, my Kiwi flower. Eat what you kill."

"'Eat what you kill'?" Fleur inquired. "Is that, like, a Ted Nugent thing? You can only eat it if you kill it yourself?"

Evan laughed. "Pretty much, actually. 'Eat what you kill' means you get paid based on business you bring in yourself. Small salary, sometimes no salary at all. But unlimited top end. Make money for your firm, make money for yourself. No unearned rewards and no unrewarded duties, as Rand taught. It's how the world *should* work."

"So, basically, you get a percentage of the money you bring in, no matter how much?"

"Or how little, yes."

"Eat what you kill," Fleur mused.

"Eat what you kill."

Fleur and Evan were sitting on his Jennifer Convertible sofa on Monday night waiting for *Seinfeld* to start. He was giving her a play-by-play of the past weekend.

"And how was the drive back this morning? Did you *bump her* in the L.I.E. *bumper-to-bumper*?"

"God, that's horrible. No. A couple of Marin's friends called needing a ride so I ended up in the backseat talking to a boring high school friend named Kaylee."

"That sucks. But, next week . . . oh . . . hold on . . . this is a good one . . . the Kramerica intern episode."

Twelve minutes later the conversation resumed.

"So, Mr. Stoess, I guess you'll be moving."

"Huh?"

"Two hundred grand? Plus the megacash before? You should be a-movin'-on-up."

"To the east side?"

"To a deee-luxe apartment, in the sky-hi-hi," Fleur sang. "Clearly I'm watching *waaaaay* too much Nick at Nite."

"You're right, though. Maybe a pre-war junior four in the East Sixties somewhere. I'll call an agent next week when the cash is in the bank. Good idea." Evan nodded contently, certain that Lydia Owen would share the name of a fashionable Upper East Side broker.

"Shhh! It's back."

Fifteen minutes later.

"What else is going on this week?"

"Let's see . . . two interviews, Fox Business and CNBC again, a short speech at some analyst's conference on Wednesday, then, on Thursday, a noon press conference with a bunch of Hollywood types about increased Alzheimer's funding before the big deal closes on Friday."

"You're kidding."

"Nope."

"*Then* you leave with Miss Perfect for your weekend in the Hamptons?"

"Yeah, I guess I do."

"Evan Stoess, you have arrived."

Evan didn't respond, couldn't respond. A strange feeling overcame him, determined yet vague. For the first time in his life, he had something to lose. *Hope.*

CHAPTER

SEVENTEEN

Drew Connor greeted Evan outside the Time Warner Center on Columbus Circle. He looked concerned.

"Thank God you're here. We're still waiting on Jennifer Lawrence and Mr. De Niro." As Executive Director of the Alzheimer's Association of America, today was Drew's big day.

"You were *amazing* on *Power Lunch* yesterday, and I heard you plugged us on Fox on Tuesday. Many thanks."

"Of course. The others are here then?" Evan inquired. Juliette Auberge, the Oscar-winning actress recently diagnosed with Alzheimer's and Medipharm's most vocal fan, was flying in from Los Angeles.

"Yes, we should have four Oscar winners before it's all over. Jennifer is actually from Louisville, so she's super-excited to be involved. And all of them—"

"Excellent. Let's do it." Evan adjusted his sterling silver Tiffany cuff links and headed toward the entrance.

Over the past few days, Evan's astonishment with his semi-celebrity status had transformed into an impatient arrogance. He relished it, the empowering feeling of fame and near fortune.

After the press conference, Evan stood arm in arm in the Mandarin

Oriental's ballroom with four Oscar winners while dozens of photographers snapped away. The group then boarded an Escalade limo for a trip downtown to a reception at the SoHo outlet of Cipriani. *"Fuck that Prius bullshit, we travel in style,"* someone said. In the limo he conversed comfortably with his famous companions, ignoring the vibrating cell phone in his pocket. Finally, irritated at the incessant distraction, he answered the phone. The display showed ECM.

"Goddammit, what?"

"It's *Andrew.* I need you at four for the Calpers conference call."

"No. You handle it." Silence.

"They want *you*, Evan."

"What part of *no* don't you understand? Handle it."

Evan tapped END impatiently and rolled his eyes. Miss Lawrence flashed a coy smile.

Evan stepped out of Cipriani Downtown at about five o'clock, semi-drunk and full-on ecstatic. The behemoth Escalade was gone but had been replaced by a half dozen black S600 Pullman sedans. He jumped in the first one.

Marin had e-mailed his BlackBerry-*crackberry* and invited him to meet her and a few friends at a new restaurant on Cornelia Street. Two of the dinner companions would be joining them in East Hampton and Marin wanted Evan to meet them. They had seen the press conference. *On the way little lady*, he texted back to her.

Traveling up Sixth Avenue, Evan looked at his watch and wondered how high Medipharm closed after the day's across-the-spectrum, CNBC to E! publicity. "How much money did I make today?" he asked the startled driver.

A thousand miles away, at the same moment, Mitch LeMaire looked at his watch, wondered the same thing, and began his run in Cherokee Park. He had to run fast to get to the airport for his flight to New York and paper millions.

CHAPTER

EIGHTEEN

During the ride north, Evan admonished himself. *Be cool. They're sober, remember. Be cool.* Climbing out of the Pullman, he put on a serious expression and buttoned the top two buttons of his Tom Ford suit coat; it was, after all, barely six o'clock.

But as he entered the shoe box–sized establishment, he couldn't help but smile. Marin and her four companions were on their feet, standing around a six-top table, clapping and cheering Evan's arrival. In Evan's mind, nothing more deserving had ever occurred in recorded history.

He held up his hands in mock submission. "Please, ladies and gentleman, hold your applause. Throw money yes, but, please, hold your applause." The group laughed, perhaps genuinely.

"You don't need any more of my family's money, Mr. Stoess." Marin said.

"So true, Miss Marin, *so true.*"

For the next ninety minutes, Marin and her friends fawned over Evan like starstruck teenagers. Gazing at Marin as she discussed the weekend's plans with Jodi and Felicia, Evan struggled to suppress the familiar pop pablum his mother served up 8-track-style over and over two decades earlier. *Before I go insane I hold my pillow to my head and spring up in my bed screaming out the words I dread I think I love you. I think I love you.*

After a few bottles of first-growth red wine, of which Evan drank little, the group entered that comfortable social zone where everyone talks but nobody listens. Six people, six conversations. Then Jodi asked Marin how she and Evan met, and the table quieted down to listen. Marin grabbed Evan's hand and recounted the story as if it were legend. *The rising star . . . East Hampton . . . Stacey Griffith . . . Nick & Toni's!* Evan sat back and wondered, *Is this what it's like to be a couple?* He had never felt more sublimely content.

After the story the group returned to all-talk mode, until their server approached suggesting an after-dinner drink.

"It's still early, why not?" Marin decided. Evan was the last to order.

"Lagavulin. Twelve year. Don't waste my time with the sixteen, okay? *Okay?*"

"Yes, sir."

The only other male at the table, an aspiring milquetoast novelist named Samuel, remarked, "You know your single malts, I see."

"Of course," Evan responded dismissively to the "man" he deemed a parasite and likened to kale.

The bill arrived and Evan presented his Platinum ECM Amex. "Please, let me." Felicia smiled at Marin and said, "Quite the gentleman." Marin rested her hand on Evan's thigh, leaned into him, and thanked him with a kiss on the cheek.

"No problem. Next time the card'll be *black*," he said so everyone could hear. And thanks to the liquid courage, Evan whispered into Marin's ear, "Where should I take you now? Home, perhaps?"

Marin demurred slightly, and with a tilted head and sly smile, hinted, "You can wait til this weekend."

With that every neuron in Evan's body fired simultaneously, a rush he likened to crack cocaine.

"If I must, Miss Marin. I can wait."

"You must. But it will be worth it. *Trust me.*" With a wink, Marin was on her feet, leading the group out onto the Village sidewalk.

Evan sat for a moment and exhaled audibly before standing to follow the boisterous friends. That vague feeling again. If the weight of hope could kill, Evan would be its first victim.

CHAPTER
NINETEEN

Sufficiently sober, Evan decided to stop by his office on the way home to make sure the conference room had been properly prepared for the Medipharm closing the next morning. The closing would, after all, put two hundred thousand dollars in his pocket and set the stage for much, *much* more.

Two dozen tall stacks of documents rimmed the massive table, ready to be signed, ready to fund Medipharm's wonder drug, ready to make a handful of people fabulously rich. If all went well, Evan would have plenty of time to pick up a case of Veuve before leaving in Marin's BMW for East Hampton. *Next time we'll take* my *new Boxster*, Evan thought as he straightened his stack of documents, to the right of Marshall's seat at the head of the table. Evan noticed Mitch's documents and wondered if his Delta flight had landed at LaGuardia on time. He thought about calling Mitch's mobile phone, but instead checked his own devices. No missed calls, no text messages, no e-mails, no IMs, no voice messages. *All's well in the world.*

On his way out, Evan passed his office. His screensaver scrolled across his flat-panel monitor, *Greed is Good Greed is Good Greed is Good,* so he sat down to check Bloomberg's "In the News" for the latest coverage of his spectacular press conference before powering down for the night.

He read the top headline and violently vomited in his wastebasket.

MEDIPHARM FOUNDER DEAD:
BODY DISCOVERED IN PARK

23 minutes ago
By Emily Thomas, Associated Press Writer

Louisville, KY—The body of Dr. Mitchell I. LeMaire, Medipharm founder and research scientist, was discovered in a Louisville park by local AP Bureau Chief Mark Seagate earlier this evening. LeMaire, who was dressed in jogging attire, is the presumed victim of a fatal heart attack.

Medipharm's stock closed today at $25.50, up $3.50. Trading is expected to be delayed on Friday.

Developing story.

As he slumped to the floor, breathless and crushed, his phone vibrated. It didn't stop until he mustered the energy to turn it off. Evan faded out. He lay there unconscious, a trickle of bile pooling by his ashen cheek.

Twenty minutes later perhaps, he didn't really know for sure, Evan managed to get up off his floor, leave his office and catch a cab for the short ride to his apartment. He looked like warmed-over offal, a pale zombie reject with regurgitated truffles on his collar. The cabbie noticed.

"You all right, man?"

"Huh?"

"You all right?"

"Cockroach," Evan mumbled to himself, barely audible through the cab's scratched and foggy security partition. "Cockroach."

"You'll be home in a sec."

Cockroach. The only thought Evan could entertain was of a cockroach he had caught in his kitchen that morning and dropped in his toilet. He watched the nasty critter struggle against the downward spiral of the flush, doomed yet determined. As the water spun, eventually the cockroach stopped swimming and accepted his fate. *Sorry, little buddy,* Evan thought now, assuming he would suffer a similar demise. *I'll be joining you soon, I fear.*

CHAPTER
TWENTY

When Evan's eyes opened the next morning, he hoped for a second it had all been a nightmare. *The mother of all nightmares, that is.* He sat up in bed, took a deep breath, and went into damage-control mode. *All those lab rats at the Louisville Medical Center. Surely Mitch had partners, colleagues, something. The deal may not close today. But Monday, yes, on Monday the PIPE will close and I'll have my money.*

His home phone rang. Andrew from his office. Evan took a deep breath, exhaled slowly.

"Andrew, how bad is it?"

"It's just breaking on FBC and CNBC, but it looks bad, Evan. *Really . . . bad.* That vulture Ben Rivera can smell blood. Get in here. Marshall wants LeMaire's team on a con call ASAP. Who's the number-two guy?"

"I don't know." Silence. Evan could hear the wail of a siren passing outside ECM's office.

"*You don't know?* Get in here. *Now.*"

Despite the sickly sour scent of alcohol and desperation, *the world's worst cologne*, Evan skipped the shower. As he dressed, he turned on CNBC and an energized Ben Rivera greeted him.

"The big story this morning is once again Medipharm. Dr. Mitchell

LeMaire, Medipharm's founder, was found dead yesterday evening in a Louisville park. Early reports are he suffered an exercise-induced heart attack. The stock closed at $25.50 yesterday before the news, an all-time high. Trading has been halted today until approximately noon, according to the NASD. We turn now to Jonathan Wilder, an NBC correspondent in Louisville. Jonathan, can Medipharm recover?"

Evan peered out his dirty bathroom at the television. Jonathan Wilder was split-screen with Ben the Jerk, standing in front of the Louisville Medical Center.

"Well, Ben, it doesn't look good. I've been talking to people here at the Medical Center all morning, and the word is Medipharm was a one-man show, and that one man is now deceased. Very sad news for Alzheimer's victims and the development of Medipharm's revolutionary new treatment."

"Sad, indeed. Earlier this morning we heard Dr. LeMaire described as a 'lone wolf.' Does that description fit, Jonathan, and what are the implications for Medipharm?"

"I won't speak for the company's stock, Ben; that's your job. But all indications are that Dr. LeMaire worked alone and preferred to keep his work . . . *confidential*, if you will. I spoke to a researcher late yesterday who asked to remain anonymous. She said Dr. LeMaire was often asked to share his research and clinical process, but he refused."

"Thank you, Jonathan. We'll certainly return to you later in the hour for an update. And we'll be back with more on this developing story."

Evan was numb. The phone rang. He answered but didn't say a word.

"Did you hear that? Evan? Evan, *what have you done*?"

It was Andrew. He sounded exhausted, like he'd just completed a marathon.

"The trading desk says the stock will open below ten. *Below ten.* Customers are calling, going berserk. Marshall is enraged; I've never seen him like this. We trusted you." Andrew sighed. Evan could feel the blood pool in his bare feet and his vision went muddy. *The cockroach had it easy.*

Unable to comprehend the events unfolding around him, he stammered, "The closing?"

Andrew's exhaustion transformed to fury.

"*Goddammit you stupid moron! Get your head out of your ass! No closing. NO CLOSING. Medipharm is done. DONE! If what we're hearing is true, ten is a fucking gift!*"

"Andrew, it can . . . it can recover," Evan stammered.

"No, Evan, Medipharm is done, a penny stock again. And we were buying at twenty dollars. All our best customers, margined to the hilt. 'One-man show.' 'Lone wolf.' What the hell was I thinking? Just get down here." Andrew hung up before Evan could respond.

He's right, Evan acknowledged. *Medipharm is done, and possibly ECM as well. Worse, I am done. The fat banking fee. My two hundred thousand.*

Riding down Second Avenue in a cab, Evan could only think of one thing.

Marin. Oh my god, Marin. My Ginevra. Poor boys shouldn't think of marrying rich girls. Poor boys are always on the outside looking in. I will die on the outside. I will never escape. I will never belong.

He wiped his wet eyes with a monogrammed handkerchief.

CHAPTER

TWENTY-ONE

Evan stood outside ECM's doors, looking in. He could sense the panicked energy. He pushed open the doors with resolve and stepped inside; the receptionist smiled meekly at him but didn't say a word.

Rounding a corner, he paused and looked across the open room of desks to his glass-walled office. Marshall, Andrew and Mark were waiting, along with a couple of men Evan recognized as ECM's attorneys. *Well, that's something at least—I finally managed to get them in my office.*

Andrew saw Evan and held up his hand, a stop sign signaling Evan to stay put. He turned to Marshall and said a few words. Marshall Owen squinted his eyes and craned his neck from behind Evan's desk to get a look at the source of his discontent. He scowled and turned back to Andrew, barking orders. Evan waited and watched.

I'll be the scapegoat. What did Andrew say a lifetime ago? Hero or goat. I killed it and now I'll choke on it.

Andrew left Evan's office, shaking his head, and quickly approached Evan.

"Let's talk in the conference room. *Now.*" Andrew grabbed Evan's elbow like he was Matthew Poncelet and directed him down the hall. *Dead Man Walking.*

"Okay, here's how it going to work. Our liability exposure is huge, Evan, *huge*. You are terminated. You mislead the firm, and you alone. You will not say a word to the media or anyone. *Not a fucking word*. Marshall is leaving for CNBC in ten minutes to pin this whole bullshit fiasco on a rogue analyst. *You*. We're holding all your files, your research, as evidence, and we will be cooperating with authorities."

"But . . . can I . . ."

"No."

"But . . ." Evan wasn't sure what he intended to ask. *Something.*

"What part of *no* don't you understand? Now get out."

As Evan turned and walked away, Andrew knew how to finish him. "And you're not going *anywhere* this weekend. Marshall spoke to Marin. I wouldn't be expecting her call, if I were you. *Ever.*"

When he staggered into his apartment sixty minutes later, Evan's television was still on, broadcasting his doom. After asking the corner liquor store clerk for a bottle of hemlock, he had settled for a pint of Jack Daniel's. Medipharm's stock had opened at $9 and was free-falling. Dickhead Ben Rivera was enjoying the bloodbath.

"In addition to Medipharm's shareholders and Alzheimer's sufferers everywhere, Equity Capital Management and its young analyst Evan Stoess are the big losers today. Our sources say at least two class action lawsuits are already in the works against ECM for its negligent research and illegal stock pumping. We'll have ECM head Marshall Owen in the studio shortly, but in a statement released by ECM's attorneys moments ago, the firm squarely placed the blame on novice analyst Evan Stoess and noted he has been summarily terminated. So unfortunate." Ben paused while the camera angle changed.

"At least one person is happy with today's events, however. Malcolm Kvamme, managing director of Contrafund, has held a large short position in Medipharm for several weeks. Mr. Kvamme?"

Malcolm Kvamme, a former college linebacker, blond and square-jawed, joined Ben on the split screen.

"Ben, let me stress to your viewers, we here at Contrafund are certainly not 'happy' with the tragic death of Dr. LeMaire, but we did question ECM's research and the stock's value from the very beginning."

"Of course. I didn't mean to imply . . ."

"I understand, and I hope your viewers understand that we mourn the tragic loss."

"Certainly. But your firm made millions today."

"Yes, we did."

Evan turned off the television, sipped the last of the Jack Daniel's, and fell back on his couch. *Well, at least someone made money today,* he thought as he slipped into oblivion.

PART II

'Tis better to be vile, than vile esteemed.

—WILLIAM SHAKESPEARE, SONNET 121

CHAPTER

TWENTY-TWO

Evan didn't bother to open his window shades, so he wasn't prepared for the nasty New York weather that rudely welcomed him to another Monday morning.

Not unusual in headache-gray January, the wind whipped snow and tiny ice pellets swirled and stung and actually appeared to fall *up*. Forgotten in his apartment, the three-dollar umbrella with the pointy black handle would have been useless anyway.

Looking pale and unhealthy, Evan was the quintessential city rat in a miserable race for nothing but the sad opportunity to run the race again tomorrow. If meaning could be found in a paycheck, Evan and his fellow zombies walking crosstown embraced the quest with the grim belief that they had no other choice.

As he walked, he daydreamed an empty room. The carpet and walls were benign beige, the folding chairs gunmetal gray. The coffin at the far end of the room was shiny steel.

In the wake of disaster, Evan Stoess spent many long hours contemplating his own death. *Who would notice? Who would care?* Just about anything could trigger it, any moment of heightened despair or a painful memory pulled from the ashes of What Almost Was.

Would there be a funeral? Would anyone say anything? Would people gather afterward over a tray of toxic cold cuts and lament the loss of Evan Stoess?

In sleep and in stupor, Evan dreamed about his own funeral and wake. In the scene he's an invisible intruder sent to measure the worth of his lost soul. The haunting image of an empty room caused him physical pain, alternatively adding to the despair and fueling his fragile resistance to fulfilling the nightmare by his own hand.

On occasion, a near-paralyzing fear would grip Evan, always a result of an unwanted reminder of his life lost. Or the image of the empty room.

Why not give in, give up, check out?

In his mind's eye he would see Geoffrey and Victoria Buchanan beaming unconditional love at their beautiful children in the backseat of a shiny silver Bentley, and he kept going.

On the street, pointed toward the subway station, Evan joined the endless queue and willingly slipped into autopilot, subconsciously aware of his surroundings yet sublimely unaware of his existence. Obligatory white earbuds provided a forlorn soundtrack: *"I'll drink enough of anything to make this world look new again, drunk drunk drunk in the gardens and the graves."* Sedated by the collective choice that swallowed them whole, Evan couldn't help but think that he and his fellow drones were marching toward their graves. *"I'll drink enough of anything to make* myself *look new again."*

Twenty minutes later, Evan stepped around a family of frigid tourists into an opulent, art deco office building, the syndicated 30 Rockefeller Plaza.

The elevator to the fortieth floor was packed with people, but Evan didn't notice. He heard the door open with a melancholy *ding. Do not ask for whom the bell tolls*, he thought to himself, stepping into an elegant reception area dominated by one word, CONTRAFUND. The young lady at the desk, blurry and faceless, offered her usual greeting, "Good morning Evan." Evan looked through her at first, waiting for her image to clear. *Ah, Maria, timid and beautiful with her short hair.*

"Hello, Rabbit," Evan whispered. The mental fog lifted, and Evan smiled, a bit of Ridgewood creeping back into his psyche.

. . .

Eighteen months prior, less than a week after the Medipharm debacle, Malcolm Kvamme called Evan and, after a two-hour sit-down, offered him a job as an assistant analyst at Contrafund. "You handled yourself extremely well before the meltdown," he said, "and you will again, someday, when the smoke clears." Evan, still numb from the soul-crushing trauma, graciously accepted, despite the thirty percent salary cut, and had spent his time at Contrafund doing equity research, primarily for Mac Kvamme.

Contrafund operated on the premise that it's easier to pick losers than winners. Its headquarters in Zurich was tremendously successful, almost prescient, at predicting major downturns in world markets. The New York office, small in comparison, focused on the U.S. equity markets and operated a well-regarded short fund that bet on stocks falling rather than rising. It, too, had been very successful, but not quite as profitable as the international operations.

Legally domiciled on the Isle of Man, Contrafund had one mysterious offshore investor, another Isle of Man corporation, the owner or owners of which was a popular topic at the water cooler. Not that Evan got involved in many water cooler discussions.

Despite having been with Contrafund for eighteen months, Evan didn't really know any of his coworkers. He kept to himself, in his isolated little cubicle close to Mac's office. Occasionally he heard people whisper about him, but even that had died down over the past year. From what he could surmise, his coworkers regarded him with an equal mix of pity and scorn, much like Evan's attitude about himself. He didn't hate them, he didn't *not* hate them; he didn't care.

Evan tolerated Mac, and they enjoyed a comfortable relationship. Mac understood Evan's desire to remain anonymous; after a few respectful rejections, he stopped inviting Evan to team lunches and other company functions, but when Mac left the office for one, he'd put a hand on Evan's shoulder and say, "Hold down the fort, okay?"

This Monday morning, as Evan entered Contrafund's open office area, an eerie silence greeted him. The appropriate number of drones were engaged in the appropriate level of ultimately pointless activity, but the sound was turned off. No mindless chatter about wasted weekends, no whiny shuffling of TPS reports, no bad jokes with accompanying fake laughter. Most important, no sickening "we're-friends-only-because-we-work-together" small talk. Evan liked it, though he didn't know why. He rounded a corner and saw who pushed the communal mute button.

Evan's cubicle sat outside Mac's glass-walled office, next to Mac's assistant. Inside the fishbowl, Evan could see Mac and another man known to visit once or twice a year and rumored to be Contrafund's mysterious European investor.

Both men sat on chairs opposite Mac's desk. Mac leaned forward, elbows on his knees, listening intently to the stranger's words. From the expression on his face, he was obviously concentrating, frequently nodding to convey attention and comprehension.

Mystery Man sat back comfortably with his left leg crossed deftly across his right. Lean and dark-haired, he wore a perfectly groomed goatee and an impressive bespoke Savile Row suit. One button on each cuff of his suit jacket elegantly remained open, a quiet testimony to its authenticity. Evan realized his look and demeanor bore a striking resemblance to Hans Gruber, the terrorist-thief character in the movie *Die Hard*. Content with this comparison, Evan decided to call the man "Hans" until his true identity was revealed. *What are you up to, Hans? Why are you in our office?*

Evan settled into his space and then pretended to rearrange files so he could stand and observe the action. As far as he could tell, Mac never uttered a word until he and Hans stood and shook hands. Mac handed Hans his cashmere Burberry topcoat and opened the office door. Evan quickly took his seat behind the thin cubicle wall, invisible to Mac and Hans. The men paused in the doorway and spoke.

Maybe Hans wasn't the best nickname, Evan mused when he heard the aristocratic British accent.

"Malcolm, I need not remind you that this war and associated economic upheaval have been very positive for our concern. World markets are down, and although some of my top coinvestors are . . . shall we say . . . suddenly *illiquid*, our global organization is forward of expectations."

"Yes, sir," Mac replied.

"Contrafund is up thirty percent for the year, but it must pull its weight. We will expect an appropriate rate of return by the end of the quarter."

Mac nodded dutifully and Hans perceptively softened.

"Unfortunately my schedule does not allow it, but upon my return we must take lunch at Per Se."

"I look forward to it," Mac replied as he escorted Hans past Evan's desk toward Contrafund's reception area and a waiting elevator.

Evan sensed a collective exhale and the sound level annoyingly returned to normal. Mac hurriedly returned to his office. Evan looked at him to say something but Mac preempted the attempt.

"Later."

Evan didn't respond.

CHAPTER
TWENTY-THREE

Three hours later, close to noon, Mac called Evan into his office.

"How are things going, chief?" Mac asked, with a paternal tone that both comforted and disturbed Evan.

"I'm okay, Mac. How are you?"

"Motivated. We have work to do. Contrafund has work to do."

"But the fund's up like thirty percent for the trailing twelve, and up—"

"Up thirty-two," Mac corrected. "Not good enough."

"Not good enough?"

"Not good enough. Our investors want our rate of return up to the level of their other ventures." Mac shook his head ruefully. "I'm sure they're aware, but they don't seem to care that here in the States our industry is under attack."

"They don't care?" Evan attempted to sound sympathetic, but in truth he agreed with Zurich. If Contrafund could pull forty or fifty percent in other markets, it should here too. No excuses.

"Evan, Contrafund *knows* things. Outside the U.S., out from under the prying eyes of all the regulators, particularly the SEC, Contrafund's principals are free to act on both what they know and what they can make happen. They're expecting and *demanding* the same performance from us."

"But that doesn't—"

"It doesn't matter to them that we're facing all these new rules and regulations . . . Rule 203 . . . Rule 105 . . . and a bunch of proposals are on the table that could actually make things *worse* for us. Have you heard that some Harvard douchebag is calling for a zero tolerance policy for nearly all settlement failures? Ridiculous!"

Evan nodded *yes*, conveying frustrated agreement with his well-meaning boss. He had read the memos from Contrafund's morose general counsel.

Securities and Exchange Commission Rule 203 of Regulation SHO, adopted just a month earlier, squelched short-term and exigent shorting opportunities by mandating "locate and delivery" requirements, functionally eradicating "naked" short-selling, or shorting shares without having borrowed them, in anticipation of quickly covering before delivery was necessary, or finding the shares later. In essence, Rule 203 made it tougher to make fast money shorting stock, betting on downturns, in the U.S. markets.

The new Rule 105 made it tougher to make money shorting stock, period. Public companies often register stock with the SEC, "put it on the shelf," and sell it later when they need cash or the timing is right. It wasn't uncommon for Contrafund to cover short sales by prearranging purchases of shares from these "shelf" registrations. This arrangement created the *appearance* that Contrafund was covering with open market shares, when in reality *new* shares were involved. The benevolent SEC deemed this strategy a "sham" and Rule 105 outlawed it.

A couple of other proposals were floating around that could further hobble Contrafund's ability to make money. One would prohibit short-sellers from withdrawing their profits from a successful position until after delivery of the underlying sold shares. Another would allow stock owners to opt out of allowing their stock to be borrowed for shorting. Brokerage firms would be forced to disclose the possibility of lending stock to the shorts and the right of individual owners to say *no*.

"You're right, Mac. Our industry is under assault from clueless ivory tower douchebags. But we'll have to get around it, find a way to make the money, find a way—"

"I know. That's why today I'm asking you to get in the game again. Time to contribute."

"Yes." Evan straightened up and squared his shoulders.

"It's been—what?—a couple of years, right? As far as I'm concerned, you're rehabilitated. Until that poor guy died, you were on top of it. A healthy young doctor has a heart attack? What the hell? You've survived long enough on a crappy base salary. It's time for you to get back in the game."

"Hell yes, it's time!" *Redemption time, that is, after eighteen months of toiling in numbing anonymity.* "I am ready."

"I know you are, Evan. And frankly, I'm desperate. When Baker and Eatherly left last month to start their own firm, well . . . they took a lot of opportunities with them. So forget about those companies that Tim and I gave you to review. Find something *new*. Get it back, Evan."

"Get it back?"

"What you had the day *before* Medipharm collapsed. I remember you on TV; it's why I hired you. Get it back, Evan. Can you do that?"

"I *will* do it, Mac."

"Excellent, because Zurich requested it directly."

"Seriously?" Evan was shocked that Hans-Zurich knew he existed.

"Seriously. Now go. Bring me an idea or two by Friday."

As Evan walked out of the office, Mac added with a smile, "Hey, Evan, don't forget—this time we *want* the stock to go down."

"And it will, Mac."

Get it back? Is it possible? Since he lost everything, Evan had been numb, surviving because he had no alternative. Or so he believed.

Get it back? Since he lost everything, Evan had been waiting for this moment. Hiding in the shadows, waiting to emerge.

Get it back? My money. My relevance. My Ginevra.

Evan left Mac's office, walked calmly to the restroom, and refunded his Cheerios in the toilet. Standing in front of the sink, he splashed water on his face and took a deep breath. He gazed into his own bloodshot eyes and exhaled slowly.

I. Will. Get. It. Back.

CHAPTER
TWENTY-FOUR

That night, Evan once again dreamt of his funeral.

But this time was different. The room wasn't empty. Live bodies filled the chairs surrounding his coffin. Faceless bodies, friend or foe, Evan did not know. But bodies nonetheless.

Deep from within his subconscious, a passage surfaced, a stray remnant from a Ridgewood French class: *J'ai eu un moment l'impression ridicule qu'ils étaient là pour me juger.*

For a moment I had an absurd impression they had come to sit in judgment of me.

Evan shifted in his sleep, fearfully doubting the absurdity.

When he awoke, only the passage remained. From *L'étranger*—*The Stranger*, by Albert Camus. At Ridgewood he was compelled to read it twice, once in the original French and once in English. He wrote a paper expressing his preference for the British translation's title, *The Outsider*. His teacher graded it a C– and told Evan to keep his preferences to himself. She kept a bottle of Jack Daniel's Tennessee Honey in the locked top drawer of her desk. With minimal effort, really an insult to his abilities, Evan had her fired.

Sitting up in bed, the winter sky still dark, Evan remembered his sophomore year, misplacing his copy of Camus' *protest against artificiality,* only to find it the next day. On the title page inside the front cover, somebody had written "Kmart's Autobiography" below *The Stranger.* Evan, predictably, convinced himself he didn't care. *Ridgewood assholes.* If he didn't care, he didn't feel the pain. If he didn't care, he beat them. At that moment, sitting in his bed, Evan vowed to report big news in the next Ridgewood alumni update. He recalled, *Et moi aussi, je me suis senti prêt à tout revivre.*

And I, too, felt ready to start life over again.

Evan shook off the fog of sleep, the words retreating to oblivion, and got ready for work. "One must imagine Sisyphus happy," Camus implored. And Evan smiled as he joined the crosstown queue.

CHAPTER
TWENTY-FIVE

By noon, Joshua Eliot Gotbaum's dealer was late. *Very* late. After a long night of clubbing, partying on Special K, Joshua desperately needed a pick-me-up. Joshua's "special" Special K was derived from a horse tranquilizer called ketamine hydrochloride; the hangover was, understandably, a problem. Joshua's dealer, Rufus, understood and always offered a solution. He paged Rufus at about ten thirty, and as a loyal and lucrative customer, Rufus usually arrived within an hour.

Joshua had been rudely awakened at ten in the morning by Ellen, his publicist's assistant, reminding him of a mid-afternoon awards presentation at the Jacob Javits Convention Center. The National Interactive Software Developers Association, "NISDA" to the nerds, was holding its annual trade show, and Joshua was receiving the Developer of the Year award at three o'clock.

As she hung up the phone, Ellen added, "And Phoebe says wear a coat and tie, okay?"

"I definitely need a little somethin-somethin," Joshua muttered to himself.

A few painful minutes later, the building's doorman buzzed him. Joshua reached for a small remote control and pushed a button, turning on a receiver and speaker built into the ceiling overhead.

"Yo!" he shouted at the ceiling.

A voice from above intoned, "Mr. Gotbaum, UPS is here. Special delivery, requires your signature."

"Finally. Send him up." He clicked the OFF button.

Rufus didn't miss a trick. He dressed in all "brown" and carried a nonfunctioning handheld device that looked like a real UPS tracking computer. With a box of product under his arm, he *was* the UPS guy. In New York's doorman buildings, Rufus had profitably surmised, discretion was a bonus and customers were willing to pay a premium for it.

By the time Joshua walked down his spiral staircase and opened the back service door of his two-story loft, Rufus was waiting.

"Rufus . . . *dude* . . . where you been?"

"Carnegie Hill, homeslice. It's a *hike* down here to Triangle Below Canal."

Rufus stepped into Joshua's spacious kitchen and helped himself to a Snapple from the Sub-Zero. Joshua sat on a stool at the kitchen's island, rubbing his temples.

"What can Brown do for you this fine morning?" Rufus asked, opening his Pandora's box.

"You should know."

"Shredded from my K blend?"

"Oh yeah." Joshua sighed loudly, with a long exhale. "I've got to be somewhere in a few hours. And in a goddam coat and tie."

Shaking a little bottle of pills, Rufus said, "I've got just what you need, my main man."

A few *speedy* hours later, Rufus-rejuvenated, Joshua stood on a stage in front of several hundred adoring fans. As instructed, he wore a black blazer, tan gabardine pants, a conservative blue dress shirt, and a striped tie. With white and black checkered Van's, fresh out of the box from Yellow Rat Bastard.

Looking out at the almost exclusively male audience, Joshua winced at the sight of the fraternity of disheveled losers who all but disappeared in the tan carpet and colorless walls. Joshua swore he could smell Vick's

VapoRub, and he sensed a panting idol worship that was borderline psychotic.

When he accepted his award, Joshua appeared to be barely half the size of NISDA's gregarious president who, at six-foot-one and two hundred pounds, wasn't exactly a giant.

"Mr. Joshua Gotbaum, president and founder of GoPostal Incorporated . . . It is my distinct pleasure to present this prestigious award to you today . . . Interactive Software Developer of the Year . . . Congratulations!"

At age twenty-five, Joshua was five-foot-seven and 145 pounds soaking wet. His bushy black hair seemingly defied gravity. His wire-rimmed Oliver Peoples shielded dark brown eyes. He was in perpetual need of a tan. His friend Cal recently told him that he looked *exactly* like Artie Ziff, Marge Simpson's millionaire prom date, voiced perfectly by the incomparable Jon Lovitz. Joshua didn't care for the comparison, but when pressed he acknowledged its accuracy.

Joshua graduated from Horace Mann, dropped out of New York University's film school at age twenty, and began developing "first-person shooter" video games. A computer genius originally backed by his father, a prominent New York entertainment attorney, Joshua's premier game was a bestseller and allowed his company, GoPostal, Inc., to go public on Joshua's twenty-second birthday. On that day, his sixty percent stake was worth $74 million.

Over the ensuing two years, Joshua created a string of bestselling "mature" video games, capitalizing on the fact that the average video game player is a twenty-eight-year-old male. Heralded by the industry and fans as the "all-time greatest video game impresario," Joshua was also the poster boy for violent games, and a frequent target of watchdog groups and congressional committees. Joshua didn't care and rarely got involved; he let the industry and his company fight the tedious and boring battles over rules and regulations. With the help of a dozen code writers, Joshua did one thing—he developed games, creating fantasy worlds where anybody and everybody was capable of horrific violence.

Perhaps because of the controversial, media-friendly subject matter, GoPostal, Inc. was a favorite of individual investors. Since its IPO, the stock had skyrocketed; Joshua had evidently mastered the foibles of the $70 billion video game industry. He had shortened the product development cycle to only six months; he produced new hits on a consistent basis; and he enjoyed strong relationships with the major platform manufacturers, particularly Microsoft, Sony, and Nintendo.

Appropriately rewarded for his virtuoso skills and industry savvy, Joshua's stock in GoPostal was now worth $350 million. When his fortune exceeded a quarter billion, he told his father that he stopped paying attention. He couldn't possibly spend it all.

GoPostal's board of directors, management team (whom Joshua called his "gray-haired suits"), attorneys, and publicists spent an inordinate amount of time dealing with Joshua's "youthful indiscretions" and "artistic sensibilities." Bouncers, club owners and gossip writers were bribed; paparazzi were menaced.

Despite his wealth and importance to a publicly traded company, Joshua refused to allow bodyguards to accompany him when he drank and drugged his way around New York. In response, a month before the IPO, GoPostal's board of directors secretly hired a security firm owned by two former Secret Service agents to tail Joshua whenever he left his apartment for "social engagements." In addition to protecting Joshua, the agents protected GoPostal, identifying those individuals who required attention and often facilitating the appropriate intervention.

About a year earlier, when Joshua's fame and notoriety increased exponentially thanks to a particularly controversial, bestselling game and subsequent congressional hearings, the agents convinced the board to fund a new "security initiative." To get Joshua out of the limelight at a reasonable hour, the agents would occasionally hire a professional to enter a venue and allow Joshua to pick her up and take her home. Not the typical sort of escort, these educated young women were expensive, but worth every penny. As paid contractors, they were manageable, unlike some of the New York bimbos who had tried to shake down GoPostal after a night with the "Emperor," as the agents code-named Joshua. The security firm generally reserved this measure for evenings when Joshua chose crowded nightspots popular with the gossip wranglers.

Joshua had no idea. He assumed if it wasn't his boyish charm and bouncy Jewfro that seduced these exquisite ladies, it was his money. In the end, he reasoned, the result was the same.

A car waited for Joshua outside the convention center to take him up to GoPostal's corporate offices just north of Times Square. Joshua worked out of his loft or at the company's design studio on Spring Street; he rarely ventured to the gray-haired suits' sterile domain.

"I hate Times Square," he once told his father, crossing Seventh Avenue at Forty-fourth Street. "*Time Out* says when the apocalypse comes, *this* is going is to be the waiting room for the damned."

But today's powwow was an important one, apparently. The suits wanted to talk to Joshua about his meeting the next day with Microsoft founder Bill Gates. Gates was coming to New York to announce the launch of Microsoft's next-generation video game system and had requested an hour with Joshua. No lawyers, no suits. Just Joshua.

After an excruciatingly interminable series of boring presentations from various middle-aged white guys, Joshua lost his patience, not to mention his amphetamine high.

"What's the big deal?" he asked GoPostal's Chief Financial Officer, Bernie Cornblum. "He writes code, I write code. I'm sure we'll get along great. I like all his people."

"Joshua, it's *Bill Gates* for God's sake," Cornblum pleaded. "He has invested close to a *billion* in this fourth-generation game system. He could break us if we're blackballed."

"*Blackballed?* Who says *blackballed?* Look, dude, I got it under control."

"Joshua . . ."

"Hey, as long as *I'm* making killer games, they'll keep coming to *me* and you and everyone in this room will get paid. I got it under control. We are done here."

Joshua looked at his dad, Daniel, the chairman of the board sitting at the opposite end of the table, who discreetly nodded. With his approval, Joshua jumped up and left the room, like a child leaving the family dinner table to play with friends impatiently waiting in the back-yard.

CHAPTER
TWENTY-SIX

Who is this punk, meeting with Bill Gates? Evan asked himself on Wednesday morning over his *Post*. The Page Six "sightings" included Gates having lunch at Michael's with "a mysterious youngster unknown to our spy." *Interesting.*

A few minutes later, Evan knew the answer. In his *Wall Street Journal*, he read that Gates was in town promoting Microsoft's new video game system and had met with Joshua Gotbaum, the "enigmatic young founder of GoPostal, Inc.," to discuss a "strategic relationship."

Joshua Gotbaum? Evan threw down the *Journal* and grabbed his *Post*. On the gossip page opposite the "sightings" mention, Evan recalled seeing that name. *You've got to be kidding me.*

"Zillionaire computer geek Joshua Gotbaum" had been spied Sunday night at Glow, partying with friends until the "wee hours." The *Post* described Gotbaum as a "frequent Glow denizen plagued by rumors of drug use and Spitzer-esque sexual proclivities."

Very interesting.

In his cubicle an hour later, Evan punched up GoPostal on his Bloomberg terminal, ticker symbol GPTL. The stock was up fifteen percent in early-morning trading on favorable rumors surrounding Gotbaum's meeting with Gates. Considering he had nothing else to offer Mac at this point, GoPostal was worthy of further investigation. But it would have to wait.

Evan had to head downtown to see Geoffrey Buchanan speak at Crain's New Venture Forum. The e-mail invitation warned that the keynote address would be standing room only. Opportunities to experience the Buchanan family were limited in the winter, so Evan couldn't miss it. He bumped into Mac on the way out.

Noticing his coat, Mac asked, "Where are you off to this morning?"

"Some venture conference down on West Broadway. I thought I might get some leads."

"*Leads?* Evan, I want—*need*—something from you on Friday. Where are you right now? Got anything?"

"I've been looking hard at one particular company for the past couple of days. Pulled the audited financials off Edgar this morning and—"

"*Audited financials?* Bullshit in a ball gown. Get the *real* story, okay?"

"Will do." *Bullshit in a ball gown.* Classic Mac-speak.

Walking to the subway and on the train downtown, to pass the time Evan focused on the faces of the people he encountered.

Joy. Sorrow. Wonder. Resolve. Anxiety. Apathy. Confusion. Awe. Fear. Guilt. Pain. Paranoia. Catatonia. Terror.

In five minutes he was sure he witnessed the entire human condition, reflected in those faces. Evan often felt all of those things in the same day, even in the same hour.

To make some sense of it all, he tried to connect the faces and emotions with characters he knew from the books he studied both at Ridgewood and as a literature major at NYU. Books allowed him to escape to worlds where he *could* belong. In addition to Rand, stories about outsiders and the absurdity of life resonated in him. He *knew* fiction's characters. They were, after all, an open book.

"This is the beauty of all literature," F. Scott Fitzgerald said. "You discover that your longings are universal longings, that you're not lonely and isolated from anyone. You belong."

．　　．　　．

As advertised, the SoHo Grand's largest conference room was filled to capacity. Despite arriving fifteen minutes early, Evan was forced to stand at the back of the room. But he was close enough.

Close enough to see and hear an inspiring speech about entrepreneurship as the foundation of American capitalism. Close enough to see and hear a relaxed and charismatic Geoffrey Buchanan hypnotize everyone in the room. Close enough to sense the enthusiasm and admiration. Close enough to want *more*.

Evan had no intention of approaching Buchanan, and he wouldn't have had a chance anyway. After the speech, during the standing ovation, Geoffrey departed via a side door, avoiding the obsequious genuflection and moronic interrogation common at such events. *Smart man*, Evan noted. *And nice exit. "When you hit that high note, you say good night and walk off."*

On the way back to his office, Evan didn't fume, contemplate, or second-guess. His thoughts turned to GoPostal.

Get it back, he told himself, *get inside*. And GoPostal was his key.

CHAPTER

TWENTY-SEVEN

This time I want *the stock to implode*, Evan reminded himself as he re-searched GoPostal the next day. The stock was up another ten percent, to $33 per share, on the Gates meeting, and the available short interest data revealed little pessimism with regard to GoPostal's future.

Unfortunately, NASDAQ only released information on the number of shares sold short on a monthly basis, so Evan didn't know if the recent price increase had encouraged anyone to bet against the stock; he checked the Yahoo! message boards, Wall Street's unofficial rumor mill.

Sure enough, the GoPostal message board was littered with talk of a short opportunity, given the speculative nature of the deal with Microsoft, but it was almost uniformly rejected. The rumor was that Gates and Got-baum got along really well—*a couple of wheezing computer geeks, two peas in a golden pod*—and a deal was a strong possibility.

After the market closed, Evan decided to call a sell-side analyst who followed GoPostal. Out of habit, he used a fake name.

"Hello, Melissa? Frank Lyman with *Investors Business Daily*. I'm do-ing a little backgrounder for a piece on GoPostal's recent activity. I'd sure appreciate your insight. Would you spell your last name for me, please, so we get it right in print?"

"Sure. M-A-R-T-I-N."

"Thanks. What can you tell me about the recent price run-up and valuation?"

"Well, the big bump the stock has seen in the past couple of days is clearly a result of GoPostal's meeting with Microsoft and the possibility of a development deal tied to the launch of the new game platform. But even if the deal doesn't happen, in my opinion the stock is fairly valued at thirty-three dollars, given the success of Manhunter. Did you see the data NPD released today after the close?"

"I did not," Evan replied honestly.

"Oh my gosh, NPD released the latest cross-platform games sales. Go-Postal's Manhunter was the leader for the sixth straight month and topped twelve million! It may be the game that knocks Super Mario Brothers Five off the top of the all-time sales list!"

Melissa was excited, almost hyperventilating. Her enthusiasm inspired Evan.

"Really? Tell me more."

"Cross-platform sales includes Sony's PS4, Nintendo, and Microsoft game systems, so it's the most followed number. Video games' popularity comes and goes—you know how kids are—but Manhunter appeals to an older demographic and has been number one for six months now with no sign of letting up. I think the free advertising from Congress helped sales, actually."

"Refresh my memory . . ."

"Well," Melissa said with a conspiratory tone, "last week the Senate held hearings *again* about violent video games. They actually singled out Manhunter, no doubt due to its popularity—it's certainly not the most violent game out there. Some of the PC games are really gross. Anyway, a couple of grandstanders demanded Tipper Gore–esque labeling and a prohibition on sales to kids under eighteen. But I think the attention just encourages kids *and* adults to buy the game."

"Gotcha. So, Melissa, bottom line. Buy, hold, or sell, and at what level?"

"Without the Microsoft deal, GoPostal is still a 'buy' at this price, maybe up to thirty-five, thirty-six, then a hold. With Microsoft, the sky's the limit for a young company like GoPostal."

Pretending to take down her words, Evan said, "Sky's . . . the . . . limit . . . I like that. What about the short interest?"

"Nobody is shorting this stock right now—less than one percent of the float is short as of the last reporting period, and much of that may be for hedging purposes. Short interest may bump up a little at this level, but I doubt it."

"And what is the street saying about the stock's prospects?" Good short-sellers never fought momentum, regardless of the fundamentals.

"No consensus that I'm hearing. Watch *Mad Money* tonight, see if that lovable nut Jim Cramer mentions it."

"Many thanks, Melissa."

"My pleasure. When will the article run?"

"I'll get back to you, without a doubt."

"Byline—"

"Thanks again." Click.

Jim Cramer. "A baffling symptom of the public's debased taste," according to Cramer himself. Evan liked the madman, who drank Lagavulin and wrote in *New York*, "The pursuit of wealth is our true national pastime." Strong words in the city of the Yankees and the Mets.

Evan called *Mad Money* and waited on hold for twenty minutes.

"Boo-yah! Mr. Cramer, care to comment on GoPostal?"

"GoPostal! AHHHHH! AK-47's everywhere! Duck and cover! But seriously I think it's too early to tell on GPTL, but I'll say that consumers can be irrationally stupid, and if they hype up this stock, it could be ripe for a fall."

After speaking with Melissa Martin and Jim Cramer, Evan was on board. As a rule, Contrafund didn't like to be late to the game or a bandwagon player. When he wasn't showering delightful clichés, Mac preached about the difficult momentum dynamics of crowded shorts. Contrafund preferred to be the first or among the first to bet that a stock would fall. Anticipating Mac's questions, Evan turned to his computer and continued his research.

GoPostal's market capitalization—the value of all of its stock—was

$1.1 billion, big enough to work with but off the radar for large cap players. Insiders owned about $500 million of that total, basically Joshua and Daniel Gotbaum, so the float was a healthy $600 million. Finally, early venture investors and long-term institutional investors held $200 million, reducing the *effective* float to $400 million. It might be tricky, but Evan was convinced that Contrafund could execute a $100 million short position in GoPostal. If the stock fell from $35 to $25 per share, Contrafund would profit about $30 million. *Not a bad day's work.*

Satisfied with the numbers, Evan turned his attention toward Go-Postal's "enigmatic impresario." He ran Joshua's name through the Nexis news database and several hundred articles appeared. Evan skipped the laudatory magazine pieces and boring business articles; he filtered out all of the Securities and Exchange Commission filings. He went straight for the dirt, immediately digging up a particularly vitriolic piece from Gawker's weekly roundup.

> What will a hundred million dollars do for a disheveled nerd accustomed to daily playground beatings? Now we know. Über-geek and mega-rich Joshua Gotbaum somehow managed to escort supermodel Kate Upton to the opening of the Ferragamo flagship store on Fifth Avenue. The stunning Upton towered over the diminutive Gotbaum . . .

Ouch, Evan thought. *Probably penned by a former jock, a has-been failure with a picture of Upton taped to the wall of his filthy apartment. Get over it, dude. You lost.* He shook his head with a quiet smile and continued down the list of articles.

Joshua Gotbaum certainly enjoyed the New York nightlife and club scene, as well as designer drugs and designer women. Not surprisingly, based on the number of "sightings" Evan reviewed, Joshua preferred the ultra-exclusive smaller venues, like StarLounge, where celebrity or big money, or both, were required for admission. The exception was Glow, the Chelsea mega-club where, if you were willing to wait on line and pay the steep cover charge, just about any appropriately attired schmuck could get in the door. Glow had VIP areas, of course, but according to reports Joshua liked to hang with the sweaty masses in the cavernous main room. Seven months ago, Evan read, while celebrating the release of Manhunter, Joshua purchased fifty bottles of Cristal for his entourage and the ten tables of lucky club-goers around him. *That should be me,* Evan told himself. *That will be me.* According to Page Six, that same night, "Two scary guys in suits carried an obliterated Joshua Gotbaum out of Glow at four in the morning."

Joshua paid $11 million for Michael Stipe's Tribeca duplex just after the IPO and has hosted a notorious Halloween party each year since. From a Cindy Adams column Evan learned that Joshua had a pair of stodgy neighbors who complained about the noise two years ago. Daniel Gotbaum managed to solve the problem last October. He put them up in Mandarin Oriental suites for the entire weekend and threw in dinner at Anthony Bourdain's super-hot new restaurant. *Only in New York, kids, only in New York.*

Just last spring, the "Gotbaum family" upgraded their Hamptons accommodations, trading in a "modest" Amagansett four-bedroom for a seven-bedroom behemoth off Further Lane in East Hampton. *South of the highway,* Evan noted with a smile, *just around the corner from the Buchanan's estate.* Over the Fourth of July weekend, Joshua left Montauk's Surf Lodge in an ambulance. The reported rumor was an overdose of Ecstasy and amphetamines, but "a spokesperson for Mr. Gotbaum insisted it was only a case of summer food poisoning." The usually loquacious club manager and staff had no comment.

Evan completed his online research with a quick review of Manhunter. Even before the Gates meeting, GoPostal's stock had more than doubled over the past six months based on the dramatic success of the bestselling video game and, sure enough, certain conservative members of Congress were none too pleased with Manhunter's sadistic and graphic violence. In addition to hearings on ratings, warning labels and sales prohibitions, Manhunter earned a "dishonorable mention" on a watchdog group's annual "Video Game Violence Report Card." Australia banned Manhunter, immediately creating a huge demand for high-priced, black market copies.

Evan shut off his computer and decided to finish his research in the field, with a visit to the GameStop on Lexington Avenue. He'd passed it a thousand times; this evening he would do a little shopping.

The five individuals inside GameStop pretty much fit what Evan envisioned as he walked east to the small neighborhood shop that exclusively sold video games. Three young boys, no more than ten years old, were excitedly maneuvering Spider-Man through a dark alley, acrobatically dispatching villains emerging from the shadows. They chirped "Get him!" and "Cool!" about every five seconds, and were absolutely transfixed with the cinematic action. Evan guessed that if the entire building collapsed around them, they wouldn't notice as long as the game continued.

The other two customers were older, probably just out of high school. Both were wearing hooded sweatshirts under heavy North Face jackets and hadn't had a haircut in months. They were silent, intently concentrating on the video screen before them, which was turned away from the windows, toward the rear of the store. To their left, Evan noticed a large cardboard display rack holding dozens of copies of Manhunter, on "special" for $59.99.

The sole employee in GameStop was a middle-aged man, probably the manager or franchise owner himself. He was removing Christmas lights from the counter area when he noticed Evan.

"Can I help you find something?"

"Yes, actually. I'd like to check out Manhunter."

"You're in luck. Those two guys back there are playing it right now. If they don't volunteer, I'll tell them to let you take a turn. They've been here long enough." He rolled his eyes and shook his head.

"Thanks. No worries."

For the next twenty minutes, Evan watched the action over the shoulders of the two young men and managed to play for a moment himself—only a moment because, as a beginner, that's how long his "turn" lasted. Once he'd taken his turn and lost, the two players acknowledged his presence and grunted out a few words.

The cleverly titled Manhunter was about hunting men, and women, in a variety of physical and historical settings, with a wide array of weapons acquired during the course of play. The graphics were amazing—just as cinematic as Spider-Man if not more so, with brutally realistic action and stomach-turning gore that would make Quentin Tarantino squeamish.

Evan could see why Congress took such interest in the ultrapopular game, at last count played in 18 million American homes. Extra points were awarded for slow, gruesome kills, and many of the victims begged for mercy in the midst of the carnage.

Evan played only the first level of Manhunter for a few minutes, but he could see it was an addictive masterstroke of in-your-face bloody fun. To move forward in the game, beyond level one, the player must hunt and kill thirteen terrified teen punks in a large, modern-day construction site. Because the player has not earned any weapons, he must make do with the construction tools and equipment available on the deserted site—drills and circular saws, sledgehammers and bolt cutters—any of which can serve up a delicious dose of oozing death.

The victims do not fight back; you lose if you don't capture and kill quickly enough. A timer in the bottom right corner of the screen counts down, reminding the player to catch his prey *now*. Once caught, the timer stops until the kill is complete, then immediately starts again.

When Evan failed to record a kill before time expired, one of the dudes asked him if he wanted to see it done right. Evan handed over the controller, and, as the massacre unfolded, the other guy told Evan that the best weapon in level one, the weapon everybody *loved*, was the nail gun, because it caused a particularly slow and gory death.

"You can't score enough points to skip to level three unless you use the nail gun," the guy playing the game commented while firing nails into the bloody back of a young woman trying to escape the construction site by climbing a fence. Although the sound was very low, Evan could hear her screams as each nail tore threw her flesh. After about fifteen shots, she slumped to the ground and the timer started up again.

"Where is he?" the player wondered.

His buddy replied, "Go right, toward the entrance." They were semi-frantic, but completely focused on the screen.

"Ah, there he is! Want to see something *tight*?" he asked, quickly taking his eyes off the action to look at Evan.

"Sure." Evan replied. *Tight is good, right?*

"This is a trick kill I learned on the Internet. I call this dude 'Melba.'"

"Melba?"

"Yeah, 'cause he's TOAST!"

Evan watched, fascinated by the perpendicular worlds around him and in front of him. The two gape-mouthed morons standing next to him were in both worlds; he was in neither.

Apparently, if the fair-haired skate rat dude with the tattoo on his back is carefully shot only in the arms and legs with exactly thirteen nails, he falls to the ground, still alive and writhing in a muddy black-red pool of tortured agony. The "manhunter" approaches the whimpering teen and, by pushing the correct sequence of buttons on the game controller, places the nail gun on his forehead, just above the victim's wide, terrified eyes and quivering lips, and fires a fatal shot. With a crunching pop, Melba's bloody gray matter explodes all over the ground and screen. Voice-over laughter is heard as the body twitches, bonus points are tallied, and the timer starts another countdown.

"Isn't that freakin' *awesome*?" the player asked, high-fiving his buddy. "Kill or be killed."

Evan replied, "But the kid didn't fight back."

"If I don't kill him, *my* game is over. Understand? If I don't *kill* him, *my game is over.*"

Walking back to his apartment, Evan's mind swirled. Tomorrow was Friday, and Mac would be waiting.

The numbers are good. No. The numbers are perfect. Okay, not quite perfect. But good enough. I can sell the numbers. I will sell the numbers.

Gates. Gates will do his homework. He'll discover that Gotbaum is a freak junkie. No way he'll put his company in bed with that punk. No way.

Manhunter. That's some fun, fucked-up shit. Congress will crack down. Congress will crash the party. If there's value to destroy, they always find a way, the sanctimonious bastards.

Something better will come along. Something always does. Plus, kids are fickle. Young and old, kids are fickle. They'll find something better. Or something different. Or both.

GoPostal will implode, and I will get rich in the process.

CHAPTER

TWENTY-EIGHT

Five miles downtown, two other young men were playing Manhunter. Rufus and Catalin sat glued to Joshua's black leather sofa, skillfully maneuvering their way through the game's seventh level, hunting and killing alternatively smug and naïve counselors in a verdant scene reminiscent of Camp Crystal Lake.

As his digital machete hacked at the perky pixelated breasts of a young camp counselor in a cropped pink tank top and shorts, Rufus yelled at the screen, "The *counselors* weren't paying any attention . . . They were making love while that young boy drowned . . . Look what you did to him. *Look what you did to him*!"

Across the loft's vast open space, past the billiard and foosball tables, Joshua was searching the fridge for beers while reheating leftover pizza. Cat laughed uproariously at Rufus's feigned rage, lost his place in the game, and his time expired.

He shouted to Joshua, "Dude, this new flat-panel *rocks*!"

"Fuckin-A it rocks. It's an eighty-five-inch Samsung UHD, cost me forty-K."

"Not bad," Cat replied. "What's the resolution?"

Joshua looked up, happy with the question.

"Res is four thousand by twenty-two hundred, quad-core processor."

"How many HDMI inputs?"

"Four, with three USB 2.0's."

"*Damn*. Does it have the RF in?"

But Rufus could no longer contain himself. He paused the game.

"Would you two nerds just *please* shut the fuck up? Can't you see I'm tryin' to *kill* here? And where are those beers dammit?"

For some reason Joshua and Cat, friends since Ethical Culture kindergarten, found this funny and both laughed out loud.

"Chill please, Pamela Voorhees. Don't lose your head. The beers are on the way. Go back to killin'. And, hey, you should see Tera Patrick on that TV. You'll learn to appreciate *resolution*."

"Now you're talkin', my main man. Now you're talkin'." Rufus turned his attention back to Camp Blood.

With the surround sound cranked, the screams filled the room. As Joshua arrived with the Stellas he discovered, he felt his iPhone vibrate. He glanced at the display.

"Shit. Pause it. It's my dad."

Rufus obeyed. He and Cat sat still and silent, listening to Joshua talk to The Man.

"Nothing . . . just heating up some pizza . . . yeah, sure . . . I'll be here . . . okay, see you in a few."

Joshua shut off his phone, pushing the END button several times, just to be sure.

"Sorry, guys. You gotta go. My dad's on the way over."

Rufus was already on his feet when Cat asked, "*The Man*? It's eight o'clock on a Thursday. What's up with *that*?"

"I don't know. He's been busy lately with the Microsoft thing and I think he was in meetings all day with the gray-haired suits. I guess he likes to keep me in the loop. It makes sense—"

Rufus, heading for the service door in his incognito Yankees cap and Bono bug-eye sunglasses, interrupted. "No charge for the weed. StarLounge special delivery tomorrow night?"

Joshua looked at Cat, who was slowly ungluing himself from the sofa, then replied, "Yeah, StarLounge around midnight. I hate the clubs on Friday—amateur night."

"Tell me about it," Rufus said as he reached his exit. Cat was making his move for the front door when Joshua noticed their untouched open beers.

"Hold up. Don't forget your road sodas. You need to-go cups?"

"Nah," Cat answered, "I'm guessin' we finish 'em before we hit the lobby."

Joshua barely had time to empty the ashtrays before his doorman buzzed.

"Yeah?"

"Mr. Gotbaum, your father is on the way up. He's in the elevator already."

"Thanks, Fernando."

At fifty years old, Daniel Gotbaum was more Jeff Goldblum than Artie Ziff. Tall and broad-shouldered with slicked-back hair just graying at the temples, Joshua often joked that he was a "Jewish Gordon Gekko on steroids." Daniel liked that description.

Joshua opened his door just as Daniel stepped out of the elevator.

"To what do I owe this pleasure?"

"I spent the whole goddam day with our team and ran late for dinner with Cecilia. She got fed up and went to the Arlington Club with girlfriends, so I thought I'd engage in some quality father-son time," Daniel said with a joking smile.

"Cecilia? Is she the flavor of the week I met at the MTV Movie Awards?"

Daniel was inside now, removing his Zegna suit jacket on the way to the living area.

"Umm . . . no. That was Danielle. You haven't met Cecilia."

"How many has it been, Dad?"

"Let's see . . . just over a year since the divorce . . . I'd say about a dozen."

"Damn. You get more ass than a toilet seat."

"And you, my son, get *less*." They shared a laugh before Daniel added, "But what can I say? New York is like a goddam Sex Disney."

"*Sex Disney* . . . I haven't heard that. Good one."

Daniel sat down on the sofa, put his feet up on the table, and turned on *SportsCenter*.

"Is the pizza ready? And do you have any of those Stellas that I brought over before New Year's?"

"Déjà vu," Joshua said under his breath. "Yes to both." Recalling seeing only three remaining beers in the fridge, Joshua grabbed his open bottle and slipped it into the freezer.

When *SportsCenter* ended and the pizza was gone, Daniel put down his second beer, muted the massive television, and turned to his only child.

"Okay, time for me to play Chairman of the Board. Let's talk some business. Big news today, lotsa news."

"All right. Let's hear it."

"First, a deal with Microsoft is looking good. Our guys talked with their guys and they're interested in perhaps a two- or three-game exclusive."

"What does that mean?"

"It means, my boy, that you will develop two or three new games *exclusively* for their new game system. They'll pay us a boatload of cash up front *and* take on almost all of the sales and marketing. We got a hefty guarantee from them, including a goddam Super Bowl ad."

"Holy shit, that's *huge*."

"Hell yes it's huge."

"What's the time frame? When can I see the specs for the new platform?"

"It's scheduled for March, but there's something else." Daniel leaned forward, drawing Joshua's attention.

"What's up, dad?"

"One of Gates's bizdev goons voiced 'concerns' about your reputation and 'late night carousing'—I believe those were his words. We told him not to believe the gossip vultures and focus instead on your game sales. It was funny—he said, 'Gossip vultures?' and we said, 'Yeah, in New York these assholes get paid to make up shit about successful people.' He's from Washington state, so what the hell does he know?"

"And . . ."

"And he dropped it." Daniel reached out and touched his son's fore-arm. "But could you tone it down a bit after we sign with these guys? I'm not asking you to join a monastery."

With a sly grin, Joshua asked, "*How much* is this deal worth to us?"

"Remember that Caribbean island for sale in *Robb Report* you were showing me? You think we should buy it? Then . . ."

"When we sign, I'll dial it down a notch."

"Excellent!" Daniel sat back on the sofa, rubbed the leather with both hands, and relaxed. Back to dad mode.

"What else happened today?" Joshua asked.

"Nothing that directly impacts you. To demonstrate our confidence in our stock, we're going to announce a major share buyback in February, a stock repurchase."

"I realize I daydream through the meetings, but we don't have the cash for that, do we?"

"Not at the moment. But in a few weeks Cornblum is closing a private placement of restricted convertible debt with a few of our favorite inside institutions. The conversion date is pushed way out and at a price around seventy percent higher than where we are now. We'll use the cash from that deal for the buyback. The street will love it, as will Microsoft."

"Cool. I knew we hired those guys to do *something*."

Daniel continued. "We heard from our consultant in D.C. Congress is going to back off until after the election in November. I guess the angry mothers don't have as much clout on the Hill as the free speech nuts. And, confidentially, our consultant just *might* have some dirt on that right-wing buffoon from Georgia. No wonder he cost so damn much."

"Hey, it's money well spent. I hated wearing a suit all day and answer-ing those uptight old farts' questions. It sucked."

"Well, you won't have to worry about it for at least a year."

"Cool. No wearing suits for a year."

Daniel shook his head, smiling in disbelief, before continuing.

"One more thing, and you'll like this. Andrea—you know, our new sales and marketing VP—reported that advance orders for Manhunter are much stronger than expected for next quarter, and big retail buyers are telling her it's because no significant competition is on the horizon. Several new sports games are in the pipeline, as always, but no new first-person shooters. I think you scared 'em away."

Joshua leaned forward and asked intently, "Did she say when I should have Manhunter 2 ready? Still summer?"

"She did. She wants to push the launch back until the holidays. Without new competition, there's no reason to cannibalize Manhunter's sales."

"Sweet!" Joshua fired an imaginary arrow at the wall.

"I knew you'd like that, my boy. But don't slack, okay? And remember what we talked about."

"Yes, sir."

Daniel tugged at his French cuff to get a look at his formidable new stainless steel Rolex Sea-Dweller Deepsea Challenge, a *titanic* gift from James Cameron.

"My car will be here in a few minutes. Care to join me for a drink at the Carlyle? A couple of my partners should still be there celebrating a big deal they closed today for Ed Pressman and Jon Katz."

Joshua sometimes forgot his dad was a prominent attorney, a rainmaker at a midtown firm.

"Dad, the *Carlyle*? That is so lame. What happened to Sex Disney?"

"Later, if I'm lucky. Cecilia lives around the corner on Park Ave." Daniel raised his eyebrows and grinned.

Walking toward the door, Joshua said, "My old man is hoping for a booty call."

Daniel chuckled. "I don't think they call them 'booty calls' on Park Avenue, do they?"

"I don't think people have *sex* on the Upper East Side, do they?" Joshua shot back.

As the elevator door closed, Daniel said, "I'll be in LA this weekend, the Biltmore downtown; I'll call you next week."

Joshua closed his door, locked it, and immediately called Cat. He could hear a thumping bass line in the background when Cat answered.

"Dude, where are you?"

"Just up Varick at Greenhouse," Cat shouted. "How'd it go?"

"Great, actually. *Really* freakin' great. Let's celebrate . . . with top-shelf tequila. Get a table and a bottle of Qui Platinum, near some women. I'm on the way."

Riding uptown to the Carlyle in his chauffeured Mercedes S600, Daniel dialed Frank Mancini, one of the former federal agents paid to protect Go-Postal's most valuable asset.

"Look sharp, Frank. He'll be celebrating tonight, and we've got a lot to lose right now. *A lot to lose.*"

CHAPTER

TWENTY-NINE

Confidently marching to the subway on Friday morning, Evan played out the day ahead, invigorated by the possibilities. At the top of the staircase, he could hear the screech of the 6 train below, and Sisyphus smiled.

He knew how Mac operated. Mac would review Evan's memo proposing the GoPostal strategy, and then he would grill Evan on the details. *I'm ready,* Evan told himself. *The numbers, Gates, Congress. I can sell this deal.*

The night before, after returning to his apartment and drafting the memo, Evan had done some quick calculations to get a ballpark idea of the only thing that really mattered—how much money *he* would take home if GoPostal's stock tanked. When he saw the result, he took a deep breath, turned off his computer, and went to bed.

Stepping off the elevator into Contrafund's opulent offices, Evan repeated his mantra, and a memory surfaced with it.

I can sell this deal. I must sell this deal. "Money demands that you sell, not your weakness to men's stupidity, but your talent to their reason."

"Indeed," he said, to no one in particular.

The morning passed slowly. The monthly short interest report was released; Evan added the good news to his memo before dropping it in Mac's in-box.

Mac spent much of his time on the phone with the unread memo waiting nearby. As he left for lunch, he said to Evan, "Don't worry, chief. I'll read it downstairs and see you later, okay?"

True to his word, at about three o'clock, Mac summoned Evan. After repeating the major points of each section of the memo, Mac said, "This is good work, chief. Very good work. Where the hell did you find this GoPostal?"

"You wouldn't believe me if I told you, Mac, but I found it, and it's right in Contrafund's sweet spot." *Time to launch a preemptive strike.*

Evan looked Mac in the eye and continued. He was in the zone, once again, *finally.*

"The short interest is practically nil, less than two percent as of today's report, up just a hair from last month. We'll be the first player in the game, we'll be *driving* the bandwagon.

"Average daily trading volume has tripled over the past quarter, and with an effective float of four hundred million, we shouldn't have a problem taking a one hundred million short position."

Mac wasn't fazed; he had read the memo.

"You think GoPostal is overvalued?" Mac said, halfway between a question and a declaration.

"GoPostal *is* overvalued. The Microsoft deal is not going to happen, and Manhunter is not only getting stale in a fickle market, Congress is poised to pounce on it."

"I know. My kids aren't allowed to play it."

"Exactly. Without Microsoft and without Manhunter, GoPostal's got *nothing.*"

Mac was quiet for a moment, contemplative. He stood up and paced behind his desk, like a lawyer preparing for a crucial cross-examination.

"Are there enough market-makers to execute—"

"Plenty. Over a dozen majors and several regional players."

"Any risk of a share buyback?"

"No cash on the balance sheet for a buyback."

"You say the effective float is four hundred million. Is that conservative or—"

"Conservative. The actual float is six hundred million. To be safe, I estimated two hundred million held by long-term institutions, like the original venture capitalists. The effective float *could* be as high as four-fifty to five hundred million."

"Good. Excellent."

Mac paced without a word or sound, his hands clasped behind his back. Evan's eyes followed him. Mac stopped and their eyes locked.

For an instant, Evan sensed a seismic shift in Mac, as if every thought Mac had entertained suddenly, perceptively, and fundamentally changed. Evan blinked and in his mind's eye, Mac stopped pacing once again and their eyes again locked. It was a strange, surreal moment, and Evan found an explanation in film, a common default when things just didn't add up. *A déjà vu, a glitch in the Matrix?* Evan asked himself. *It happens when they change something.*

Mac took a breath as his mouth opened to say something, but then he hesitated. Again he looked Evan in the eye, squinting as if to sharpen the image.

"Time frame and price target?"

"Before the end of the second quarter, June, GoPostal will be a twenty-dollar stock at best. We should start covering at twenty, and ride her down."

Mac sat and worked his calculator. He was back to business.

"*If* we manage to cover the *entire* position at twenty . . . our performance fee would be roughly nine million." He looked up at Evan. "And at thirty-three percent, you would make close to three million bucks, Mr. Stoess."

As Evan heard the words, the temperature in Mac's office seemed to spike and he felt dizzy. The cool zone of articulate confidence abandoned him.

"Uh, yes. I am aware of that, Mac."

"You know, you only get one second chance."

"I know."

Mac relaxed and leaned forward, resting his elbows on his desk.

"Evan, I'm not one to give speeches, to put the fear of God in you. But Contrafund does not like to lose."

"Neither do I, Mac. I lost everything once; it will not happen again." *And I certainly don't fear your god*, Evan wanted to add, but he held his tongue.

Mac sat back in his chair. "Okay, let's go downstairs to the trading floor and talk to Kennedy. If he thinks it's doable, I'll clear it with Zurich on Monday."

"Holy shit." Only Evan knew those words had a double meaning. *Holy shit this just might happen and holy shit if I stand up too fast I just might keel over.*

"Damn straight, 'holy shit.' Let's go. You, too. You should see how he works."

They walked together down one flight of stairs to Contrafund's small trading area. Kennedy Phillips was the firm's head trader, renowned on the street for his ability to get trades done discreetly and at the right price. Mac reverentially called it "execution discipline."

Evan expected to hear what Tom Wolfe described as "the rousing sound of the greed storm," but, nearing the market's close on a slow Friday, the trading floor was quiet, and Kennedy was reading *Sports Illustrated* when Mac entered his office. Evan waited in the doorway. Kennedy spoke first.

"You again? I just put that position to bed an hour ago. Eighty million. You got another dead soldier already?"

"I do, but first let me introduce you to our newest assistant portfolio manager, Evan Stoess."

Kennedy stood and said, "Ah, Evan Stoess, the *infamous* Evan Stoess." Evan stepped in and extended his sweaty hand. Kennedy continued, "We've met before in passing. Thanks again for Medipharm. We made a *shitload* on that sick puppy."

Evan felt rage rushing up his throat, a powerful growl, but he smiled and spoke.

"Yeah, I recall. And we're going to make even *more* on GoPostal."

Kennedy sat back down and turned to his terminal. He was off to the races.

"GPTL," Mac advised, GoPostal's trading symbol.

"GPTL," Kennedy repeated. "Have a seat, gentlemen."

As he sat, Mac reached out and grabbed Kennedy's *SI*. Evan looked around and spied a tattered *Maxim* on the floor.

While Mac read, Evan flipped the pages and studied the action around him. Kennedy was a bear of a man, with a sizable beer belly under his blue button-down. His sleeves were rolled up and, in his wrinkled Brooks Brothers chinos and sockless Sperry Top-Siders, he looked like a bespectacled *Preppy Handbook* reject thirty years late for a sail. Or, alternatively, a clone of Philip Seymour Hoffman.

But instead of duct-taping his venerable LL Bean moccasins, he was typing, obsessively scribbling notes, his face just inches from the yellow tablet, and then typing some more. Outside the office, the noise level increased as the market closed and the traders removed their telephone headsets and prepared to depart for the weekend. Colleagues. *Friends.* Evan listened to their insipid banter. One of them was leaving directly for Killington and wouldn't be back until Tuesday.

In mid-scribble, Kennedy looked up at Mac.

"How much?"

"A hundred million, in the thirty-six range."

Kennedy rolled his eyes, gritted his teeth, and went back to scribbling, but with even more feverish fervor.

Mac quietly said to Evan, "He loves a challenge," before returning to his magazine. Mac was calm. Evan's heart has beating like a hummingbird's and his only coherent thought was *three million, three million, three million*. It played in his head in rhythm with his tachycardic heartbeat.

After what seemed like an eternity, or five minutes, Kennedy turned to Mac and waited for him to look up from his article.

"It may take a coupla weeks, but we can get it done," Kennedy said with a confident nod of his head.

Evan was silent, stunned. His heart rate dropped to fifty and he once again felt dizzy as hot blood pooled in his feet.

Mac asked, "Do you need to call around to see if the shares are out there to borrow?"

Kennedy looked at one of his screens. "I don't think so. Volume, float and market-makers look okay. I already have an idea how we'll start."

"*You*," Mac said.

"Huh?"

"You, Kennedy. I want *you* to handle this personally."

"Of course, Mac. I'll start slow, keep it real quiet. I'll spread the trades over a bunch of firms and brokers, and I'll probably buy a coupla small blocks to confuse the market, make 'em think we're short-term or covering already. When I get close, maybe the last five million, I'll go loud and use one talkative broker, just to get the word out on the street. When it's done, you'll decide how to proceed, but with that aggressive position, you may want to tip the odds a bit by calling some sell-side analysts and leaking it to the media."

"We'll see." Mac wasn't a fan of spreading doom and gloom.

"Your choice. But I'll get you the position, at the price you want."

"That's what I want to hear!" Mac exclaimed, suddenly standing up, shocking Evan's heart back to normal. "What did Gordon Gekko call his guy, *the Terminator*? We've got one right here!"

Kennedy laughed appreciatively as Evan stood, then said, "I'll get it done for you guys. *Execution discipline*." To Mac he asked, "*When* do I start the assault on GPTL?"

"I'll get confirmation for the strategy on Monday."

Looking around his office in an exaggerated, suspicious manner, Kennedy replied, "Don't you think they already know?"

Evan detected an unwanted wince on Mac's face, but Mac quickly recovered and laughed it off.

"Yeah, Kennedy. *They* already know."

But Evan couldn't help but question the sincerity of the sarcasm.

CHAPTER
THIRTY

Rufus arrived at StarLounge a few minutes before midnight, hoping to complete a transaction with another customer before Joshua showed up. Eudora Signoret, the owner of the ultra-exclusive venue, was Rufus's best customer and the only person allowed to purchase in bulk for resale, but only to patrons visiting from outside New York.

StarLounge had a simple door policy—only Eudora's celebrity and megarich "friends" gained entrance, and when the FOE had entourages in tow, Rhino, Eudora's manager/enforcer, often vetted them, turning away the lesser members. Rhino was particularly fond of wielding his power to shun uptight personal assistants. He sent them to the corner diner to wait out their *fabulous* employers.

Rhino liked the nerdy little guy, Joshua Gotbaum, even if he did get out of control on occasion. Joshua's entourage was generally a reasonable group of two to five people, and he tipped very well (and when he was too wasted to tip, his buddy Cat fished out the little guy's cash and spread it around).

Inside, StarLounge was more miniresort than bar. With seating for only eighty in ten separate areas, each group of guests enjoyed their own fully stocked bar with personal service. The atmosphere was Jetsons space lounge with a retro twist; the ceiling sparkled and danced with stars and celestial bodies created by a multimillion-dollar planetarium software system sophisticated enough for most flyover museums. The menu included Tsar Imperial Osetra caviar for $1,600 per portion, but the stunning European staff was just as willing to order in pizza or Chinese food for their elite customers.

Rhino spotted Rufus as he approached and waved him around to the side alley entrance. He called an underling on his headset to unlock the door for Eudora's favorite dealer. He also notified Eudora, who met Rufus at the door.

After the obligatory double air-kisses, Eudora placed a large order, her first since the holidays, and asked Rufus if he had any other business to do "in the house."

"Yes, of course, our little Joshua, *très bien*. Rufus, my dear, you're lucky I don't charge you commission. But he's not here yet. Why don't you wait in my office and I'll have Rhino let you know?"

"Sure, works for me. Is the PS4 hooked up?"

"But of course, *mon ami*."

Just minutes later, a shapely member of Eudora's staff escorted Rufus to the back service bar where Joshua Gotbaum was waiting. He was drunk and happy.

"Rufus, *duuude*, what have you got for us tonight? Methinks we'll be needin' some Ecstasy. Yeah . . . Ec-sta-sy! Four of us. But enough for eight. No, ten. Yeah."

"You got it." Rufus counted out the pills, each one bright red and stamped with Ferrari's famous stallion, and dropped all but one in a small envelope. He held out the remaining pill, waving it like a treat. Joshua closed his eyes and stuck out his tongue. As he swallowed with a satisfied grin, Rufus asked, "Charge it to your account?"

Joshua giggled and swayed on his feet. "Yeah dude, charge it to my account." He swung around and returned to his table; Rufus disappeared out the back door, into the night.

Joshua twirled awkwardly on the square table separating the banquettes and overstuffed chairs, his head tilted back so he could see the stars. Cat laughed and clapped; Becky and Leslie Hornsby, Cat's next-door neighbors and Joshua's guests at StarLounge, also looked skyward, mouths agape at the entrancing cosmos above them.

When Joshua finally sat down, he was sweating profusely, the beads running down his clammy forehead and catching on the frames of his glasses. Cat too felt perspiration on his brow and worried they were overheating from Rufus's psychoactive "love drug." He called for ice water just as Joshua exclaimed, "Let's go to Glow! Now!"

The Hornsby sisters squealed with delight and danced in their seats. Pretty Leslie knocked over her lukewarm beverage, a healthy pour of Little Black Dress vodka with just a splash of soda. She didn't notice.

Cat was no fan of amateur night at the clubs. Neither was Joshua, ordinarily.

"On a Friday? Are you kidding? It'll *suck*."

"Naaah. Call. Tell 'em to set us up. No line, no waiting. Tell 'em we'll *pay*."

"Why? Why tonight? We're just hittin' our groove here."

"'Cause in a few weeks I'll *hafta* stay outta trouble. Big crowds are . . . bad," Joshua said, shaking his head and enjoying the resulting dizziness.

"Ah, shit. That's right. Okay, Joshua, I'll make the call."

"My man . . ."

Cat stood up and headed to the exit to talk on his cell phone. Joshua put his arm around Leslie and together they swayed to the music while gazing at the stars.

"It's beautiful, isn't it? So real." Leslie marveled with the wide-eyed wonder of a child.

"Like a dream," Joshua said.

To Frank Mancini and his brother Doug, StarLounge *was* a dream. GoPostal paid their agency big money to keep Joshua out of trouble and out of the press; StarLounge's obsessive exclusivity and small size made their job relatively easy.

They or their two employees, a pair of former New York Police Department detectives, would park their beige Oldsmobuick halfway down StarLounge's quiet block of warehouses. They'd park, and they'd wait.

Glow, in stark contrast, was a nightmare. The bulk of the megaclub was located in a former subway depot, an expansive cavern subdivided into six huge rooms with sixty thousand square feet of party space. Labyrinthine corridors, always crowded and lined with "VIP chambers" and dark vestibules, connected the rooms. On an average weekend, fifteen thousand people eagerly paid a fifty-dollar cover charge to experience Glow's twenty-dollar cocktails and two coed restrooms.

One of Glow's major attractions, each coed restroom featured its own bar for those people waiting to enter stalls with clear glass doors that automatically fogged over when latched shut. Tourists paid the cover charge just to see them, never realizing that the club also had "normal" restrooms on a mezzanine level, more convenient facilities for the club's in-the-know regulars that also served as "offices" for drug dealers, whores, and hustlers.

Although each room was different, Glow's common denominator was its vicious assault on the senses. The thumping music played so loud that employees were required to wear earplugs. In the area featuring trance music, special machines pumped in a phosphor dust that coated everything in the room and everyone who entered. Ultraviolet black lights, the only illumination in the subterranean space, revealed a surreal scene, itself an inebriating hallucination.

The main room, Glow's largest at fifteen thousand square feet, coupled earsplitting pop club music with hundreds of seizure-inducing strobe lights, luring clubgoers into a cacophonous consciousness that virtually required chemical intervention to survive. At the far end of the room, the upper level overlooked four dance floors and a huge horseshoe-shaped bar. This crowded mezzanine, close to the relatively private restrooms, was Joshua's favorite spot, and he wasn't averse to slipping a hundred-dollar bill to a manager to "free up" one or two of the half dozen tables with a bird's-eye view of the undulating masses below.

On this particular visit, Cat had made the call and therefore handled the requisite remuneration. After bypassing a long line of over two hundred freezing wannabes, he and Joshua, accompanied by Leslie and Becky, were escorted to a waiting table on the mezzanine. A complimentary bottle of champagne sat in its center, protected from interlopers by two massive men in black.

Snaking through the frenzied mob, Cat sensed a do-or-die ferocity he hadn't experienced, even on an amateur night. He tapped the manager on the shoulder and screamed, "What's the deal tonight?"

"Haven't you heard? There's a rumor the mayor wants to shut us down. I guess people think it's now or never. Like I said, I can set you up in a VIP chamber if you'd prefer."

"No. No thanks. Joshua likes the mezzanine. Will it happen, the shut-down?"

"I doubt it. Our owner has too much money."

They arrived at the table and the manager addressed Joshua. "Can I get you anything else?"

"Ice water," Joshua shouted. "And lots of it."

Outside Glow, Frank and Doug Mancini stood on the sidewalk, across the street from the long line of wannabe revelers, their hands pushed deep into the pockets of their London Fog overcoats. Forced to park their car two blocks away and stand in the cold at two in the morning, they weren't the happiest former feds in New York.

"I hate this place," Doug said. "Should we call in the cavalry and get him out of there?"

"At this hour? Nah. He'll leave at four when they stop serving booze. Plus he's already with two women. It might be tough for the cavalry to drag him away."

Doug looked at his feet and frowned, then looked up with a resolute grin. "The little Emperor will probably have whiskey dick anyway."

The brothers laughed, and Doug said, "You're right. Let's get the car, double-park, and wait him out."

Two hours later, a pair of sedans pulled up displaying Elite Car Service signs in their front windows. Frank put down his coffee. "Bingo. Elite. The Emperor's favorite chariot service."

Moments later, Frank and Doug were following one of the cars downtown to Joshua's Tribeca loft. Joshua was alone in the sedan; the other car departed with Cat and the Hornsby sisters. Once they had seen Joshua stumble into his attended lobby, the brothers yawned in unison.

"Another day, another dollar."

CHAPTER

THIRTY-ONE

Like clockwork, Fleur knocked on Evan's door a few minutes before eleven on Sunday. She had her own television now, a gift from a long lost boyfriend, so she and Evan didn't see each other much anymore. Sunday night was the exception.

Evan greeted her at the door, happy for companionship after a lonely winter weekend.

"How are you this dreary evening, Mr. Stoess?"

Evan grinned. "Oh, I'm percolating, Fleur. I'm telling you, I have never felt so fertile. I'm mossy, my Kiwi flower. My brain is mossy."

Fleur fake-chuckled. "Funny. Is that one on tonight?"

"I don't know, but it's true. I had a good week at work, and this week could be *huge*."

"Well it's about time," Fleur said with a maternal tone. They sat on opposite ends of the sofa and Evan instinctively clicked to Fox.

Fleur continued, "It's great to finally see you excited about something again."

"Thanks. Yeah, I found the perfect stock to short, and if it gets approved and goes the way I want, I'll make a lot of money. *A lot of money.*"

Evan noticed a deep look of concern on Fleur's face, and he sensed the trepidation leap out of her and into him.

"It's a *short*; I *want* the stock to go down."

"You *want* it to go down? And you make money if it does?"

"That's right. My firm borrows shares of the stock from other firms and sells them on the open market. When the stock price falls, we buy 'em back, then return the shares to the firms we borrowed from and pocket the difference. Get it?"

"Umm . . . I think so . . . maybe not. I *am* at F.I.T. you know."

"Say you think Apple is having troubles and its stock will fall next month. You borrow a thousand shares from Merrill Lynch and sell them for twenty dollars per share, or twenty thousand dollars."

"Okay, I have twenty thousand cash and owe a stack of shares to the breed apart."

"Exactly. So the stock falls to fifteen per share. You buy them back for fifteen thousand, return the shares to Merrill and keep the five thousand. Easy money."

"What if there's good news and the price goes up?"

Evan would have preferred if she hadn't asked that question.

"Well . . . then basically you're fucked."

"You sure are. Fucked, fired, and broke. *Again*." Fleur flashed a devilish smile and added, "But fucked is not necessarily a bad thing," then turned to see George Costanza extol the prospects of a young Steven Koren. *"He's going to be everything I claim to be, only for real. That's my dream."*

"Hilarious!" Fleur exclaimed. "I love Jerry's next line."

"I had a dream last night that a cheeseburger was eating me!" Fleur said it with him.

Minutes later, the Van Buren Boys thwarted, Evan turned to Fleur.

"I had a dream last night."

"Do tell," Fleur replied, sipping a Peach Snapple through a bendy straw.

"At first it was great. I was sitting behind the wheel of a new Bentley convertible. My wife and kids were in the car with me. I turned the ignition, but the car wouldn't start.

"Then it was pitch-black and I was trapped in an old wooden coffin, buried alive. I pounded and scratched on the lid until my fingernails ripped off. There was a soil smell in my mouth and I choked on it. I can still smell and taste it, like a wet greenhouse. I broke open the coffin lid, tore through the soil and escaped. Then I was walking toward the Bentley. But I was *in* the Bentley, or at least my façade, my outer shell was. The rest of me, my inside, was covered in dirt and blood.

"I opened the door and sat *in myself*, clean and whole again. I pulled a gold key out of my pocket and started the car. It was beyond vivid, Fleur. It was *real*."

"How awful. What does it mean?"

"I don't know, but I think I'll find out."

CHAPTER
THIRTY-TWO

"It's a go, chief."

Evan looked up from his *Wall Street Journal*; it was just before ten on Monday morning. "Excellent," he replied. "The stock is at thirty-six, ripe and ready."

"*Ripe and ready,*" Mac repeated. "You want to tell Kennedy, set him loose?"

"How did it go down, Mac? With Zurich?"

"You don't need to worry about that. It's a go."

"Do they know it's from me, Mac?"

"They do. And that sealed it."

Evan opened his mouth to ask why, but Mac stopped him. "You. Downstairs. Kennedy. Now. Go."

Kennedy was standing over the shoulder of a rotund trader with a thick New Jersey accent. They were profanely happy, watching a NASDAQ Level II screen full of numbers, some of which were blinking. When Kennedy noticed Evan, he put on a serious face and patted the trader on the back. "Keep at it."

"You got it, boss."

Kennedy walked several steps to Evan, extending his hand.
"GPTL?"

Evan gripped his hand firmly and demanded his eye.

"GPTL. Make it happen."

"A hundred million?"

"Correct."

Kennedy nodded and loosened his grip. Evan held firm.

"Mac says you love a challenge."

"I'll make it happen, Evan. It's what I do."

Evan relaxed. "Thanks, Kennedy. Mac also says you're the best."

"Mac doesn't lie." Kennedy took a step back. Evan stepped forward.

"What's your estimate on timing?"

"I'd say ten to fifteen trading days to get it done. It's an aggressive position."

"It's an excellent opportunity."

Turning toward his office, Kennedy said, "Good God it had better be."

CHAPTER
THIRTY-THREE

Early on Tuesday morning, Bernie Cornblum, GoPostal's chief financial officer, was sitting in Albert Higgins's office, the company's CEO. The top two suits had Daniel Gotbaum on speakerphone.

"Where are you, Daniel?" Bernie asked.

"Just got back from LA. I'm in a car coming in from JFK. How're things goin'?"

"All's well," Bernie replied. "We're on schedule to close the private placement in two or three weeks. No rush, really. Everything's lookin' good."

Al spoke up from behind his massive desk. "And we're proceeding nicely with Microsoft. Looks like the timing will coincide with the buy-back announcement."

"Perfect," Daniel said. "Anything from Felix Kahn in D.C.?"

"He's a piece of work," Al answered. "Apparently the son of a bitch *does* have some dirt on that homophobe zealot from Georgia. He's probably another wide-stance toe tapper. Let's just say Congress won't be bothering us for a while."

Daniel laughed. "Felix *is* a piece of work. He's merciless, which is why he does *very* well in D.C. How will we get that info out, that Congress is backing off?"

"The industry will take care of it for us. The International Game Developers Association. I'll see to it."

"Good man, Al. Anything else?"

"Daniel, did you have an opportunity to speak with Joshua?"

"I did. We reached an understanding. He promised to calm down once we've put ink on the Microsoft deal." Daniel took a breath. "Why? Any problems over the weekend?"

"Not really. Frank Mancini reported in yesterday. Late night at Glow on Friday."

"Yeah, I'm sure he'll want to do it up over the next coupla weeks. But he knows the score, gentlemen. Just have Frank and Doug keep a close eye while we wait for MSN."

"They always do," Al said.

"And they should, for what they cost us," Bernie added, always the finance guy.

Daniel and Al ignored him. "When do we meet again? On Monday, correct?"

"Yes. All hands on Monday."

"Until then, gentlemen." Daniel clicked off his phone and smiled at the sight of midtown's skyline. "All's well," he said to himself.

"Excuse me, sir," his driver replied, peering at him in the rearview mirror.

"Fifty-third and Park. You do have E-ZPass, I presume."

"Yes, sir."

"Good. Let's go."

CHAPTER

THIRTY-FOUR

Evan stepped out of 30 Rock into a bearably chilly evening, the ghost of Noël's Norway spruce hovering over him. Walking the city's streets was free therapy, and he decided to take advantage of it.

Heading north on Fifth Avenue, Evan resisted the urge to window-shop, to spend his three million—*three million*—prematurely. He didn't spot a must-have Jil Sander virgin wool overcoat in a Saks window, nor a pair of suede Ferragamo shoes, nor a sweet Hugo Boss suit, nor a de rigueur Louis Vuitton valise.

Crossing Fiftieth Street, Evan was relieved that Saint Patrick's Cathedral sold only salvation, and he wasn't buying. He could see light pouring out of the main entrance, the colossal portal open after an evening Mass. A warm rectangle of illumination extended across the sidewalk almost to the curb; Evan stepped around it.

Turning right, temptation behind him, the blocks passed quickly, effortlessly, as he made his way east and north. When Evan reached the Seventies, the chill caught up with him, coincidentally accompanied by his appetite. He stepped inside J.G. Melon for a cheeseburger, waffle fries and a few beers.

Comfortably seated at the far end of the bar, beer in hand and pensively contemplating whether the image in front of him was a cantaloupe or a honeydew, a voice from the dining room cut through the warm monotone din.

"*And then he three-putted! I laughed so damn loud . . .*"

Evan shivered, and a childlike instinct told him to *run*. His skin crawled, his lips went numb and pale with dread.

A voice from the past, buried deep but not forgotten.

Where does your trailer trash mother buy your clothes, at Kmart? Yeah! She buys 'em at Kmart! From now on, your name is Kmart, you poor sack of shit. Kmart! Kmart! Kmart!

Their blurred faces snarled a hatred that Evan couldn't possibly comprehend. He was trapped on a playground merry-go-round, a frightened fourth-grader at Ridgewood Academy. The three boys had forced him on it and were now spinning him around, faster and faster. The centrifugal force smashed his face on the cold metal bar he held in a death grip. *Kmart's poor, Kmart's poor, Kmart's poor.* Why? What did I do? Why me? The bullies spun him faster, violently, and faintness joined young Evan's fear. They were chanting, frenzied, like rabid animals. *Kmart! Welfare! Food stamps! Trailer trash!* Willoughby, we played blocks once in first grade. What did I do? Evan pictured a pack of Mutual of Omaha hyenas circling a wounded wildebeest. Please make them stop. Please. Evan's eyes closed and his thin body went limp. The force pulled his legs to the edge of the spinning merry-go-round. His tormenters smelled blood. *Kmart! Die you worthless piece of shit! Die! Die, Kmart, die!* Spittle flew from their mouths as they screamed. When consciousness escaped him, Evan's body spun off the merry-go-round like a rag doll, landing in the wet grass outside the muddy rut formed by children running around and around the playground toy. Triumphant, the three fellow fourth-graders ran off to play on the nearby jungle gym.

During his first three years at Ridgewood, Evan enjoyed a peaceful coexistence with his privileged peers. He and his classmates were *children*. But something had changed over the summer. The children had evolved, become consumer beasts, their entitlement realized and unleashed, hell-bent on being just like mom and dad, echoes wed to idolatry.

When Evan woke up, he was quite sure he was in heaven. An angel looked down on him, beautiful and clean. For an instant, he was happy.

Then he blinked, and the angel was his teacher, debutante Brown graduate Miss Lockwood. *You're okay, Evan,* he heard her say. *The boys said you
fell, but you're okay. Your blazer is torn, but you'll be just fine. Just rest here
until your bus arrives.* Evan closed his eyes and touched her arm. Hopefully I'll die before that happens. Will you say nice things to me in heaven?
Please?

*You goddam piece of worthless shit! Do you have any fucking idea how
much that cost?* When Evan got home, George immediately noticed his
rumpled clothes and torn blazer. After a few beers of cursing to himself, he
beat Evan with a heavy wooden hairbrush.

After the beating, as Evan lay quietly sobbing on his bedroom floor,
Faye snuck into the room. *It's okay, baby, it's okay,* she said, cradling him
in her arms. *I'll fix your blazer for tomorrow. It'll be fine. You just do good
at that school, and you'll have what those boys have. Do good, and someday you'll have money. You'll have money, baby. No one will hurt you
then.*

Evan endured twelve years at Ridgewood, the childhood equivalent of
the Bataan Death March. After about the seventh grade, the physical ha-
rassment and beatings subsided and Kmart faded into the background,
generally tolerated if not ignored. Few students ever spoke to him. He was
a ghost, wrapped in a cloak of indifference. The last to arrive and the first
to leave, Evan learned how to all but disappear.

*You belong in their world, baby. Yes, you do. You don't belong here, in
this place. Calm . . . calm . . . belong.* Faye whispered to Evan with anxious
hope, the polar opposite of resentment.

Of course, in the later years Evan was still subjected to the occasional
vitriolic remark—*You don't belong here, Kmart. Why don't you just leave?*—
and the stares and snickers constantly reminded him that he was *different*
from his classmates; he was *poor.*

When freshman year began and he moved across the building to the
upper school, two scholarship students joined his class of sixty, and Evan
thought he might gain an ally, if not a friend. No such luck. Ridgewood
munificently covered the boys' tuition because they were superior athletes,
one soccer and one golf. They stuck together the first year and were even-

tually accepted by the ruling elite, the clique of dominant "lifers" who passed judgment on all others. Evan accepted his fate; he was alone.

"It is a fearful word, alone," Evan read in a book that year, a book, a *prayer*, that would give him the strength to march on.

"Holy shit, it's Kmart!"

Evan was sitting at the bar, still in the nightmare, when he heard the words. He languidly turned to his right to see a stout young man walking toward him from the back restaurant area. Willoughby Andrews, the ringleader on the playground that day, wore a gray suit and carried a Brooks Brothers topcoat as he approached Evan with a big buzzed smile on his rich round face. Evan took a sip of his Pilsner Urquell just as Willoughby put a heavy hand on his shoulder.

"How the hell are you?"

"Hello, Willoughby. What brings you here?"

"Oh, my buddy back there just got engaged, so I drove in from Darien to celebrate with him and another guy. Heading back now."

Aryan Darien, who would have imagined? Evan thought before actually asking, "How's life?"

"Perfect! Couldn't be better. My dad and I moved the business to Connecticut three years ago and he just retired, so it's all mine now." Willoughby rubbed his thumb and first two fingers together, palm up. "Major cash cow, which keeps my wife and kids happy." Evan could see the alcohol in his eyes, and in the eyes of his two friends who now stood behind him.

"Oh, hey, this is Jackson Peters and Chris Wilton. Chris just got engaged."

They nodded hellos and Evan said congratulations.

"This is Evan Stoest. He graduated with my class at Ridgewood."

"Stoess, Willoughby, *Stoess*."

"Yeah, Stoess. Rhymes with 'mess.' Back then we called him Kmart for some reason . . . Man! Those were the days."

Jackson and Chris offered fake smiles; Evan did not. Willoughby had a question.

"How long were you at Ridgewood, anyway?"

"Twelve years, Willoughby. I was a lifer, just like you." The irony of the statement escaped Willoughby, but not Evan.

Willoughby removed his meaty, manicured hand from Evan's shoulder with a look of genuine shock.

"A lifer? No shit?"

"No shit."

For a moment Willoughby's face went blank and he stared into space. If he was capable of unearthing the past, Evan chose to spare him the revelation.

"Hey! Let me buy you guys a shot, to celebrate the engagement . . . and old times."

Willoughby shook his head. "I really shouldn't. Gotta drive back to Darien."

"C'mon! Just one shot. Jackson? Chris?"

"Sure, why not?" Chris said.

Willoughby looked at his friends, then at Evan. He was shellacked in self-confidence. "Okay, what the hell? One shot." Willoughby slapped the bar. "Let's do it!"

Evan ordered four tall shots of Gentleman Jack, and the men threw them back.

"Good stuff," Jackson said.

"The best."

Willoughby man-hugged Chris and announced it was *definitely* time for him to go. At least an hour's drive to Darien, what with construction on the Triborough Bridge. The other guys lived in the neighborhood; they could walk home.

After the perfunctory good-byes, Evan watched the three friends step out onto Third Avenue. Observing them closely, he took a tip quarter off of the bar and, because the bartender was eyeing him, replaced it with a dollar bill from his pocket. Chris and Jackson walked south; Willoughby walked north.

"I'll be right back," Evan said abruptly to the bartender. "It's time to worship at the altar of schadenfreude." J.G. Melon was a cash-only establishment; Evan didn't have a credit card holding his tab, but the barkeep spied Evan's topcoat on his stool, so he squinted his assent. Evan didn't notice and didn't care.

He stayed about twenty yards behind Willoughby, following him as he ambled north on Third Avenue. At Seventy-sixth Street, in the light coming from Haru, Willoughby fished keys out of his pocket and pushed a button on the key chain. Evan saw the taillights of a Mercedes blink. Willoughby's standard-issue *Aryan Darien* car, parallel parked behind a yellow Mini Cooper. Evan watched him cautiously pull away from the curb, Willoughby MacLean Andrews planning to return to his perfect life in rich people's Connecticut. *Not tonight, asshole. You're done.*

Evan ran across Third Avenue to a pay phone on the opposite corner. He dropped the tip quarter in the slot and dialed.

"9-1-1, what's your emergency?"

"Uh, yeah, a really drunk guy just got in his car and drove off. I tried to stop him, but he said to fuck off 'cause he had a *gun*."

"Can you describe the—"

"Silver Mercedes E500 sedan. Connecticut license plate CMS-903. Heading north on Third Avenue toward the Triborough, probably around Eightieth Street right now. The drunk driver is white, mid-thirties, wearing a suit."

"He said he had a gun?"

"Yeah. I told him he shouldn't drive, and he said fuck off mind your own business, so I said no, really, and he said he had a gun, nine millimeter. I was scared, so I let him go and called you."

"One moment while I dispatch officers."

Evan looked around for a convenient bodega, considered buying a Twix for dessert.

"Okay, sir? Can I have your name? Officers are intercepting."

"I don't want to get involved. The guy could be in the mob or something. *Sopranos* shit. No way."

"But sir—"

"Thanks for helpin' out."

Evan hung up and walked calmly back to his waiting barstool, cheerfully humming Pearl Jam's "Jeremy." *Clearly I remember . . . pickin' on the boy.* In the event the cops stopped by the pay phone, he didn't want to be buying his Twix nearby. *Seemed a harmless little fuck.* He'd get it later, the only candy bar with the cookie crunch. *But we unleashed a lion . . .*

Safely back in J.G. Melon, he celebrated with another beer and wondered if he'd be reading *that* news in Ridgewood's alumni newsletter.

CHAPTER
THIRTY-FIVE

"Have patience, chief."

It was Friday, just after the markets' close; Mac and Evan were meeting in Kennedy's office for a progress report.

"That's right, Mac, *patience.* We had an excellent week. We're halfway there, fifty million in, and GPTL is holding up. I've found the shares and the buyers, and when word leaked on Wednesday that smart money was short, I bought a small block from a well-known loudmouth to confuse the street, then on the uptick I hit the bid and dumped a large block with my best quiet guy."

"That's beautiful, Kennedy."

Kennedy beamed; this was his nirvana.

Evan asked, "How does next week look?"

Kennedy straightened up and cracked his knuckles. "Next week is going to be too much fun."

Mac raised his eyebrows. Kennedy acknowledged Mac's skepticism.

"Well, at least for *me* it is. Might be a little stressful for you girls upstairs."

"Why is that?"

"Well, Mr. Stoess, buyers are getting thin. I'm not worried about

finding the shares, but with fewer players lifting the offer, I'll probably
have to create my own opportunities, and we might have to step back and
wait for a few days."

"Create your own opportunities—"

Mac interrupted. "He'll buy more small blocks to create an uptick and
then short with another broker."

"Exactly. And I'll put out five or six offers to buy on different ECNs,
aka *dark pools* because they are completely anonymous, so not only will
we get the uptick, we'll create the impression that buyers are out there. We
want GPTL to tank *after* we've closed our position."

"Amen to that," Mac said as he stood, signaling an end to the sit-down.

Evan sensed that the men wanted to say something else, some clever
cliché or pithy bon mots, to just perfectly capture the "band of brothers"
moment. *Point of no return. We're in this together. It's now or never. Let's
win one for the team. If Evan fucks this up, we'll skin him alive. We'll dump
his worthless corpse in the East River. Win-win!*

But not a word was spoken.

Back at his desk, Evan refreshed his memory of the SEC's venerable uptick
rule. Adopted in 1938, in response to "bear raids" that allegedly crushed
the market in '37, Rule 10a-1 forced short-sellers to sell borrowed shares
only after the price had gone up a "tick" from the previous sale price. The
goal was obvious—prevent shorts from causing a stock's downward spiral
with their own successive sales of borrowed stock.

The rule worked; the "ghoulish characters" who started nasty rumors
and hoped for catastrophe lost a powerful weapon, the unrestricted selling, or "raids," that could devastate a company's stock and send the shorts'
profits soaring.

Evan laughed out loud when he read about an earlier attempt to dis-
courage short-selling. In 1932, the United States Senate published the names
of those people and firms holding the largest short positions. The goal? To
shame them as immoral, evil, and unpatriotic.

Immoral? Bullshit. It's immoral not *to make money.* Evan's mind flashed
and he quickly googled Francisco's money speech, a passage he memorized

long ago for an NYU literature class. As he read it, a certain comfort washed over him, warm and soothing, like a true believer reciting the Lord's Prayer.

Money is your means of survival . . . When you have made evil the means of survival, do not expect men to remain good. Do not expect them to stay moral and to become fodder for the immoral. Do not expect them to produce when production is punished and looting rewarded. Do not ask who is destroying the world. You are.

"Amen."

CHAPTER
THIRTY-SIX

When Daniel Gotbaum walked into GoPostal's boardroom, everybody was in their seats, waiting patiently, munching on catered H&H bagels and sipping strong coffee.

"Am I late?"

"No, sir."

"Right on time."

"We just got here."

"Perfect timing."

"Hell yes. Where you been?"

Daniel smiled at his son and savored the irony. He grabbed an everything bagel as Albert Higgins's secretary handed him a cup of coffee, "regular."

After an hour of boring company bullshit, Albert closed his black leather portfolio, sat back and crossed his arms.

"Okay, that concludes the formal agenda. The minutes for the meeting will now end. But we have something important to discuss, off the record, so how about we take five minutes and then unofficially reconvene?"

Joshua looked at Al, raised his eyebrows and telepathically inquired, *Can I go now? Please?*

As the others headed for the facilities and coffee pot, Albert said, "Stick around, Joshua; you'll enjoy this."

Ten minutes later, the curious group waited to hear the news. Kathy Fiscus, in charge of investor relations, had joined them, pulling up a chair next to Albert.

Albert made the most of his moment. After clearing his throat and a dramatic pause, he announced: "Ladies and gentleman, a bear, *or bears,* is hunting us. They smell blood, but I promise you, the blood they smell is their own."

After two seconds of silence, the room erupted in excited and inquisitive murmurs. Only Daniel was still. He stared at Albert, who refused to meet his eye. While Daniel appreciated Albert's moment in the spotlight, he didn't like surprises.

"Al, tell us what you know."

"Kathy?"

Kathy, a confident and extremely competent Wharton graduate, stood up to address GoPostal's board of directors.

"Last Friday afternoon, after the markets closed, I received a phone call from a trustworthy contact who works on the trading desk of a major Wall Street bank. This person, and her firm, of course, must remain anonymous."

Kathy stepped back from the table and began to walk around the room, drawing everyone's undivided attention. Albert beamed; she was his protégé.

"Last week our stock was off a few dollars on unusually high volume. According to my source, a talented firm or firms is taking a large short position in our stock. We don't know which firms, and we won't have the numbers for a couple of weeks, but my contact called around and guesses it's *at least* a million shares, with indications it will continue next week."

Kathy explained that apparently the short-selling was spread out over many brokers and was accompanied by anonymous ECN activity, "dark pools," she intoned ominously. She believed the shorting would continue because it ended quietly on Friday, and "the bears will want to show their claws when the time is right." After fielding a few questions on the mechanics and implications of the activity, Kathy returned to her seat and asked, "Any other questions before Albert takes over?"

"I've got one," Joshua said. "Why are these assho—*people* after us? All's well, right?"

"I have *my* theories, but I also checked the chat rooms for gossip and rumors. First, the short interest in our stock has been *nil,* so that's attractive to bears. Beyond that, it's pure speculation, a big gamble. There's lot of chatter about the Microsoft deal. Congress. The industry. From the outside, in this market and industry, I can see why there's interest. But they're wrong." Kathy looked to Albert.

"Perfect segue, Kathy, and thank you. Absolutely they're wrong, and we're going to nail them to the wall. This very well could be great for our stock price."

"How's that?" Joshua asked.

Bernie Cornblum answered. "All the stock that has been sold short was *borrowed.* If the share price goes up, the bears will be forced to cover, to buy back the shares at whatever price. Their own buying could drive our price even higher."

"A short squeeze," Kathy said.

"Exactly. A short squeeze."

Daniel knew the gist of the answer, but he asked anyway. "What's the plan, Al?"

"Okay. Bernie, Kathy and I have a multipoint strategy that covers the next three weeks."

Albert explained that during the current week, GoPostal would remain quiet and see what transpired. *Let the bastards dig their own graves,* he said.

Second, Bernie had spoken to the institutional investors and would close the private placement on Friday, two weeks ahead of schedule.

"With the cash in the bank, on Monday of week two, seven days from now, we'll publicly announce the share buyback. The street will love it and that alone could panic the shorts."

Also next week, Albert informed the group, the International Game Developers Association was meeting in Denver and would announce that

Congress had shelved the idea of further regulating the industry. "That's great news for us and the entire industry."

"Finally, in week three, if all goes as planned, which it will, we and Microsoft will announce positive news about our development deal. That, my friends, will be the coup de grâce." Albert leaned way back in his chair, his fingers laced behind his head.

"With all the news and the squeeze, our stock could *easily* double, maybe top eighty bucks," Bernie said. Kathy nodded in agreement.

Daniel looked around the table, watching his fellow directors digest the information. John Barnard was one of GoPostal's ostensibly independent directors, an accomplished securities attorney.

"John, your thoughts, please."

"As a group, we must remain absolutely silent on this issue. Do *not* discuss it with *anyone* until NASDAQ releases the official short interest data at the end of the month. Proceed as if we knew *nothing* of the shorting activity because, officially, we do not."

He looked specifically at Kathy, who would field inquiries from the press.

"After the NASDAQ release, all of our corporate actions were long-planned and occurred and are occurring in the regular course of business. Although we've upped the timetable, we have truth on our side with that one, fortunately."

"Good advice, John. Anyone else?" After a moment of silence, Daniel motioned to Albert, deferring the corporate benediction to the man of the hour.

"Great! This nonmeeting that never happened would now be adjourned if said nonmeeting had occurred and was thereby adjournable."

The group laughed. They had good reason to be happy. They all owned stock and most had options vesting in February. If the stock doubled, they'd be rich, if they weren't already.

CHAPTER
THIRTY-SEVEN

Bernie Cornblum did his job, as did Kennedy Phillips.

On Friday, in a law firm's conference room in the Freedom Tower, GoPostal closed the private placement of convertible debt that would provide the cash for its stock buyback. On Monday, as planned, the company would announce its intention to purchase its own shares on the open market, a strong signal that it believed its stock was undervalued.

A few blocks away, as the ink dried on GoPostal's deal, Contrafund closed its $100 million short position. In total, Kennedy managed to borrow and sell almost 3 million shares of GoPostal's common stock. For every dollar that GoPostal's stock dropped, Contrafund would make three million dollars. Of course, for every dollar the price went *up* . . .

"What's the word, Kathy?" Bernie was engaged in a cell phone walk-and-talk, returning to his office after the closing.

"Is the money in the bank?"

"Yes, indeed it is. I have the wire receipts right here to prove it."

"Fantastic," Kathy said. "Volume is up again today, big blocks selling left and right, but we're only down seventy-five cents."

"What's the word?"

"According to my sources on the street, it's one major player, Bernie. Someone is taking a *huge* gamble, we're talkin' two or three *million* shares."

"Good. They're fucked," Bernie quickly replied, his competitive spirit riled by the audacious position. "We'll press release the buyback on Monday after the close, file the 8-K. They'll choke on it, the stupid bastards."

"It's done, Mac. GPTL. A hundred freakin' million." Kennedy had him on speakerphone, an hour before the markets closed for the week.

"You're kidding. Already?"

"I'm surprised too. On Wednesday a bunch of shares became available through the DTCC's Stock Borrow Program, the Depository Trust and Clearing Corporation. I jumped on the opportunity and the price held up. We'll pay a fee to the clearing division for the shares, but it's done. And by Monday the street will know it."

"You told some guys to talk it up?"

"I sold the last fifty thousand shares with an obnoxious schmuck who *will* talk it up. You'll see on Monday; I guarantee it."

"Good job, Kennedy. I'll let Evan know."

"You did *what*?" Albert Higgins couldn't compute what Daniel Gotbaum was telling him.

"I fed the bear."

"How, exactly?"

"On Tuesday, I transferred half a million shares of my stock to my broker's unpledged account at the Depository Trust. Then I had him tell the DTCC that my shares were available for borrowing. Sure enough, the bear took the bait."

"You clever bastard. We gave 'em the noose to hang themselves."

"You got it. And get this—I'm earning *interest* on the full cash value of the borrowed shares as long as they're out. Can you believe *that*?"

"Beautiful, Daniel. Absolutely beautiful."

"Okay, Mac, what do we do now?"

"You know the drill, chief. We sit back and let nature take its course."

"Kennedy mentioned calling analysts and the media, letting them know we think GoPostal is overvalued."

"You know my stance on that—only if absolutely necessary. That sort of thing is what gives short-sellers a bad name. If GPTL's price goes up on rumors, we'll counter; but until then, we'll let the fundamentals work themselves out." Mac paused and looked Evan hard in the eye. "*Patience . . . okay?*"

"Okay," Evan replied, but it stuck in this throat. He could think of only one thing, his mother's words, so long ago. *Someday you'll have money. You'll have money, baby. No one will hurt you then.*

Someday was now.

CHAPTER

THIRTY-EIGHT

On Friday afternoon word spread that smart money was short GPTL. By late Monday morning, the rumor had amplified and some brokers began warning their best clients of impending downgrades.

After lunch, the selling began.

Kennedy called Evan when the price hit $30.

"Well, whaddaya say?"

Evan was beyond ecstatic, but he tried to keep his cool. "Bid is below thirty now. Down four bucks today. Word is out, huh?"

"Yep. And if limit orders kick in . . . stand back."

"So what's happening out there, with the traders?" Evan asked.

"Just a lot of talk. Our short position got 'em talking. People think somebody knows something. What are you seeing?"

"The usual—rumors and speculation," Evan replied.

"Of course. The engines that drive the Street."

"You got it. Let me know if you hear anything interesting, okay?"

"Will do."

Evan punched up GoPostal's Yahoo! message board, fertile ground for hearsay and rationalizations. *Smart money. Microsoft. New regulations. Sales forecasts.* They were all there. One post discussed Joshua Gotbaum's "drug problem" and claimed that Gotbaum had entered a rehab program in Arizona. Intrigued, Evan scrolled down the thread. *Find out tomorrow if it's true,* he read. *Gotbaum is supposed to speak at NYU. If he's there, he ain't in rehab in AZ.*

Evan googled it up. Sure enough, Joshua Gotbaum was scheduled to appear on Tuesday at an entrepreneurship conference sponsored by NYU's Stern School of Business. The shiny new Kimmel Center, 60 Washington Square South. Evan made a mental note.

Sitting on his sofa three hours later, an almost empty bottle of Woodford Reserve resting on his knee, Evan fought the panic laying siege to his psyche.

GoPostal's "encouraging" buyback announcement hit the news wire at five o'clock. Shortly thereafter, an industry mouthpiece in Denver declared victory over censorship—Congress had blinked, postponing consideration of new video game regulations that could hurt sales. GoPostal's stock would undoubtedly recover on Tuesday, and possibly worse.

Two minutes after the news hit the wire, Evan was in Mac's office. Staring at his bottle of booze, he replayed the proceedings.

"What's going on here, chief?"

"Well, Congress—"

"Forget about Congress. They could change their minds tomorrow. The buyback. Tell me about the buyback. GPTL doesn't have the cash for it."

"They *didn't*, Mac. They filed an 8-K *today*, 'entry into a material definitive agreement and unregistered sales of equity securities.' On Friday they closed a private placement of convertible debt with institutional investors. They plan to use the cash for the buyback." *Right there, that was it. The moment the panic mobilized to attack.*

"Could be bullshit."

"What?"

"I've seen it before. GPTL knows smart money is short, and they know a buyback announcement could trigger a quick cover, so they announce it but never follow through. They back off the deal, *based on market conditions* or whatever."

"Bastards."

"Exactly. I've seen companies do some crazy shit when they're under the gun."

Crazy shit. Suddenly feeling empowered, Evan capped the bottle tightly, set it aside, and dialed Mac's direct line. Voice mail, as anticipated.

"Hey Mac, it's Evan. I won't be in until around noon tomorrow. A GPTL executive is speaking at a conference downtown; maybe he'll field a question about the buyback. I'll let you know what I hear. See you around noon."

Like a patient enemy, the panic withdrew, just out of sight. Evan leaned back and closed his eyes.

One hundred and twenty steps. The gauntlet from bus stop to screen door. Evan's Via Dolorosa, a terrifying path from purgatory to hell.

It wasn't until years later that Evan counted the paces at the other end, from bus stop to freshman home room, the ghost walk from cradle to grave. One hundred and twenty steps.

The Jeffersonian symmetry did not escape Evan. A veneer of genteel serenity, an antebellum utopia, conceals the ugly truth: Within, the Sage of Monticello rapes a slave in the parlor.

CHAPTER

THIRTY-NINE

A somber sky overhead, Evan walked under the Washington Square Arch and started across the park. He could see NYU's Kimmel Center rising ahead and to his left, its windowed façade shining brightly in the late January gloom. Staring at the many windows, Evan recalled reading about a rash of student suicides and wondered if self-defenestration concerned the school. *Probably not. Once the tuition check clears, let 'em jump.*

He crossed Washington Square South at La Guardia Place, the red-brick law school on his right. *Where English majors learn to lie for a living*, he mused with a smile as he entered the Kimmel Center for the Stern School's annual Entrepreneurship Conference.

After the cold and quiet solitude of the park, the humid warmth and noise surprised him. The lobby area was crowded with groups of students and young professionals, friends, acquaintances and colleagues, standing in circles, sipping coffee and babbling meaningless bullshit. Evan hated all of them. He approached the registration desk.

"Your name?" She was cute. Young. Probably a work-study undergrad.

"Valerius Babrius."

"Cool name." She looked down at a multipage list of attendees, then up at Evan. He smiled as she spoke.

"Are you registered?"

"Actually, no. I'm a work-study student at City College just hoping to hear the ten o'clock speaker. I'm a big fan of his video games."

The young lady looked to her left and right, before saying quietly, "Okay. I'll give you a name tag, but if you try to attend any of the seminars or get the box lunch you'll be asked for your registration, so don't—"

"No worries. I'll be outta here right after the ten o'clock, I promise."

Evan entered the crowded room and found a lone seat on the left side, near the stage. Normally he sat toward the back, but he wanted—*needed*—to get a good look at this guy.

The morning's program was running behind; the nine thirty speaker was due up next. Evan frowned, vaguely recalling his voice mail promise.

Finally, after suffering through twenty minutes of some asexual dork's breathless dreaming about nanotechnology, the time came to meet Joshua Gotbaum.

As the conference chair began his glowing introduction, Evan shifted in his seat, nervous. Not with anticipation, but with *fear.*

And then Joshua Gotbaum took the stage. *So much for rehab.*

Behind the outsized podium, Gotbaum was five foot nothin', weighing in at a buck-o-five, max. Evan thought that probably wasn't too far from the truth. After taking in the scene, he was drawn to Gotbaum's inexplicably familiar facial features.

The bushy Jewfro. The glasses. The prominent beak. *Holy shit, he looks just like Artie Ziff, Marge Simpson's prom date!* Evan laughed out loud, drawing the glares of several assholes in his vicinity.

Gotbaum spoke of the excitement of being an entrepreneur and launching a new company at age twenty, and of the trials and tribulations of going public. Evan yawned, looked at his watch. He spoke of the importance of corporate innovation, the pursuit of dreams, flying higher, and other ridiculous clichés that pissed off Evan to no end. Then Joshua turned his attention to GoPostal, its rapid growth and strategies for future success.

"Yesterday we announced plans to repurchase a significant amount of our company's stock . . ." With each word, Evan felt a fresh dollop of sweat emerge on his forehead.

"We learned that Congress will not censor our products or regulate our sales . . ." His clammy hands left stains on his trousers.

"In the coming weeks, we're anticipating favorable news on a development deal with a major platform provider . . ." Evan's vision faded as if covered in gauze. He fought the faintness.

He leaned forward, chin down, clenched his eyes tightly shut and gritted his teeth. *"You too have the power to become a successful entrepreneur. Follow your dreams!"* Joshua finished his speech to loud applause.

Evan raised his swollen head, eyes still closed, and exhaled through pursed lips. Slowly opening his eyes, he watched Gotbaum exit stage right, an excited group of attendees waiting for him, a menagerie of video game geeks and budding entrepreneurs. As Gotbaum stepped off the stage and shook hands with the conference chair, a long receiving line formed, the unwashed masses waiting to kiss the Pope's ring.

Fucking putrid supplicants, Evan snarled to himself. *I'd kill them all if I could.*

Walking east on Fourth Street toward the Astor Place subway station, Evan considered his options.

With Mac's approval, he could officially call some retail analysts and perhaps even the media, but with all the positive news, what good could it do? Contrafund's efforts would be transparent—the desperate move of a bear fund obviously stuck in a bad position. The same unfortunate reality applied to any report Contrafund issued to support the short, or any attempt to influence independent research providers like CFRA or even Behind the Numbers. Without a doubt, the ethical options were already foreclosed.

But a little thing like ethics never stopped Wall Street. Evan was well aware of *his* ethical obligation, *to make money.*

Turning north on Lafayette, Evan switched gears, slowed his pace, and considered his *real* options. He could see the Kmart up ahead, adjacent to the subway entrance. The sight of it inspired him.

Bullshit Internet rumors were an easy choice, à la Conrad Black. Weak. Ineffective. He could leak rumors directly to some hedge fund managers and GoPostal's competitors. But from an anonymous or fictitious source? Lame. Pedestrian. Pathetic.

The problem was all the *goddam* good news. Buyback. Congress. Microsoft. How to creatively circumvent the good news and effectively torpedo the stock? "How to circumvent the machine and learn if the inevitable admits a loophole?" Evan asked himself, quoting Camus' imprisoned Meursault as the guillotine loomed. He looked up at the leaden sky, letting his mind wander. The guillotine certainly loomed. He searched the clouds for a loophole.

Where English majors learn to lie for a living. He stopped. Looked around to see if anyone else heard his mental inspiration, grinned broadly, and continued. So simple. So obvious.

Those fucking bureaucrat lawyers with their endless rules and regulations. Sarbanes-Oxley. Dodd-Frank. I'll capitalize on the morons' knee-jerk paranoia. Fucking beautiful.

An anonymous employee sends a letter to GoPostal's audit committee and CPA firm. Whistle-blower. Internal accounting irregularities. Fraud. Make-believe revenue. Worse than Take Two Interactive. Something must be done, before it's too late.

Definitely an option, Evan mused, spitting on Kmart's display window as he passed, startling an employee inside.

"Evan . . ." Mac's voice was an octave lower than usual, rising with every word. "What the hell is going on with GoPostal?"

Evan was taking off his coat, the heady glow of destruction still warming his soul. He raised his eyebrows at Mac.

"It's up three dollars today. What's the story? Did Gotbaum say anything about the share repurchase?"

"You were right, Mac. *Crazy shit.* A steaming pile of hype, probably so the insiders can sell."

"You sure this stock'll tank?"

"Oh yeah, quite sure. I'd bet my life on it."

CHAPTER

FORTY

Back at his apartment, Evan drafted an anonymous letter to the audit committee of GoPostal's board of directors. He thought it was effective, if not particularly articulate. *Remember, an accountant-type is writing this,* he said to the wastebasket next to his desk. Weak, passive voice. Fear in the words, but also conviction. Not disgruntled. Slightly self-righteous. No spelling errors, too meticulous for that. One grammar mistake, easily overlooked. A math or econ major, after all.

But Evan had his doubts. GoPostal was a relatively small company. He worried the accusations could be quickly investigated and dismissed. *And,* from what he had heard today, he didn't have much time.

Anxiety crawled into his gut, accompanied by fatigue, and he decided to call it a night.

Maybe the SEC is the way to go. Force a Wells Notice. He committed to investigating the criteria and timetable the next morning. But he had his doubts.

The vivid dream came quickly, like a powerful tsunami. The funeral home was packed to the gills, hundreds of tearful mourners gathered to celebrate a life lost, to confront their own collective fate and defy their own fears.

Evan walked among them, from room to room, in awe of his power to attract. Faceless women with slumped shoulders, sniffling into their handkerchiefs. Unknown men standing tall, too proud to emote. He happily lingered in the dream. The main room, dark and larger than he expected, was majestically decorated, flowers everywhere. Crystal chandeliers and gold leaf. A magnificent funeral. An expensive proposition. *I did it. I won.*

For a moment he rose above the crowd to see the casket in the distance. It was surrounded by a halo of warm light. Drawn to it, he slowly threaded his way through the worthy congregants, reveling in their grief. The prospect of viewing his peaceful corpse emanated tremendous comfort. He was calm, reassured, adored. Such a moment of sheer joy, unencumbered exhilaration, he had never felt before.

Evan filtered through the dark crowd of mourners and stepped into the warm halo of light. Silence, utter and complete, embraced him.

The golden casket was open, a resplendent sarcophagus fit for a pharaoh. He stepped toward it, victory defeating a flood of painful memories, a quick slideshow before his watery eyes. George, Ridgewood, Willoughby, Gus. Marshall Owen, Mitch, Marin. *Powerless.*

The coffin called him forward, in it, his Victory Complete. He turned to the spectral mass behind him in the darkness. They were still. He sensed they could see him now, encouraging him to take the final step. *They know,* he recognized. *One more step,* they whispered. *One more step.*

Evan turned back to the golden glow, its radiating warmth enveloping him. He savored the quiet inner peace that surpassed his understanding. He stepped forward and looked inside the casket.

Joshua Gotbaum lay before him.

Evan blinked in disbelief and looked again. Joshua Gotbaum. More thin and fragile in death than in life.

Evan closed his eyes, in his dream a curtain drawn across a bright stage. The peace, the calm, the reassurance, the adoration—the soothing warmth stayed with him. The curtain opened.

Joshua Gotbaum lay before him.

A gentle whisper, *You did it. You won. Your Victory Complete.* He turned again to face the haunted memories, now standing in the light. As one, they retreated into darkness. Only the warm glow remained. Evan felt it settle inside him, occupy his body and soul, crowding out pain and anxiety, fear and doubt. Motionless he stood before Redemption. Fade to black.

In one motion Evan leaped out of bed and landed on his feet, like a marionette clumsily called into service, the cold floor a rude return to consciousness.

So simple, so obvious.

Joshua Gotbaum must die.

CHAPTER

FORTY-ONE

As usual, the Sprint store on Eighty-sixth Street was a complete cluster-fuck. Evan left his office early and, after changing into baggy jeans, a sweatshirt, and a hideous ghetto-red Yankees cap, arrived chez Sprint at peak rush hour. He waited twenty minutes for a salesperson, during which time he stood quietly in the window, watching the people on the busy sidewalk outside.

The pay-as-you-go phone, with one hundred minutes of talk time, cost ninety-nine dollars. No contract. No bills. No nothing. Evan paid cash and walked two blocks south to a public phone on the corner of Second Avenue and Eighty-fourth Street. He dropped in a quarter and dialed the activation number for his new cell phone.

He found the electronic serial number under the battery. When his "customer care specialist" asked for his name and address, Evan became William "Bill" Jones, shelter resident.

"You're *homeless?*"

"Yeah, but I'm lookin' for a job and need a phone where I can get calls. Spent my last dime on this'un."

"Uh, credit card?"

Evan snorted. "No credit, no card, no credit card. That's why I got this here phone."

"I understand, sir. We're happy to accommodate you. One moment."

Evan smiled, looked across the street at Dorrian's. *Robert Chambers met his quarry there. Perhaps history could repeat itself . . .*

"Okay, sir? Your number has been assigned and your phone will be active in approximately thirty minutes. You have one hundred prepaid minutes that expire in ninety days."

"Plenty of time."

"Super. And you can add minutes by purchasing a Top-Up card at any retail store, and then calling us with the serial number on the card. Top-Up cards come in denominations of twenty dollars and you may pay cash for the cards."

"Perfect."

"Have a great day, Mr. Jones, and good luck."

"Yeah, thanks."

Evan walked home, whistling a tune.

CHAPTER
FORTY-TWO

The Paslode Model #900420.

On Saturday, Evan decided to check off this key item from his mental list.

With six hundred dollars cash in his pocket, he headed to Penn Station to catch the 1:14 P.M. train to Deer Park, Long Island. Once again, he chose clothes he would not ordinarily wear. An old pair of 501s, faded and stained. A heavy New York Jets sweatshirt purchased at the Second Avenue Goodwill for seven dollars. Boots he bought in business school for snowy winters, outdated and workmanlike. And a black ski cap, pulled low over his ears.

The LIRR covered the forty miles in about seventy minutes. Evan sat alone in the last car, gazing out a north side window as the train passed through an endless parade of suburban death traps. A few reminded him of the hellhole he grew up in. At one point, as the train slowed to a crawl, he watched dirty children playing in the backyard of a shitty shotgun house, oblivious to the pain that awaited them. If they knew, he was certain, they would dutifully lay down on the tracks and accept their fate.

Seeing them, Dickens's urchins blissfully unaware of their own hopeless fate, Evan knew he was the same, but different. He heard a voice from his past. *"You're different. Not typical Ridgewood Academy."*

Yes, Ridgewood was the difference. A twist of fate. A cruel, wonderful promise offered to a child who had no choice but to accept. Evan closed his eyes and remembered the promise.

Money. Power.

Wall Street.

For the *sprezzatura* incarnate, Ridgewood was the first step. They were silver-spoon pickpockets born to exploit the lazy, the feeble-minded, and the naïve—the Pleasant Grove denizens who had neither the sense nor the will to join their ranks. The indoctrinated insiders easily mastered the deadbeat outsiders, protecting society's incestuous birthright. Kmart knew the truth. Richie knew the truth. He *lived* it, a fugitive in both worlds, ostracized and reviled, always struggling to belong. But the struggle would soon end. He would join the ranks of the Winners, forever abandoning the wilted Losers.

Evan sat back, smiled as the train accelerated. *"When force is the standard, the murderer wins over the pickpocket. And then that society vanishes, in a spread of ruins and slaughter."* He whispered the prayer to himself, over and over again.

The Home Depot was about a mile from the train station, a treacherous walk along a busy Long Island Avenue to Commack Road. When he saw the P.C. Richard up ahead, he knew he was close.

As planned, Home Depot was jam-packed with Saturday shoppers, Evan's just another unremarkable face in an unremarkable crowd. He spotted an employee walking away from a satisfied customer holding a heavy-duty sander. A black gentleman, older, name tag said IKE. *Perfect.*

"May I help you, sir?"

"Uh-huh. I'm looking for a Paslode model number 900420."

"Good choice. We have it, right over here." They walked together toward a Paslode display area. "*Excellent* choice. Cordless, fuel cell powered. Lightweight. Well-balanced. *Powerful.*"

"Powerful?" Evan asked.

"The most powerful nail gun on the market. She'll drive a three-inch nail into solid concrete." They stopped and Ike removed the bright orange Cordless Framing Nailer from the pegged wall. At first glance it looked like a cross between a handgun and a Wagner Power Painter, with a grip and trigger like a pistol, but with the heft and utility of a power tool. About a foot tall and five inches thick at its thickest, the nail gun would slip easily into an over-the-shoulder messenger bag.

"Here she is. On sale for three forty-nine." He handed the nail gun to Evan.

"Hey, it's lighter than I expected."

"About seven pounds fully loaded with fuel, battery, and one strip of forty-four three-and-a-quarter-inch nails, ring shank or smooth, depending on use." Ike looked at Evan, anticipating an answer.

"My buddy an' me are building a deck on the back of his house."

Ike smiled knowingly. Lots of do-it-yourself decks in Deer Park. He nodded. "Smooth nails will do the job, then. She'll fire three nails per second, and twelve hundred with one fuel cell."

Fuck me, Evan thought. *In three minutes I could kill the entire fucking company and half the shareholders.* He asked, "Does it have any childproof safety crap that might cause us trouble or slow us down?"

"Just the standard double trigger mechanism. You have to pull the trigger *and* press the gun against a solid surface to fire a nail." Ike lowered his voice. "Most of the pros keep the main trigger depressed all the time and use the safety catch as the actual trigger. Just press the gun down and she'll fire automatically."

Evan nodded, expectantly. Ike continued. "I'll show you how to do it, but don't tell no one and don't hurt yourself or your buddy, okay?"

"Yes, sir. We certainly appreciate the tip."

"With the main trigger disabled, she'll fire *on contact*. With *anything*, including your expensive flooring, or your *leg*." Ike lowered his chin and raised his eyebrows.

"Gotcha. We'll be careful," Evan said seriously.

Ike took a step back and looked intently at the nail gun in Evan's hands.

"*Really* careful," Evan promised.

"Okay. We'll go to the counter and get the nails you'll be needing. How many to start?"

"I'm not a hundred percent sure, but it's a small deck, so let's go with two hundred to get us started, and one fuel cell."

"Sounds about right."

Ike took the display model from Evan and put it back in its place on the wall. He opened an adjacent cabinet and removed a heavy plastic carrying case, also an eye-catching bright orange. "Everything's in here, 'cept the nails and the fuel cell." They walked over to a counter-cum-workbench where Ike quickly showed Evan how to disable the safety mechanism before packing up the nails and fuel cell.

"There you go. You pay up front. Good luck with that deck."

Evan thanked him and, as he walked away, he heard Ike greet his next customer. *A thoroughly unmemorable encounter,* Evan told himself. *In an hour grandpa will have completely forgotten about me.*

After he paid cash for the nail gun and accessories, the checkout girl began to tape the receipt to the can't-miss-it carrying case. Evan winced.

"I'm sorry, I'll need to have this bagged up."

"But it's easier to carry by the handle . . ."

"It's a gift, actually, a surprise for a friend."

"Oh, okay. I'll bag it and then put it in a coupla shopping bags. No one will know whatcha got."

"That's the idea," Evan replied, taking his merchandise and returning to the train station.

CHAPTER

FORTY-THREE

Evan stood on the sidewalk outside of Glow, the long line of Saturday night wannabes stretching down Twenty-seventh Street to his right. Huddled with some other randoms, he watched the bouncer work his clipboard. Groups of guys waited forever or were summarily turned away. Decent-looking chicks and couples waited and paid. Hot chicks without male baggage walked right in—but they too paid the ridiculous cover charge. Only the ultrahot, scantily clad club chicks immediately gained free passage.

Finally, after twenty minutes of watching, a man in a crisply pressed black suit with a matching crew cut stepped out in the cold and spoke privately with the doorman bouncer. Evan studied the interaction. The well-dressed Marine-looking dude was definitely a manager, a boss man, the alpha dog. Alpha studied the long line, patted his minion on the back, and retreated into the crowded club.

Evan didn't smoke, but he dropped his cigarette on the sidewalk and bug-squashed it. He walked fifty yards west and turned down an alley that separated the Chelsea megaclub from an empty warehouse awaiting conversion. *Where are they?* he wondered, navigating the deserted alley. Just before he reached Twenty-eighth Street, the block behind Glow, he heard them. He stopped, pulled his ski cap low on his head, and donned a pair of shiny silver aviator-style sunglasses, with mirrored lenses. Corey Hart suddenly played in his head and he chuckled.

Evan took a deep breath and rounded the corner to see four Glow employees standing next to an overflowing Dumpster, trying to enjoy a cold smoke break. *Bingo.* Since New York's bars and restaurants went smoke-free in '02, employees were relegated to alleyways and backdoors to satisfy on-the-job nicotine cravings. Evan knew he'd find them *somewhere* on Glow's isolated perimeter. He walked toward their smoky, garbage-scented sanctuary; they fell silent and stared at the unexpected intruder.

Evan flashed his most charming grin and said, "Hey, sorry to bother youse. A guy out front said I might find Millicent back here havin' a smoke." A worn-out redhead dressed like a cocktail waitress answered.

"No Millicent here. She work at Glow?"

"Uh, no, but her sister or cousin or somethin' does and I think she hangs here with her. The guy out front said to look back here behind the club, just in case." *C'mon, people.*

"What guy out front?"

Finally. Thank you.

"Didn't catch his name. Big guy. Black suit. Crew cut. Looked like a fuckin' hardass drill sergeant."

The group laughed and an oily dishwasher spoke up. "Uh-huh, Anthony Venona."

"Anthony? Is he the owner?" Evan asked the man, casual yet curious, drawing a cancer stick of his own from the pack in his coat pocket.

"Shit no. Anthony just a floor manager. Real prick too."

The redhead added, "Ego, man, ego. Anthony loves the attention."

Evan began to step backwards toward the alley; he had what he came for. He said thanks, turned, and left them to their anti-Anthony bitch session. The pack of smokes landed in the first corner garbage can. Evan figured they'd be fodder for a bum fight or two.

On Sunday, at about eight o'clock in the evening, Evan stepped off the L train in Williamsburg, Brooklyn. He walked a few blocks, following the crowd to Sixth Street, where he spotted a pay phone on the corner of Berry, outside the Sea Thai Bistro. He called Glow. Someone answered on the second ring.

"Glow. Go."

"Hey, I'm trying to reach Anthony Venona."

"He's right here; hold on a sec . . . *Anthony . . . phone . . . I don't know . . . didn't ask.*"

Evan cleared his throat.

"This is Anthony."

Evan spoke quickly, with no pauses. "Hey, Anthony. My name is John and I'm a freelance photographer for *People* magazine and we're putting together a layout on club-goin' executives and I understand that you are *The Man* to talk to at Glow about getting, shall we say, special accommodations regarding patrons' comings and goings."

"What do you want?" Anthony was short. Evan's window of opportunity was closing. *Ego, man, ego.*

"People tell me that you know *everything* that goes on at Glow. One of your bartenders told me you'll probably be *the* general manager soon." Evan paused. Silence. He had him. "Anyway, I need a photo of that rich video game guy, Joshua Gotbaum, havin' a good time at your establishment. Good PR for Glow, and I'll try to get your name in the piece if you'd like. Plus, I'll make it worth your trouble by—"

Anthony interrupted. "My name in *People*?" Evan momentarily recalled a favorite movie quote, "*Vanity, definitely my favorite sin,*" before replying.

"Sure. Something like 'Glow manager Anthony Venona says that executives make great customers.' Hell, I don't know, I'm just a photographer, new to the business. But my girlfriend is the executive assistant to the senior editor in charge of the story. If you help me, she will make it happen."

"You also said you can make it worth my trouble?"

Evan could sense Anthony trying to contain his excitement about the quote, so he reduced his intended offer. "I'm poor, but this photograph could really help my career. How 'bout two hundred?" He *wanted* Anthony to take money. Employees who accept cash bribes are more likely to keep their mouths shut.

"You got a deal. How do we do this?" Anthony could no longer contain his enthusiasm.

"You'll be there on Tuesday?"

"After four o'clock."

"Okay. I'll send over the cash. When Gotbaum comes in, you call my cell phone and I'll do the rest. Don't worry, I'll be discreet. No one will even know I was there."

"He's not exactly a regular. It could take a week or two or longer."

"Yeah, I know. The layout isn't scheduled to run until April, so no problem."

Evan gave Anthony his homeless guy cell phone number and confirmed the spelling of *Venona*. "You know, for *People* magazine and all."

As they were about to hang up, Anthony said, "Maybe you should send the cash to my home address in the Bronx." *Great idea*, Evan thought, copying down the address where, forty-eight hours later, a Kinko's computer-printed envelope arrived with two crisp C-notes, a Queens postmark, and no return address.

CHAPTER
FORTY-FOUR

Evan turned up the volume on his Bose SoundDock. Loud. He had no idea how much noise his nail gun made when it fired, but he had to find out.

His weapon of choice fit perfectly in the solid black Gap shoulder bag he bought on Eighty-fifth Street. With the strap shortened and worn across his chest bandolier-style, the bag rested snugly on his lower back, the bulk of the nail gun invisible in the mirror image before him.

Following Ike's instructions, he had disabled the double-trigger safety mechanism, and "the world's most powerful framing nailer" now fired on impact. Its popping sound would not be heard over the thumping music and hazy din of Glow's brain-dead revelers, and the recoil was certainly manageable. The brochure did say "Work all day with less arm fatigue," Evan recalled. But he didn't need all day.

One minute or less. Fourteen nails, thirteen in the skinny limbs and the coup dc grâce in the forehead, right between the eyes. One minute or less, and he was rich.

Who would be the first to figure it out? The cops? Bloggers? The real press? The wealthy father? Killed by a crazed fan of Manhunter, probably a "good boy" inevitably driven to gruesome murder by the horrific violence of a popular video game. Oh, the humanity!

The right-wingers and Jesus freaks—Rand's *mystic parasites*—would have a field day. While one side of the face humbly expressed despair over the senseless tragedy, the other side would self-righteously bellow, "See! See! We told you so!" The industry's poster boy, killed by his own creation. Mary Shelley would approve. And Congress would go ballistic.

"We should short the industry."

It was Monday, and Evan was in Mac's office.

"*What?*"

"Mac, we should short every company that makes significant revenues from violent video games. Activision, Take Two, Midway . . . all of them."

"Evan, *please* tell me you're joking. We're already getting hammered on your GoPostal play. You say it's noise, but—"

"A friend of mine from college lives in D.C., works on the Hill. He *assures* me that Congress will be back *soon* with a crackdown. Public pressure. It's an election year. I mean, have you seen the cover of this week's *Economist*? The *cover* story is 'Breeding Evil, the real impact of video games,' with a demonic little kid holding a joystick. The *Economist*! And last month the American Psychological Association called for new laws—they say violent video games cause violent behavior. They *breed evil*. Congress *will* act, Mac. Strict ratings, labeling requirements, sales restrictions, the works. It's our chance to leverage our GPTL position and make *bank*."

Mac slowly shook his head, leaned back in his chair. "You're serious. I can't believe it."

"Hell yes I'm serious. Talk to Zurich if you have to." Evan knew Mac would bristle at the notion that he needed permission to make the decision.

"That won't be necessary. I involved Zurich with GPTL because it was a huge position, not to mention your first call." Mac looked up at the ceiling. "What are you thinking, specifically?"

"I'm thinking we take very reasonable short positions in three, maybe four companies. Take Two, Midway, and Activision immediately come to mind. Mac, we can *double* our profit, we *will* double our profits when Congress gets involved next month—"

Mac sat up and interrupted. "Next month? Your friend was *specific*?"

"Yeah, he was." Evan paused and turned his gaze to the ceiling, pretending to contemplate how much of his *inside info* to reveal to his boss. "Look, my buddy works on the committee staff that deals with this kind of thing. He's *personally* involved with the preliminary planning. He was in the city over the weekend and—"

"That's enough, I don't need to hear more. The answer is no."

Evan took a deep breath. "Mac, if I'm wrong, you'll have my resignation on your desk the next day. This is my . . . *our* . . . chance."

Mac glanced at a random spreadsheet on his desk, stared at his computer monitor, gazed out of his fishbowl at the Monday morning malaise, then looked at Evan. "We covered two substantial positions last week, both Barry's, and did very well. I may regret it, but let's put twenty million in it."

"Thirty?" Evan asked, raising his eyebrows.

"You're killing me, chief." Mac considered it for a moment. "Okay, thirty million. But only if the numbers make *perfect* sense, and tell Kennedy to hedge half of it dollar for dollar."

Evan jumped to his feet. "You won't regret it, Mac."

"I already do. Get out of here."

CHAPTER

FORTY-FIVE

Kennedy was beaming. "Mr. Stoess, what do you have for me today?" His eyes did not leave the monitors in front of him as he spoke.

"Why are you so happy?"

"Haven't you seen? Markets opened off two percent and are falling through twelve-month lows. An *idiot* could make money today. We're covering three positions as we speak, surfing the tsunami." Kennedy paused, hit a key with a theatrical flourish, a virtuoso's final note, and looked up at Evan, perhaps expecting applause.

"Wow," Evan remarked.

"Hey, you take the good days when you get 'em."

"I've been in with Mac. GPTL?"

"Flat on low volume. Not so good."

"Its day will come," Evan quickly replied. "Speaking of which, we want to leverage the opportunity. Thirty million total, spread over three companies."

Kennedy readied his fingers over his keyboard, a look of boyish anticipation on his preppy round face.

Evan continued. "ATVI, TTWO, MWY."

Kennedy typed the stock symbols as the letters exited Evan's mouth, then leaned back and focused on the screen. "We made good money on Take Two a while back; accounting scandal, I believe. Let's start there."

Evan took a seat in one of the battered chairs in front of Kennedy's desk. As Kennedy typed, studied, and scribbled notes on a yellow legal pad, Evan zoned out for a moment. In mid-scribble, Kennedy asked, "You think these three will take a hit with GoPostal?"

Still in the brain pause, Evan replied, "Even the guiltless meet reproach."

Kennedy stopped abruptly and gazed at Evan, his expression one of complete confusion. *"What?"*

Evan snapped out of it, his head twitching and pupils narrowing as he focused on Kennedy. "Sorry. 'Even the guiltless meet reproach.' Iago's warning that destroying the innocent can be as pleasurable as destroying the guilty. It's from *Othello* and, yes, I'm confident these three stocks will fall with GPTL."

Kennedy said nothing, went back to work, and, a moment later, he whistled.

"What's up?" Evan asked.

"Take Two might be tough. Twenty-five percent of the float is short with the stock at a fifty-two-week high. Major squeeze possibility." He looked at Evan, anticipating comment.

Evan didn't speak, didn't move, didn't breathe.

Kennedy continued. "Okay, I'll see what I can do, maybe six to eight million worth. Let's take a look at the other two."

Evan waited, silently calculating the possibilities.

If the thirty-million position yielded a fifteen-million-dollar profit, the math was nice and tidy. His take of the performance fee would be a cool million, almost to the penny, the down payment on his new condo. *Another million dollars. Must have it.*

"Activision will be easy enough. Nice float, low short interest, near highs. Probably do half the position." Again Kennedy sought comment.

"Okay, you're the man, whatever you say."

"Midway will be much tougher. Small cap. Low float—insiders own fifty percent of the shares. Stock's taken a beating lately. But all things considered, the volume's good. Probably split the second half of the position between TTWO and MWY."

"Sounds great, Kennedy, as long as we get the *entire thirty million done*, okay?" *Must do thirty to get one.*

"Okay, thirty million."

Evan began to stand. "Couple of days?"

Kennedy consulted his screen. "Give me until the end of the week."

"We don't want this ship to sail without us," Evan replied. *Or eager Alpha Anthony to call before we're ready to maximize our profits.*

"End of the week. Guaranteed."

CHAPTER

FORTY-SIX

"End of the week?"

"That's what I said, numbnuts. 'End of the week.'"

Joshua was in his SoHo design studio, talking to Cat on the landline. He continued, "By the end of the week I'll have this proposal done for Microsoft. I've been working on the fuckin' thing night and day—"

"What's it all about?" Cat asked, genuinely interested.

"They want an outline for a new game, what could be the first joint venture if and when we sign this exclusive deal. Storyboard, screen shots, technical specs, *everything*. It's a shitload of work." Joshua took a breath. "But you'll fucking love it. It's better than Manhunter."

"No way. You *gotta* tell me. I can keep a secret."

"I know you can."

"What's the premise?"

"*Gladiator* meets *Bill & Ted* meets *Fight Club* meets *Blade Runner*."

Cat was silent, contemplating the meaning of this richly textured and subtly nuanced Netflix description. Suddenly, the proverbial light bulb. "Dude, that's *brilliant!*" Then darkness. "Huh?"

"Okay, pay attention, Einstein. You play a badass Roman gladiator who time-travels to fight other badasses. You start in the Colosseum. If you win, you move forward in time to the present and into the future. Some-where around level three, for example, you'll fight a knight, *Excalibur*-style, then a samurai in Japan, Tom Cruise–style. Different settings, different weapons—historically accurate, so very, *very* bloody. Truth is gorier than fiction, right? That's what we'll tell Congress and the rabid right-wingers."

"Dude, you are a freakin' *genius*! Slaughter *and* learn!"

"Exactly."

"So at the end of the week we'll go out and celebrate?" Cat asked.

"Yeah, sure. I'm thinking Buddakan for dinner and then Glow. You wanna set it up? Also call Becky and Leslie; I'll talk to Jenna and Eric."

"Six for dinner and Glow, mezzanine table?" Cat could barely contain his enthusiasm.

"Perfect. And I'll talk to Rufus."

"Friday it is then."

"Friday it is."

CHAPTER
FORTY-SEVEN

A man on a beach, a hazy mirage.

Blistering heat, an oasis beckons.

A sea of molten lead, gasping and fetid. À l'horizon, un petit vapeur.

Blinded by sweat, a shimmering form is smiling.

Time stands still. Time stands. Still.

A single step. Un seul pas en avant.

Cymbals crash, the sky splits open.

A motionless corpse.

Lying on his couch with the TV blaring, Evan slipped in and out of restless consciousness, enjoying the twilight state between asleep and awake, replaying the vivid scene frame by frame. *A man on a beach . . .* Vaguely visceral, the images are tattooed with subtitles and conjure up a comforting, dreadful hope. *A man on a beach. A stranger. An outsider.*

Friday's midnight approached. If tonight was the night, he would soon know.

Evan was ready. Kennedy had closed the short positions, as promised, and Evan had bought as many options as he could afford in his personal account. The money was on the table, waiting to be claimed, a just reward for time served.

Earlier in the evening, Evan had dressed for the highly anticipated occasion—all black, from head to toe. Club and crime appropriate. The nail gun was loaded, charged, fueled, and discreetly placed in its Gap-brand holster. If the phone didn't ring, he would do it all over again tomorrow. He would prepare. He would wait. Meanwhile he would welcome the man on the beach.

"Get it back," he whispered to himself, peering through his eyelashes at Conan the Barbarian, kicking ass on TNT.

Then, for the first time since he bought it, homeless Bill Jones's cell phone rang. Evan about fell off the sofa reaching for it.

"Hello?" He could hear horrible house music in the background.

"John, it's Anthony. Your boy is on the way. He just called, requested two tables on the mezzanine."

"Great. Thanks for the call."

"You'll let me know about the *People* article?"

"Absolutely."

Evan grabbed the shoulder bag and three hundred dollars cash, leaving his wallet and all identification behind. Before clicking off the TV, he paused for a moment to hear an all too familiar voice. *"Now they will know why they are afraid of the dark. Now they learn why they fear the night."* He nodded his approval, and twenty minutes later he was standing near the end of Glow's side alley, facing Twenty-eighth Street.

Although he couldn't see them, Evan could hear the Glow employees sharing a cigarette break around the corner, on the sidewalk by the Dumpster, just outside Glow's back door. They were bitching and moaning, of course.

"Okay, we should get back inside. Carl'll be wonderin'."

"Fuck him."

"Yeah, you say that out here . . ."

Evan heard the door open and the music spill out into the night. It sounded distant, but remarkably loud. When the door closed, peace was restored.

He stepped out of the alley onto the wide sidewalk. The dingy block of warehouses was deserted. He approached the door, pulled it open, and stepped inside.

Evan moved quickly through a dark corridor, lit only by one bare bulb, toward another door that arced out with each thump of the bass line raging on the other side. The door was breathing, *breathing,* like it might explode, forced off its hinges by the powerful expiration of communal angst.

Just as he reached for the knob, the door swung open toward him and he was punched square in the sternum by the full force of Kanye West. He almost fell backwards on his ass, like a child new to ice skates. A short Hispanic man stepped in and quickly closed the door behind him. He looked like a teenager, growing his first thin 'stache. Evan recovered and smiled. "Are the bathrooms back here?"

"Bathrooms? No. Door say *'employees only.'* "

"Shit. Sorry." Evan stood with his hands at his sides, palms facing outwards, Friendly Man. "Can you help me please?" He reached in his pocket and pulled out a twenty.

The little guy paused for a second, eyed Evan suspiciously, looked around him down the dim corridor. "Just you?"

"Just me. My friends are dancing inside." Big harmless smile.

"Okay. Bathroom's 'round the corner to the left."

"Muchas gracias," Evan said, simultaneously sidestepping the little man so he couldn't see the shoulder bag resting snugly on his lower back and handing over the bribe. As he opened the door, he watched the young dishwasher walk away, fumbling for a pack of cigarettes in his hip pocket. He felt the hot blast of music as he slipped into the club.

Safely inside, Evan leaned against the wall next to the door, emptied his lungs of the acrid, adrenaline-laced air, and surveyed the scene.

He was at the back of a long, fairly narrow room, the focus and purpose of which was a bar on his left. More lounge than club, it was obviously a room frequented by patrons in need of liquid courage before hitting the dance floor. Ignoring Pink's plea, *Don't be fancy, just get dancey,* the crowd consisted primarily of guys-who-hate-to-dance, slamming drinks to become invisible, accompanied by increasingly exasperated females with a fondness for ruby red lipstick and hair spray. *Poor bastards,* Evan thought. *Forced to make fools of themselves, and they'll end up too drunk to schtup.*

A young woman dressed like a Hooters waitress approached him from the right. She was carrying a tray of eerie green glow-in-the-dark glasses and her baby tee said EVERGLO. She leaned in close so Evan could hear her.

"Complementary Everglo?"

"Free booze? Excellent. What is it?"

"It's new—a mixture of tequila, vodka, caffeine and ginseng."

"*Really?* Is it strong?"

"Strong enough," she replied, lowering the tray and reaching for a glass.

"Can I have two?"

"Sure. Enjoy."

Evan was double-fisted for only a moment, sipping from the first tumbler of Everglo before abandoning the cup in a dark corner. He chased after the Everglo girl, putting his hand on her shoulder. She turned, her face transforming from a scowl to a smile. "You like it?"

"It's great. Another?"

"Sure. The sooner they're gone, the sooner I go home."

"Can you point me toward the mezzanine?"

"The mezzanine? Yeah. It's downstairs, in the old subway station. Go through there," she said, motioning with her hair to the wide portal opposite the smoke-break door, "and follow the noise down to the main room, the huge one with the horseshoe bar. Then look up. You can't miss it."

Evan nodded and, with an Everglo in each hand, began to make his way toward Joshua Gotbaum's mezzanine.

Evan stepped out of the Lounge and, after one more gulp, threw the full glasses into a garbage can. He was now in the rear of an impossibly chaotic "reception area" where clubgoers who had made it past the velvet rope showed their ID, enjoyed a quick pat-down, paid the cover charge and were then herded like Disney families toward and down a wide staircase, from which emanated an unholy cacophony, both human and otherwise. The bouncers' and managers' focus was on the entrance; Evan was looking at their backs, including Anthony Venona's. He had safely and surreptitiously reached the inner sanctum. He joined the shuffling queue, swearing to himself that he smelled Drakkar Noir.

Slowly descending the stairs, he reached a landing and turned a corner, each step now feeling like another into a sweaty wet furnace. Thick waves of music-noise carried heat and electricity up the stairs, simultaneously energizing and silencing the fresh meat soon to join the circus. Evan sensed the crowd's anxiety and adrenaline. The collective anticipation was palpable and, he speculated, intentionally orchestrated.

The destination itself, however, was anticlimactic. Four dark corridors awaited him at the bottom. The crowd split up and Evan followed the bulk of the revelers straight ahead, down the widest corridor, drawn to the roar.

He stepped out of the dark conga line and entered the Depot, as it was called. It could easily house a football field. Four large dance floors, each separated by dividers and high bar tables, surrounded the monstrous horseshoe bar. There was no seating on the main floor, but there were plenty of strobe lights, disco globes, and other anime flashes of retina-burning brilliance, the sources of which Evan could not discern. Sweat ran down his forehead, settling in his eyebrows. If he was at all subject to epileptic seizures, he would quickly find out.

High above, overlooking the swollen boil of humanity, Evan could just see the mezzanine that ringed the room. Blurred silhouettes rhythmically wobbled in the rising heat haze, spectators enjoying the show below. He wiped his wet brow with his sleeve before choosing the metal staircase on the left, and he climbed the open-weave steps.

As Evan emerged into the mezzanine's sharply contrasting darkness, a different Everglo girl approached. He asked her to point him toward the tables. "Straight ahead, but they're all reserved tonight," she shouted. "You might find a seat at the bar," she added, motioning over Evan's shoulder in the direction she was heading. At that moment a space opened along the railing; Evan filled it immediately. Slowly his senses adjusted to the onslaught and he began to comprehend the alien environment surrounding him. If the Depot was a football field, Evan was overlooking the twenty-yard line. To his right, close, was the mezzanine bar. To his left, in the far end zone obscured by distance, darkness, and haze, he would apparently find the VIP tables, and his redemption.

Redemption. The word frightened him, knotting his gut, and the taste of tequila and bile soured his throat. He choked it back, white knuckles gripping the railing.

He closed his eyes, concentrated, and slowly the warm glow of his dream enveloped him, a soothing bubble. Then his heartbeat quickened, pounding fiercely with the beat of the music. *"You only get one shot, do not miss your chance to blow."* Waves of heat bounced off of him. A tingling rivulet of sweat flowed down his back. *"This opportunity comes once in a lifetime."* He opened his eyes. Everything in focus, Evan pushed back from the railing and stood for a moment with his back against the mezzanine's coal black wall. He walked toward the tables, staying close to the wall, passing quietly behind countless witnesses, all dulled by a thick drunkenness and unaware of his presence, if not their own. He recited from memory:

"Subtly, subtly, I become invisible.

Wondrously, wondrously, I become soundless.

Thus I hold my enemy's fate in my hands."

Instinctively he reached back and felt the nail gun. About thirty feet short of the end zone mezzanine, the crowd of spectators shifted and Evan once again filled a space on the railing. The music played. *"This world is mine for the taking . . . Make me king."*

To his left he could now see the tables. Starting at the far end across the club, he studied the occupants. Like a desert mirage, the figures wavered in the jackhammer noise rising spasmodically from the dance floor. He could feel it inside him, striking the soles of his feet, hammering up his spine and exploding in sweat from his scalp.

The Very Important People at the reserved tables stood and sat in tight groups, friends laughing and sipping drinks from bottles of vodka and champagne. Evan couldn't hear them of course, but he knew what they were saying, and he despised them. Every one of them *deserved* to die, but only one of them *had* to die, and he was sitting at the corner table closest to where Evan stood.

Joshua Gotbaum. He had two four-top tables pushed close together on the right angle, his entourage consisting of two other guys and three cute girls. Evan was looking down the rail at Joshua's profile. His 'fro was wilder than it had been at NYU, and he appeared to be breathing out of his open mouth. His head bobbed gently to Eminem's beat and occasionally he turned to one of his cohorts to speak. Joshua Gotbaum was obviously wasted.

Evan decided to find a better vantage point to observe his quarry. He slipped down the sideline past the tables to the back wall of the end zone. He found a spot in the shadows just twenty feet from Joshua's tables and waited for his opportunity to close the deal. *If I don't kill him, my game is over.* He'd follow the little fucker home if he had to.

Seconds later the skinny blond girl at Joshua's table stood up and walked straight toward Evan. She turned, passing within three feet of him, walked parallel to the back wall and then turned again, disappearing down a dark corridor that Evan hadn't even noticed. When she reappeared five minutes later, Evan opted for a quick recon mission. *"You can do anything you set your mind to, man."*

He discovered two small, single-stall restrooms, unmarked along the lightless, dead-end corridor. One reeked of ether; the other sported a used condom on the side of the sink. Both had dead bolt locks on the inside. He returned to his spot on the rear wall and waited.

The booze. The heat. The goddam noise. Feeling his temples throb, Evan focused all his energy on tuning them out. He stared at Joshua, seeing and sensing nothing else, like a telescope with Joshua at one end and himself at the other. *Towards thee I roll, little man . . . to the last I grapple with thee, from hell's heart I stab at thee, for hate's sake I spit my last breath at thee.* "Melville or Khan," Evan said to no one. "Both work for me."

Minutes passed, measured only by empty glasses and changing songs. When Joshua and his friends happily danced together in their seats to what was obviously a crowd-pleaser, Evan considered stepping up and popping him right there, just to put an end to it. But it would be tough to spend his money from a jail cell.

Mercifully the song ended, blending into another, a club remix of an overplayed pop favorite Evan had heard a thousand times the previous summer. It was only the second tune he actually recognized. *"Wake me up inside . . . call my name and save me from the dark."*

Joshua clumsily slid off his seat and slammed a full flute of champagne. Evan tensed and shifted forward, his weight on the balls of his feet.

Joshua looked toward the corridor, shouted something to the guy next to him, and took a few staggered steps directly at Evan before veering to his right.

Evan followed Joshua into the dark hallway and watched him enter the second restroom.

He waited about five seconds before turning the knob. Unlocked. Evan stepped in the bathroom, distinctly hearing *"without a thought, without a voice, without a soul . . . don't let me die here"* as he bolted the door behind him. *No such luck, Joshua. You die here, now. Business is business.*

Joshua was inside the stall, sitting on the toilet. Evan could see his shoes and ankles; his pants were pulled up. He was just sitting there.

Evan shifted the messenger bag forward on his right side and removed the nail gun. It was warm to the touch, solid and reassuring. After two deep breaths, he approached the stall door and paused. He didn't want to hurt the little guy, just kill him. A struggle wouldn't be pleasant, something he hoped to avoid. One more deep breath. He could hear the music. *Bring me to life, motherfucker.*

Evan kicked in the door with his right foot, stepped forward and held it open with the back of his left hand. He pointed the nail gun at the person inside. "Hello," he said reflexively.

Joshua looked up at him, his glazed eyes outshone by a huge, drug-addled grin.

"Heyyyyy . . . you wanna bump?" A clear vial of something rolled off of Joshua's lap onto the grimy tiled floor. "Ohhhh . . . no gooood." Joshua looked down, first to his left and then to his right, searching for his lost treasure. "My precious . . . nooo gooood."

Evan stepped forward and held the nail gun where Joshua's forehead had been seconds earlier. "Joshua," he said, with no response. "Joshua, look at me." Nothing.

"JOSHUA!" Evan shouted with his teeth clenched.

Joshua called off the fruitless search and tilted his head up toward Evan, the loopy grin returning to his face despite the Paslode Model #900420 gently touching his forehead, right between his eyes.

Evan pushed forward and the gun fired. The nail penetrated Joshua's skull and lodged in his brain. His head and shoulders snapped back for a moment, then slumped forward. For a second Joshua returned to exactly the same position he had been in before he had a three-inch nail in his frontal lobe. His glazed eyes didn't flinch, but his grin melted and his head fell forward, his chin resting on his chest. Blood dripped from the small hole in his forehead onto his belly and crotch. Joshua Gotbaum was dead. Evan fired thirteen more nails into Joshua's lifeless limbs. A few of the nails struck bone, making a sickening splintering noise. It was a surprisingly bloodless experience, however, unlike the newly deceased's Manhunter. Joshua's shirt and pants absorbed most of the blood—very little fell to the floor.

Evan closed the stall door and returned the nail gun to the messenger bag, securing it on his back. He unbolted the restroom door, opened it a crack, and peered outside. The corridor was empty. He stepped out, closed the door, and left the club the way he entered. Around the corner, he crossed behind Frank and Doug Mancini's Oldsmobuick as he hailed a cab.

PART III

What good is it for a man to gain the whole world, yet forfeit his soul?

—MARK 8:36

CHAPTER

FORTY-EIGHT

"Il fait chaud," the waiter said as he wiped his brow. Evan nodded his agreement as he deciphered the menu at Les Deux Garçons on le Cours Mirabeau.

Nicole had invited him to Aix-en-Provence in the South of France for the Festival International d'Art Lyrique, and they could certainly afford to dine anywhere, but *he* had chosen tourist-laden Les Deux Garçons for *le déjeuner* because it was Albert Camus' favorite haunt during his time in Provence.

Nicole protested, but when Evan told her he took a class at university devoted entirely to the Nobel Prize–winning author-philosopher, she acquiesced. And now Evan was free to commune with Camus, to search for transcendence while knowing none can be found.

Unlike Camus' Meursault, Evan *had* the golden key, and he had opened the terrestrial door. But despite his high-priced coronation, he faltered on the threshold. His access now unfettered by an infusion of funds, crossing over inexplicably eluded him. But he would not discard his key. Despite his still unrequited desire to belong, he would not give up, and he would not give in. Perhaps Camus would inspire him, and he could step inside—inside with Nicole and the bake sale mom and Ridgewood and the people who *mattered*. Inside the painted sepulcher, the Golgotha of money.

"They offered us an *English* menu, for god's sake," Nicole fumed. "How embarrassing! *Je suis humiliée.*"

"Oh *relax*. It's just one lunch. Look at the fountain, the statue," Evan replied, waving his hand dismissively.

Nicole's eyes followed Evan's motion toward the stately frog king standing triumphantly on a pedestal in a small circle of dingy water, but her gaze settled beyond the frequently photographed fourth fountain. "Maybe I'll go across the street to that Lacoste store while you eat your *ham and cheese*." She was already on her feet, the sight of a passing fanny-pack causing her to noticeably shudder with contempt. "We *must* get back to the festival," she said, walking away.

"Do you want some money?" Evan asked.

Nicole looked over her spa-perfect tan-in-a-can shoulder with a coy smile. "No thanks, I have my own."

"Yes, you do," Evan said under his breath, enjoying the view of the sculpted figure underneath her colorful Provençal sundress. A French literature major at Harvard, Nicole worked at the United Nations. Evan wasn't exactly sure what she did but he assumed it was *something* to prolong briefly the doomed "lives" of Third World Darwinian roadkill. She found it important—Evan pretended to—but somehow she *did* manage to open the checkbooks of influential and wealthy do-gooders, Bono-style. Evan was sure her weapon was shame, but succumbing to it was the donors' malfunction, not Nicole's. She wasn't exactly a heroine, Evan once told Mac, but she was definitely not a brainless looter either.

Ironically, Evan mused while watching her cross the famous boulevard, men like him wage war and make money so they can marry women who don't need it. Sure, they'll fuck the ones who *do*, but they *marry* the ones who *don't*.

Indeed, Nicole Marie Vandevelde had money, a fat trust fund that kept her blissfully entombed in Chanel, Prada, air kisses and urban guilt. It pained Evan to admit that Rand would dismiss her as "*the quintessen-*

tial random female with causeless income who flitters on trips around the globe."

Evan, too, had money, but without the guilt. Adjusting his background to serve himself, he had *earned* his money, enough to get him to the threshold and dissuade Nicole from asking too many questions about his net worth and lineage. For the time being.

Sixteen months ago, about thirty days after Joshua Gotbaum's death torpedoed GoPostal and unhinged the video game industry, Evan cashed out eight million dollars, his share of Contrafund's performance fees, plus some extra he collected from his own stock options.

Joshua's "deranged crucifixion" made the cover of Sunday's *New York Post,* and on Monday GoPostal's stock nose-dived to two dollars as the *Times* reported "the shocking similarity between Mr. Gotbaum's murder and Manhunter, a popular video game of his own creation." *As if I'd written the story myself,* Evan thought with a satisfied grin. It was quite obvious to the enlightened: An alienated and misguided youth, transformed psychotic by senseless video game gore, had predictably re-created his favorite colorful scene, but with real nails, real blood, and real death. The anticipated consensus: Society was to blame—unbridled and unregulated consumerism. As *The Economist* foretold, video games had indeed bred evil. Numerous warnings had been ignored. The murder was an inevitable tragedy. Mammon had triumphed over morals, another casualty of *affluenza.* And Evan's arm hurt from patting himself on the back.

Investigators had plenty of leads. GoPostal, and Gotbaum personally, had received hundreds of pieces of psycho fan mail and innumerable e-mails, many of which were disturbing enough to warrant follow-up. For months the authorities tracked down postmarks and IP addresses, comparing names and faces to Glow's credit card receipts and the footage from the surveillance camera over the main entrance. The misunderstood, victimized youth-murderer did not materialize, but the NYPD caught an ill-tempered pedophile, a surly hacker, and a sixteen-year-old identity thief who used geriatrics' credit cards to buy Clearasil, porn passwords, and graphic "novels." About a year ago, three months after Evan's triumph, when the media lost all interest, Daniel Gotbaum offered a half-million-dollar reward for the apprehension of his son's executioner, with the solemn promise that the troubled soul *would* get treatment and would *never* face the death penalty. Not even a segment on *America's Most Wanted* yielded results. One anonymous investigator blamed the *CSI* phenomenon for creating "savvy bad guys." GoPostal had to fire most of its suits before a rival company acquired it for about a buck a share.

Of course the guiltless met reproach as well. Every company that produced a video game with so much as an angry scowl took a hit when the politicians promised "immediate action to stop the senseless slaughter." Outraged pontificators, most facing reelection, demanded quick action on sales restrictions, "parent-friendly" labeling, rating requirements and, Evan's personal favorite, "an immediate prohibition on graphic, sadistic, and pornographic content likely to cause antisocial behavior." The ACLU pitched a world-class hissy fit, but it was too late. The industry tanked; Evan Stoess made *bank*.

"Let's play *American Psycho*."

Nicole was back, France's meager GDP enhanced by her disgust with Evan's choice of eateries.

"What?" Evan asked. "*Here?*"

"Yes, here. *American Psycho*. Now. I bought you two shirts by the way." Nicole was scanning the crowd as she spoke.

"Well, in that case . . . Who shall be our hapless victims?"

"That distinguished-looking couple across the street, walking this way, each carrying a bag from Cave du Félibrige."

Evan followed her gaze to the only targets who could possibly merit their attention. "Yep, they've earned the *American Psycho* treatment," he said, licking his lips.

Nicole reached beneath the Garçons' wobbly bistro table and opened her Hermès Etrusque crocodile Kelly bag, retrieving a stray correspondence card, Crane's in Cambridge blue with a white border, no doubt from Kate's Paperie, and an S.T. Dupont pen in platinum and black Chinese lacquer.

"Okay," she said. "I'll go first." Resembling Kristen Bell's determined doppelgänger, she sat up straight, cleared her throat, and adjusted the straps of her sundress.

"*Madame* is wearing a ruffled mauve satin blouse by St. John Couture, skillfully pairing it with Oscar de la Renta's fuchsia silk-taffeta skirt and a vintage Hermès foulard. Her sling-back, embroidered Champagne heels are also by de la Renta, and her multizipper yellow lizard bag is by Tod's. Her sunglasses, obviously, are Chanel."

"That's *it*?" Evan asked, rubbing his hands together in mock anticipation.

"Well, I can't see her lingerie, but her ring is impressive, looks like black diamonds and an emerald cut blue sapphire, most likely de Grisogono."

"Yes, I believe that's correct."

"You do?"

"You'll see," Evan replied with an eyebrow raised mysteriously.

Nicole smiled and looked at the tick marks on the improvised Crane's score pad.

"Six points. Your turn."

"The sartorially resplendent *monsieur* is wearing natural cotton pants by Brunello Cucinelli and a subtly striped dress shirt by Ermenegildo Zegna. His sunglasses are vintage Ray-Ban Aviators. His magnificent custom shoes, until recently available *only* in Paris but now available on Madison Avenue next to the Cucinelli boutique, are by Berluti, specifically, the 'Andy Warhol' loafer, in the bold color choice of cashmere."

Evan paused, took a dramatic breath, before continuing.

"And his timepiece, my dear, a spectacular Instrumento Grande in white gold with an alligator strap, is *definitely* by de Grisogono."

"*Chantmé*," Nicole replied, impressed. "So they shop together . . . for more than just wine."

"Indeed. Together, they shop."

"*Jamais en vain, toujours en vin.*"

As if under a spell, they watched the enviable pair walk hand in hand down the crowded sidewalk, effortlessly parting the sweaty H&M sea. Without taking her eyes off the disappearing couple, Nicole spoke first.

"Is Berluti really on Madison now?"

"Yes. It is," Evan intoned.

"Fascinating," Nicole replied, pondering the revelation.

In New York City, you *are* where you *live*. Embracing this truism, after he deftly closed the GoPostal deal, Evan wasted no time subletting an apartment in Frank Gehry's shiny new tower at 8 Spruce Street, cleverly named "New York by Gehry" and the tallest residential building in the city at seventy-six stories. His three-bedroom A-line unit had recently leased to an "undisclosed Russian businessman," but a prenup deadline divorce left it vacant. Less than a month after cashing out, Evan rented it for only fifteen thousand dollars a month. His favorite amenity was the Morphosis series Alpha Jacuzzi, a damn fancy soak-and-poke designed by Peninfarina, from which he had a spectacular view of the Brooklyn Bridge and midtown Manhattan. Sitting in his pricey tub, smoking a cigar, he felt like Tony Montana. Occasionally a blimp would pass over Manhattan, on the way to a baseball game. *The world is yours, indeed.*

Gehry's tower, with its undulating Bernini folds, would do for now. Evan had his eye on a much more exclusive prize—one of Santiago Calatrava's cubes, the "Townhouses in the Sky," an alternating stack of twelve, four-story homes scheduled to rise a thousand feet over lower Manhattan's South Street. Evan tipped the sales director ten grand to stay in the loop, knowing he would need to amass a fortune of at least fifty million dollars to have a shot at residential immortality. *A fortune well spent*, Evan told himself, recalling the words of Giovanni Rucellai, an obscenely wealthy Renaissance Florentine and costar of a Ridgewood term paper. *"I think I have done myself more honor by having spent money well than by having earned it. Spending gave me deeper satisfaction, especially in the money I spent on my house in Florence."* Well said.

"Hey, can we go now? The Berlin Philharmonic starts soon, at the foot of Sainte-Victoire." A pair of neon Crocs, with tube socks, had caught Nicole's attention and frightened her back to reality.

"Camus died on a Monday. January 4, 1960. Car accident."

"Yes, I know," Nicole replied. "In Villeblevin. I've seen the monument.

While on exchange at the Sorbonne I wrote a paper on his feud with Sartre." Nicole paused for a moment, looked at the sky.

"He wasn't driving the car, you know," she said, her voice flat, emotionless.

"What?" Evan asked, suddenly rocked by a visceral dread, like learning a lump might be cancer.

"*What?*"

"Camus, when he was killed," Nicole finally replied with vigor. "He wasn't driving the car. Michel Gallimard, his best friend and publisher, *was*. Camus was just a passenger, along for the ride." She pushed her spindly chair back from the café table. "Hey! Can we go now?"

"Yes, we can go now." Evan hid his anxiety, attempted to ignore the stirring panic.

"To the festival? To Sainte-Victoire?"

"Yes. And then back to New York. The sooner the better."

CHAPTER

FORTY-NINE

Evan stood in the shadow of his favorite Dutch elm, across from 940 Fifth Avenue. Living downtown, the Ritual had grown more complex, and therefore less frequent. To tip the scales in his favor, Evan paid one of the building's young porters to send a text message to an untraceable cell phone when he knew that Geoffrey and Victoria Buchanan were on the move. He told the guy his name was Joe and he liked the Buchanans' car.

Geoffrey had accomplished the seemingly impossible, upgrading the Bentley, to a Bugatti Galibier, the latest "Royale." Evan assumed the birth of his third child demanded the Bugatti's spacious "rear cabin" for the three-hour ride to East Hampton. He was correct.

Evan stepped into the sun as the one-and-a-half-million-dollar fastback sedan rounded the corner. Again, silver. Victoria's favorite color. He calmly watched as the family stepped out from under the currency-green canopy. He pictured himself carrying the baby, driving on 27 with an appreciative Geoffrey riding shotgun, cracking jokes with Victoria, promising Ashley and Tyler he'd help build a sand castle before supper. He blinked, and they were gone.

•   •   •

Thirty minutes later, Malcolm Kvamme was sitting in Evan's office.

"Thanks for walking up, Mac."

"No problem. It still feels weird not having you right outside my office, but this new space is great. Nice view, huh? How was France?"

But Evan wasn't in the mood for small talk. The distressing Camus revelation, the Bugatti—anxiety was inevitable, and a welcome motivator. Since his ascension, Evan constantly fought the seductive salve of money, the complacency that having a *little* can engender. He fought the pitiful but all too common weakness of premature satisfaction.

"Listen, Mac, the year is half over, and I'm not satisfied with where I stand. I need more capital, I need to take bigger positions, I need more freedom, *I need more money.*"

Mac turned his head from the window with a look of amazement.

"Are you kidding? You've made—what?—about a million this year?"

"It's not enough," Evan replied with conviction.

"Not enough? We were the first on the street to short Bear. And our Apple call was worth half a million alone. You said Apple was arrogant, couldn't sustain its innovations, couldn't convince consumers a four-hundred-dollar *toy* is disposable. We crashed the party. We rode her down from eighty to fifty, then we—"

"Mac, Apple was a no-brainer, a goddam *New York Times* article about 'outraged howls from dead iPod owners.'" Evan stood up, walked to his window, stared out at the mid-afternoon haze. "People hate feeling pressured to replace their gadgets every year, and for no good reason. *Duh.*" He exhaled audibly, obviously frustrated.

"And I *asked* for three hundred and fifty thousand shares, not one seventy-five. I *should* have walked away with a *million,* not a half. And now this fucking bull market is making it tough to earn a goddam penny."

Mac shifted in his seat before speaking.

"Listen chief, *relax.* We're doing great. We got lucky with GoPostal, had a huge year because of it. This year we're ahead of Zurich's expectations, but it *is* a tough environment, so we need to be patient."

Evan spun on his heels, stepped forward, and stood before his genial boss. Stood *above* him.

"'We,' Mac, *We*?" Evan's guttural growl was just above a whisper, primal and fierce.

Mac shivered and his jaw dropped as he looked up at his self-proclaimed protégé.

"Have you read *Anthem*?" Evan's voice had returned to normal, but he held Mac's eye with his own.

"Huh? Uh, no," Mac replied.

"*We* is a monster, the root of all evil on Earth, the root of man's torture by men, the root of an unspeakable lie.

"*We* is the word by which the weak steal the might of the strong, by which the unwilling lay claim to the efforts of the willing. I am done with the monster of *We*, the word of servants, of misery and shame. I reject *We*'s tyranny of mediocrity and cowardice.

"Mac, *I* will not relax. *I* will not be patient. *I* will not go along for the ride. *I can not*."

"What do you want, Evan?"

"I want more money. I want what I *deserve*."

CHAPTER
FIFTY

Betting against Apple *was* a no-brainer. So was shorting the shit out of those ugly-ass Crocs, and that Amway-NuSkin ponzi scheme the FTC finally shut down. But a half million here, a quarter million there was not going to cut it. No doubt, the cash was great, but it was a palliative distraction. To be free, to be secure, to step inside, *to get one of Calatrava's cubes*, Evan needed *wealth*.

Somebody might have to die.

The wholly unoriginal idea came to him, not in a dream or vision or even a fortune cookie, but at his desk while he was surfing the Internet, searching for companies to upend despite the bull market.

Somebody might have to die. Somebody a helluva lot more valuable than Joshua Gotbaum. The first time was easy enough, why not a second?

Death had proved to be good business for his firm, first Medipharm and then GoPostal. And, let's face it, nailing Gotbaum was a gift to society. Joshua's death forced the callused gamers to think up their own revenge fantasies, the pathetic intellectual plagiarists, although most of them couldn't pull themselves away from Pornhub to bother.

Two hundred and fifty million, Evan had told Mac in his office earlier. "I want two hundred and fifty million dollars, committed to my calls, no questions asked. Give me six months. You won't regret it."

Mac had looked at his hands, out the window, at the ceiling. He had started to say something then stopped, looked out the window again.

"Okay."

"Okay?"

"Okay, we'll name you the solo portfolio manager of a new fund, commit up to two hundred and fifty million dollars of the firm's capital."

Now, in the evening's late-summer sun, Evan sat under the awning on the sidewalk at Nello with Nicole and six of her coworkers from the U.N., a group Evan called the "International House of Pancakes." A trio of Italians, a Spaniard, a Frog and an escapee from Greece, the IHOP crew were the type of people who order unusual gelatos and expect passersby to burst into spontaneous applause.

Evan and Nicole faced Madison Avenue, on the back edge of the sidewalk just outside the open café, a tick north of what Nicole called "Hermès corner." Air-conditioning cooled their shoulders as Evan sipped a Ricard. Nicole looked beautiful, perhaps because she was blissfully chatty about his "promotion." IHOP gushed in a dizzying blur of languages, encouraging Evan to invest only in socially conscious companies. "Good for you and good for others are not mutually exclusive." Evan didn't have the patience to explain that he *shorted* stocks, and his ebullient mood precluded the necessity.

Somewhere in the midst of a spirited conversation about the USA's insane obsession with fracking, disappointing drone assassinations, the Porsche 918 Spyder, and a divinely louche Balmain minidress, Nicole looked outward at a striking blonde waiting to cross the busy avenue.

"Oh, I like her Jimmy Choo sandals. Very *Rome*," she said quietly to Evan.

The striking blonde was Marin Owen. She crossed Mad Ave and noticed Evan, who casually looked away. He brushed some stray tendrils from Nicole's shoulder, leaned back, and rested his arm on her cushioned chair. The group laughed at a lame SUV joke. Evan joined them. *Fuck her*, Evan said to himself. *She had her chance.*

Marin walked into the restaurant, passing about five feet from Evan's table, presumably conferred with the maitre d', and then reappeared on the sidewalk, outside the café's boundary, an impenetrable row of potted plants, a magical force field that separated the haves from the have-nots. *She* was on the outside, looking in.

Opening her leather iPhone cover with "beam me up Scotty" flair, Marin paced the curb in front of the café, dramatically gesticulating while she spoke. She glanced repeatedly at Nello's seated patrons.

"*Quel cinéma!* Who is *she* trying to impress?" Nicole asked when it became superbly obvious that the show was intentional.

"I know her," Evan replied nonchalantly. "We used to go out. Haven't seen her in years."

"Ah, I see . . . like Café Momus. Am I right?"

Café Momus. Evan recognized the reference, scanned his Ridgewood and NYU memory banks. No luck. Then he remembered an incredible meal at Masa . . . and *the opera afterwards.*

"Yes, you're right," he said, relieved.

"Musetta?"

"She's a nobody, a nonentity. Don't look at her."

Nicole smiled at Evan, opened her legs a bit so her short skirt slid up her thighs, and leaned in close with the warmest, wettest, most precoital look she could muster.

"But I *do* like her outfit, *especially* her sandals," she whispered in what must have appeared to be a touching moment of couples intimacy.

"All the *angels* go naked," Evan replied.

"So true," Nicole said at full volume, laughing and turning to one of her IHOP friends. "Bernardo, act two of *La Bohème*, at the café, Musetta's prancing around in her finery, so desperately trying to impress, and Rodolfo says 'all the angels go naked.' *Ricordate*?"

"*Gli angeli vanno nudi*," Bernardo replied with appropriate flair.

"That's it!" Nicole said, raising her glass of white burgundy, a lovely Bâtard-Montrachet.

The group followed suit, triumphantly lifting their drinks.

"A toast to *gli angeli vanno nudi*."

"All the angels go naked!" They exclaimed in unison, turning nearby heads despite the crowd and street noise.

Defeated, Marin Owen pocketed her phone, hailed a cab, and disappeared.

Evan finished his pastis, closed his eyes, and savored the sweet, sweet victory.

CHAPTER

FIFTY-ONE

Evan never would have guessed that *BusinessWeek* would graciously offer up a blueprint for murder, a roadmap with destination Cash. But there it was, a headline on page thirty-two, so practical yet so glorious: *"Hard Luck Hayward—Daredevil CEO Beats the Odds . . . and the Street."*

The Movers & Shakers feature was an unmistakable treasure trove, a veritable invitation to a man of unborrowed vision. To *reject* its gift would be a crime. Surely, Hayward's hard luck could be Evan's easy fortune.

Thomas Hayward was the undisputed Father of New Economy Synergy, the man responsible for countless cross-promotions, from the ludicrous to the sublime. His company, Canyon Holdings, owned majority stakes in more than a dozen public companies, and Hayward's conception of twenty-first-century synergy drove them all. Old media, new media, wireless, satellite. Consumer products, supply chain management, automated on-demand manufacturing. Soup, nuts. Remarkably, Hayward found profitable ways to link them all, to unleash the synergies hiding in, say, your smartphone and your microwave oven. A sidebar to the article listed, including Canyon, fourteen "beat the street" public companies interwoven by Hayward's unique, synergistic strategy. *Fourteen companies. Say it with me, brothers—Synergy!*

Hayward was also a "capitalist on steroids," a daredevil who preferred extreme sports to golf. He lived in the ultraexclusive Yellowstone Club, a zillionaire's conclave where he biked with Greg LeMond and shredded double blacks with the club's developer, Tim Blixseth. Hayward earned his "hard luck" nickname by breaking his back at Tommy Moe's "Steep and Deep Ski Camp" and shattering an ankle while skydiving over the Keys. "The heli-skiing accident, I only cracked three vertebrae, and the ankle thing . . . well, let's just say I didn't stick the landing," he told *BusinessWeek*.

The article also quoted a Hartford Life manager who said he insured several "adrenaline junkies" whose "testosterone-scented air of invulnerability" compelled them to take chances—and made them better leaders. Hayward agreed. "Fast, or you lose. First, or you fail. Right, or you die. In my business, the rules are the same."

Leslie Alexander, a member of Canyon's board of directors, also commented: "Since our days at the University of Colorado at Boulder, Thomas has been a risk taker. We try to point him toward less dangerous activities such as scuba diving and surfing, but, in the end, he does what he wants."

The article closed with Evan's marching orders. Next month, Hayward would be the keynote speaker at a conference in the Cayman Islands, "Unlocking the Value of Mixed Media, 1 + 1 = 3." "The east end of Grand Cayman offers some of the best deep wall diving in the Caribbean," Hayward told *BW*. "I can't wait."

CHAPTER

FIFTY-TWO

Evan stood outside the Village Dive Center on Bleecker Street. Just as he reached for the door, he spied a pay phone on the corner. *Might as well double check before I get wet*, he said to himself while pulling the folded *BusinessWeek* article out of his suit jacket's inside pocket.

"1-1-R, how may I direct your call?" She was young, Hispanic, sounded like Rosie Perez.

"I'm calling for information on the 1 + 1 = 3 conference next month," Evan replied.

"Who are you with?"

"Venkman, Spengler and Stantz—public relations firm."

"One moment . . ."

Who ya gonna call? Evan silently sang with a smile, showing his age.

"This is Jessica." Caucasian. Also young.

"Hello Jessica, Ray Stantz here." Evan spoke rapidly, like he didn't have time for bullshit or questions. "Venkman, Spengler and Stantz PR, trying to confirm that Thomas Hayward will be speaking at the 1 + 1 = 3 event at the Cayman Ritz on the third of August."

"Yes, he's a confirmed speaker and will appear on several panels throughout the conference," she replied with the breezy insouciance of a carefree teen, which she might have been. "Will you be attending?"

Evan relaxed. "Someone from my firm will, probably that pederast Venkman, the lucky bastard. You?"

"Yes! The Ritz is amazing. It's *so easy* to register online. You should come. Grand Cayman is great!"

"What about hurricanes?" Evan asked earnestly.

"It's definitely the low tourist season in August, but too early for hurricanes. For a conference this size at the Ritz, my dad had to schedule it in the summer. It'll be hot, but everybody's encouraged to dress very casually. Even nice golf shorts are okay!"

"Well, that's certainly a refreshing attitude. Thanks for the info. Maybe I'll see you there."

"May-be . . . you will!" Jessica exclaimed in a distinctly nepotistic, singsong voice.

They said their good-byes and Evan turned his attention to the dive shop. *Three weeks. No time to waste.*

The guy behind the counter was holding a beaten-up relic of a clipboard and talking on the phone. He was pretty much exactly what Evan expected. Young, probably mid-twenties. Lean. Tan. He was wearing khaki O'Neill board shorts and a white T-shirt that read GONE DOWN LATELY? in a large red font. He had longish blond surfer dude hair and brilliantly white teeth. Undoubtedly, he fucked more NYU coeds than Sallie Mae. He was talking about sharks off North Carolina when he waved to Evan and offered the "one minute" signal.

Evan glanced at his ceramic Panerai Luminor wristwatch, a gift from Nicole. She was expecting him at the Gagosian in thirty minutes for a friend's opening. *Installations,* Evan recalled with a bubble of unamused dread. *Very* important *installations.*

He had begged Nicole to skip the "repurposed" junk and opt instead for the new Greenbergs at ClampArt, but Larry had personally extended the invitation, so they were stuck. "I love Jill's portraits," Nicole said. "We'll go next week. Brian will understand." And that was that.

When scuba dude's conversation transitioned to "drift diving Santa Rosa," Evan cleared his throat and shot him an impatient glare, and scuba dude got the message, ending his call.

"Sorry about that . . . What can I do for you, my main man?"

"How quickly can I get certified?"

"Well, that depends." Scuba dude looked at his clipboard. "Our next open water class starts on—"

"It's a simple question," Evan interrupted, more anxious than angry. "Cost doesn't matter."

Scuba dude looked Evan up and down. "Yeah, I can see that." He put down his clipboard and crossed his muscular arms before continuing.

"If I set you up with a private instructor and you do the DVD this week at home, you could probably have most of it done by the end of this weekend, with three lessons in the pool on Saturday and two on Sunday. How's that work for you?"

"Most of it?" Evan softened his tone, raised his eyebrows.

Scuba dude dropped his arms, and his defenses.

"We'll need to schedule your written exam, and your four required open water check-out dives . . . What's your hurry?"

"I'm going to Bermuda in three weeks and my buddies are all certified divers, plan to dive every day, and I want to join 'em."

Scuba dude glanced at the clipboard, then back at Evan. "You *could* do your check-out dives down there, finish your certification."

"No," Evan replied emphatically. "I want to go down with my C-card." He looked around the store, conspicuously eyeing the many expensive toys. "And I'll need *all* the necessary equipment, too."

Scuba dude grinned, calculating his commission. "Okay, no problemo. Next weekend we can get you to Dutch Springs for your check-outs."

"Dutch Springs?" Evan had never heard of it, but he assumed it wasn't in Holland with the potheads and hookers.

"It's a fifty-acre quarry lake just north of Bethlehem, Pennsylvania. Not a bad spot to check out. Viz used to be horrible, but the zebra mussels have cleaned it up—"

"Perfect!" Evan interrupted again and reached for his wallet.

Scuba dude looked pleased. "Okay, here's what we do . . ."

Evan arrived at the Gagosian right on time and found Nicole at the make-shift card table bar. The gallery was mostly empty, with only a few shaggy friends-of-the-artiste having shown up unfashionably early, undoubtedly for the free wine and unsalted mixed nuts.

"You're in a good mood," Nicole said with a hand on her hip.

"Yes, I am," Evan replied, kissing her cheek after appropriately admiring her new strapless Lanvin ruffle dress. "But there's a change of plans for this weekend."

"No Hamptons?"

"No Hamptons for me at least. I'm getting scuba certified for a business conference in the Caribbean. This weekend is the only time I can do it. Next weekend, too."

"Scuba? Really?"

"Sure, I think it'll be fun. Excellent networking opportunities, you know." Evan presumed that was ninety-nine percent a lie, but the magic word "networking" went a long way with Nicole.

"Should I get certified with you?" She scrunched up her perfect Diamond nose when she asked.

"No rush for you. Later, before Eden Rock in the winter. I'll be really busy this weekend, so why don't you go out east and I'll see you early next week?"

"I do have a tee time with Auntie Emma at Maidstone . . . and an appointment with Hamptons Tanning . . . the owner, Rachel, is coming out to the house at noon . . . Joey and Marc invited us to Twilight Thursdays . . . Sunday brunch at Babette's . . . So I'll be quite busy, too."

Nicole paused, sampled a nut. "Sure, go do your scuba thing. I'll be fine without you."

The next morning, Evan phoned the Cayman Ritz directly. The reservations manager had a lovely British accent, like Madonna's, but without the troubling Michigan undertones.

"I'm afraid all of our oceanfront rooms are booked for the conference, sir, but I do have waterway rooms available."

"Waterway? Ouch, I don't like the sound of *that*. How bad are they?" Evan asked playfully, hoping to score points, forgetting with whom he was conversing.

"Sir, it *is* Ritz-Carlton. A raised walkway affords convenient access across West Bay Road to Seven Mile Beach, and the North Sound pool is just steps away."

"Any other options?" Evan asked, heard an impatient sigh, then typing.

"I do have an oceanfront one-bedroom residence with private terrace overlooking the Caribbean, a separate living area, marble bath, and full kitchen. *Quite* extraordinary."

"I'll take it."

"The rate, sir, is *eighteen hundred* U.S. dollars per night, not including the ten percent service charge, ten percent tax, and other fees. Will you *take it*?"

Take it in the rear, bitch, Evan thought, not particularly caring for her tone, or her attitude.

"My Amex is *black*. What do you think?" He didn't wait for her reply before reading the account number and expiration date.

"Splendid. Your total for five nights is eleven thousand sixty-two dollars and fifty cents, American."

"*Splendid.*"

CHAPTER
FIFTY-THREE

"Let's go to Paris, *today*!" Nicole said breathlessly.

"*What*? Are you *insane*? You're going out east." Evan replied. It was just past eight on Thursday morning. They were on the street, pointed toward their uptown subway station. Nicole had slept over and exhibited far more energy than Evan cared for at this semi-early hour. When she complained about the anticipated furnace-like conditions of the subway platform, Evan perplexed her with a devilish quote: "*Learn the subways, Kevin. Use them. Stay in the trenches. Only way I travel.*" As they crossed the street, she annoyingly circled him like the little dog Chester circled Spike the Bulldog in the old-school Looney Tunes cartoons. She spoke staccato, eager and sincere.

"I'm *craving* oysters. Marennes, actually. *David Hervé*'s Marennes. From L'Ami Jean. Stéphane Jégo. We can stay at the Ritz. Coco Chanel suite. Like last Christmas. Remember?"

Evan was unimpressed. "We can have Totten Inlet Virginicas at the Oyster Bar, get a suite at the Plaza."

Nicole ignored him.

"And I'm absolutely *dyyyying* for Gregory's royale de foie gras. His barbeque palette de cochon? *Soooo* yummy."

"We can go to wd-50, ask Wylie to custom-make his aerated foie gras for you, and I'll get Brett Ottolenghi to fly in some truffles, bellota too."

Nicole stopped circling, held out her arm like a teasing porn movie traffic cop, and made Evan stop walking. "I'm *serious*. Alain Ducasse took over Le Meurice's kitchen! Three Michelin stars! And remember last December?"

Evan remembered last December. Le Bal Crillon des Débutantes. The culmination of three months' work.

In September, nearly a year ago now, Evan read in *Town & Country* that Victoria Buchanan's sixteen-year-old niece, Andie Calumet, would be coming out, making her international debut on the first Saturday of December in Paris. Family members and several escorts would accompany her, including her uncle, Geoffrey Buchanan. Only twenty-four privileged young ladies were extended invitations to the aristocratic fairy tale fête, and the guest list reflected the exclusivity.

First, Evan called the international for-more-information number listed in the article and asked about purchasing a ticket. The person at the other end literally laughed at him.

Obviously to relieve some blue-blood guilt, the haute couture debutante ball also served as a benefit for Lauren Bush's FEED Foundation, so Evan called the foundation and offered to make a sizable donation, with the expectation that he could attend Le Bal Crillon. "Sorry," the woman said, "unless you work for *Vogue* or are an *invitee* of one of the young ladies, I'm afraid you will not be extended an invitation." *Fair enough,* Evan thought, angrily admiring the elitism and relishing the challenge to crash the party.

Next he called the ball's venerable sponsor, the Hôtel de Crillon, commissioned by Louis XV in 1775 but now owned by a Saudi prince, and asked if reserving a suite might result in a ticket to the big show. *"Pas possible,"* he was told impolitely.

Next Evan did what everyone does when they don't know what to do—he googled the damn thing, and the solution appeared.

The Web site of the New York Social Diary listed the names and New York connections of that December's lucky twenty-four. Number three on the list, after a French *comtesse* and Tallulah Willis, was Miss Augusta Vandevelde, who would make her debut in Chanel Haute Couture, following in the footsteps of her sister Nicole, a New York socialite who came out nine years ago. Evan googled Nicole Vandevelde.

Forty-eight photos on Style.com. Endless "party pictures" courtesy of the New York Social Diary. Nicole cochaired the Neue Galerie Winter Gala and a handful of other big-money charity extravaganzas. She worked for the United Nations. She ran in some sort of potato chase 5K in Bridge-hampton three years ago. Evidently, she loved all things French. She lived on Park Avenue in a building owned by her late father. Cancer had killed him a year earlier. *He* was a renowned connoisseur of fine wines. She was on the host committee of a cancer benefit being held *the next evening* at Michael White's Ristorante Morini.

Evan met Miss Nicole Vandevelde thirty hours after googling her. He also met her "boyfriend," a Zorro-esque Spanish investment banker named Roberto Vargas. *Quién es más macho?* Evan thought to himself, noticing Zorro's wandering eye. At the open bar, Zorro told Evan that the Friday happy hour chicks at Ulysses were hotter than "these weepy cancer party chicks." Evan listened and nodded. Zorro rambled on. Zorro was a butt man.

The next day, Evan called an escort service and hired two junk-in-the-trunk hookers to dress like gold-digging secretaries and meet Roberto at Ulysses at six o'clock on Friday. He ordered up one white and blond, the other Latina and brunette. Beyond the ass, Evan doubted Zorro had a pref-erence, but he covered his bases nonetheless. The escorts' company-owned apartment on East Fifty-seventh Street was wired for video—blackmail was good business for New York escort services and a favored "negotiation tactic" for high-priced New York divorce lawyers, who paid handsomely for the footage.

Nicole dumped the randy Spaniard on Monday, minutes after she re-ceived a DVD of him lustily humping the brunette, doggy-style. She as-sumed her family trustee or attorney had hired a private investigator to check out Roberto, whom she'd known only for a few months, but the pro-tective whistle-blower preferred to remain anonymous, to avoid any *un-dignified* conversations.

Evan gave her time to grieve. He called three days later and invited her to a ridiculously expensive tasting of Adrian Murcia's French cheeses at City Winery in SoHo. She was thrilled, and she particularly enjoyed the

Époisses from Burgundy and the doughnut-shaped Couronne Lochoise, a goat cheese from central France, Evan presently recalled to his immense satisfaction. *A fellow turophile,* she'd remarked. *What a refreshing change!* He'd replied, *I practically live at Murray's!*

After a few more effortless, well-researched dates, he closed the deal with a "heralded" 1985 Sassicaia, a two-thousand-dollar bottle of wine, an "explosive yet velvety soft" Super Tuscan. *One of my father's favorites,* Nicole had said with a sad sniffle and watery eyes. *Really?* Evan had replied, skillfully conveying empathy and shock at the same time, knowing full well that her father had purchased a rare case from Sotheby's shortly before his death. Nicole had sniffled one last time, composed herself. *What are you doing the first weekend of December?* she asked.

"Evan? Hello? Earth to Evan? Do you remember last December?"

"Of course. Augusta's debut in Paris. *Incredible.* But I have to *work.* I'm a PM now, and I've got that scuba thing this weekend. I can't run off to Paris on a whim."

Nicole softened and they resumed walking.

"Are you working on something big?"

"*Huge.* I've been researching an idea that could earn me millions, *tens* of millions, maybe *more.* Part of my research involves the *networking* conference in the Caymans. Timing is tight. I can't slack off right now." He has used the magic word.

"Okay," Nicole replied with a smile. "The Marennes and foie gras royale can wait." They walked half a block in silence, and then Nicole suddenly said something that reminded Evan why he kept her around after Le Bal Crillon, other than the ubiquitous male inertia, Hamptons connections, and uninspired sex (but *sex,* after all).

"Hey! My discretionary account has several million in it right now, I'm not exactly sure how much. Maybe more? Can I get in on your deal? I'll split the profits with you fifty-fifty, Monsieur Stoess."

Evan let a smile cover his face, reached for and squeezed Nicole's hand, and pushed forward, counting his money and contemplating Calatrava immortality.

CHAPTER
FIFTY-FOUR

While the subway platform was like a sauna on the equator, the uptown 6 train itself was nice and cool.

"Topic—the downfall of Merlot. Did it begin with the corrosive derision it received in *Sideways*, or before?"

"'Corrosive derision' . . . damn, Nicole, that's beautiful."

"Wish I could claim it. Eric Asimov wrote it in the *Times* in a brilliant piece on the topic."

"Well, what did Asimov conclude?"

"I don't remember."

"That's ironic."

Nicole didn't reply, and Evan allowed the rhythmic rocking and womblike white noise of the subway to carry him back to Paris, back to Le Bal Crillon. . . .

Geoffrey and Victoria Buchanan radiated effortless elegance, sophistication and class. Evan watched them from across the opulent ballroom, hypnotized by the long-planned encounter. He even considered approaching Geoffrey, saying something, *anything*, but what? He did not know.

The Ritz's Coco Chanel suite was impressive, as it should have been for ten thousand euros a night. Evan could see the Vendôme gardens from the window in the *bathroom*. Nicole's mother and Auntie Emma hosted a bittersweet reception in the Salon Psyché. They toasted the tragically absent patriarch under the Aubusson tapestry, which depicted the room's namesake, with an *impériale* of 1986 Château Lafite Rothschild, the incredibly rare six-liter bottle. The Almas white Beluga caviar was delicious. At least Evan *told* himself it was delicious . . . or did it actually taste like over-salted shit served on a crusty shingle? When Nicole told him that only a few kilograms of "the roe" were produced each year and then sold in tins made of twenty-four-carat gold, he concluded that, yes, it was indeed delicious.

CHAPTER

FIFTY-FIVE

When he finalized the list of twenty companies to bet against, Evan shredded the *BusinessWeek* article on Hard Luck Daredevil CEO Thomas Hayward.

Including Canyon Holdings, twelve of Hayward's super-synergized companies made the list; Evan excluded two because their stock had already been hammered by outside economic factors, plus it was smart to be not so obvious. *Hayward? Who's he?* Evan said to himself, chuckling in his quiet office.

He selected eight independent companies with strong ties to Hayward's dirty dozen, and he drafted a clever narrative that made some sense of his strategy, *without* Hayward's final bit of hard luck.

New Economy Synergy? Bullshit. Just another post-bubble attempt to revive unsupportable valuations. Do people really want to be able to turn on their microwave ovens with their smartphones?

Just in case anyone viewed his profit from Hayward's tragic but he-died-doing-what-he-loved accident as a tad suspicious, Evan made a list of research items to find or fabricate, and then backdate—evidence supporting his non-dead Hayward master plan. He assumed the Cayman investigators, if any appeared, would be as slow-witted and incompetent as

Aruba's and, as in Aruba, there would be no body. At least, that was the plan.

Kennedy perused Evan's spreadsheet, typed feverishly, scribbled notes, all the while oblivious to the drying splotch of mustard on his Thomas Pink shirt. Evan knew the drill and sat in silence.

"On the phone you said two weeks max, right?"

"Correct," Evan replied. "I'd like it done in two weeks or less, before any sell-side analysts start commenting on anticipated third-quarter earnings."

"Shouldn't be an issue, twenty companies, two hundred fifty million. They're all heavily traded, so we won't have the problems we had last time with your little guys."

"No problems? Even Canyon Holdings, the seventy-five million short position? That's my priority."

Kennedy carefully eyed his computer screen. "Not a problem."

"And my options strategy, the underwater puts?"

"Very aggressive, but doable." Kennedy looked at the spreadsheet again. "You sure about these? If you're right, you could make like ten times your money, but if you're wrong . . ."

Evan nodded after putting on a look of appropriate but confident concern, which Kennedy acknowledged with a half smile.

Given the regulatory constraints imposed by self-loathing cowards and frightened ivory tower idealists, Evan's options strategy *was* aggressive, but given the future he would create in the Caribbean, it was *weak*. He knew, however, that option contracts were thinly traded, and disproportionate positions would result in computer-generated red flags and an SEC investigation, which he did not care to suffer. Evan didn't want to end up like the Goldman Sachs morons who traded eighty percent of the options the day before Adidas bought Reebok, information they had purchased from a coconspirator at Adidas's investment bank. The feds seized their cash—and threw them in jail. The salivating *Times* concluded "they got greedy." *Wrong,* Evan knew. They got *stupid*. So, acknowledging the constraints he could not overcome, Evan decided to be prudent and leave some money on the table. He certainly wasn't happy about it, but it was the smart thing to do. He reassured himself with a graphic reminder from Rand: *"Your self is your* mind; *renounce it and you become a chunk of meat ready for any cannibal to swallow."*

"If you're right . . ." Evan replayed in his head, staring at the ceiling above his bed, Thursday becoming Friday. After his meeting with Kennedy, he secretly filled in the final column of his spreadsheet, by hand, for his eyes only. If the twenty stocks behaved the way they should without Mr. Synergy, Evan would bank fifty million dollars, *after taxes.*

Fifty million.

Ignoring his philosophical objections, he would donate half a million or so to a charity, if not for the inevitable party invitation, then for the blurb in Ridgewood's alumni newsletter, Nicole's admiration, and the plaque on the wall bearing his name.

Evan closed his eyes and fell asleep.

Over the past many months, his recurring nightmare has changed. Evan is no longer a spectral visitor at his own funeral, unseen and unheard, an estranged cosmic auditor.

Now he wanders through seamless scenes of his past life, amongst his friends, enemies, family, coworkers, even Nicole. He's *with* them, at the table, in the car, on the playground . . . but they cannot see or hear him. He's there, *right here goddammit!*, but imperceptible to them all. They ignore him, can't see him, don't sense him. It's excruciating: Replaying his life is worse than haunting his death.

Frustrated and furious, he screams at the top of his lungs, tries to reach out to touch, but they cannot hear, and he cannot feel. The air is always cold and suffocating. He slams shut his eyes, clenches his jaw, fists so tight his forearms burn, every cell of his being freighttraining one thought, one epic wish. *To belong.*

But he cannot. The hurt is so visceral, the isolation so total, it must be hell's crescendo.

CHAPTER
FIFTY-SIX

Evan's private scuba instructor was a soon-to-be fifth-year senior at NYU. A typical college student, he was as naïve and mentally malleable as an unremarkable kindergartner. A semiprivileged son of a Hartford insurance executive, when he informed Evan that "the rich don't pay their fair share," Evan literally laughed in his face. It was Sunday afternoon; they were shootin' the shit poolside, talking politics while preparing their gear for a final training dive.

"Yeah? Ya think?"

"Absolutely. The rich don't pay enough, the rich . . ." *Blah blah blah.* The regurgitated nonsense of pseudointellectual frauds—soft, tenured, and dangerously oblivious.

"Tell me, do you ever plan to make real money?" Evan asked casually, when Junior finally shut up.

"Sure."

"How?"

"I'm not sure yet. Law or business. I'm taking the GMAT *and* LSAT next semester, just started a Kaplan—"

"Okay, I get it," Evan interrupted, signaling *stop* with both hands.

"So, a few years from now, you're a lawyer or a businessman. Do you want to earn a million dollars?"

"Of course. *More.*"

"Why? What do you want to buy?"

"A place on Ambergris Caye so I can dive whenever I want." The youngster paused. "North of the cut. And maybe my own dive boat, for me and my friends."

"Perfect. So you've graduated from law school or B-school, worked hard, earned your first million, and you're looking at new condos north of the cut. How much of that million do you want to pay in taxes?"

"Huh?"

"*You*, my friend, are rich now. You're the one percent. What's your 'fair share'? A third? Half? *Half a million?* More? You'd better be looking at shitty little shacks on the wrong end of the island."

Junior's eyes went vacant as he stared off into space. He stopped fiddling with a worn regulator hose.

"*Half*?" He finally said, a look of childlike but I-should-have-known shock on his face, as if he just found out the unavoidable truth about Santa Claus.

"Many of your enlightened jealous brethren want more than half."

"Shit. I've never really thought about it." Junior's voice trailed off and he added, under his breath, "Half."

Evan patted him on the shoulder. "It's different when it's your money, huh? 'The rich' pay too much already."

"Yeah, I guess you're right." After a few seconds, he nodded resolutely and said, "Maybe I'll hide some of my money in the Caymans or something, not pay *any* taxes on it."

"*Now* you're actually *thinking*," Evan concluded with satisfaction, a job well done.

The pool training complete, Evan asked Junior if he wanted to grab a beer or two, "on me." Evan was nervous; he needed insider intelligence to ensure his upcoming performance was believable.

They walked to Peculier Pub, an NYU institution on Bleecker Street with a beer list longer than the dictionary. Evan told Junior—what was his real name? *Ian*—that if he ordered a Coors Light, he'd beat him like a bastard stepchild. "And trust me, you don't want that."

They found a malodorous booth near the jukebox and, after Ian was lubricated with two Lambics, Evan pulled a pen and notebook out of his storm blue Hermès Arion weekend bag.

"Okay, here's the deal. I'm going to Mexico in a few weeks to dive with some old high school buddies. I kinda told 'em I was an experienced diver, and that's what I want them to think."

Ian's beer arrived, he smiled dreamily at the stormy-weather waitress, then turned to Evan.

"Piece of cake. Slice of strudel. First, you already have your own mask-fins-snorkel. Rent the rest of your gear in Mexico. New stuff is a dead give-away. Tell your friends you flew in from somewhere else and couldn't bring your own regs and BC. If they ask about your computer, tell 'em you only use tables, don't trust a bend-o-matic."

Evan stopped scribbling notes. "Bend-o-matic?"

"It's slang for a dive computer."

"Cool." Evan added it to his notes with an asterisk. "What about a dive knife? What do experienced divers carry?"

"Ah, good question. Newbies love big, flashy knives, fuckin' Samurai Jack swords strapped to their legs. Don't do it. I carry a little folding Ocean Master, three-inch blade, easy to open with one hand, even with gloves. Stick it in your upper BC pocket where it's easily accessible."

Three-inch blade. Perfect.

"Good advice. Maybe tell me some more slang?"

"Sure," Ian replied, tipping back his peach beer-syrup. "A 'Christmas tree' is a diver with lots of unnecessary gear dangling from him like orna-ments. Newbies are usually Christmas trees.

"A 'CN' is a clueless newbie.

"A 'hoover' is an air hog, usually a CN or an out-of-shape diver who's the first person back on the boat with an empty bottle, which is slang for your tank.

"Let's see . . . a 'braille dive' has low visibility, but you won't have to worry about that where you're going.

"Lobsters are called 'bugs,' and if you get seasick and hurl over the side, you're chummin' like Chief Brody.

"Finally, always remember: A good diver is a *calm* diver. Do everything methodically, efficiently. Newbies get nervous, get too excited, end up in trouble. *Not you.* You don't want to be a hoover . . . or a statistic, and that starts *on the boat.* Get it?" He concluded with a satisfied nod and a hiccup.

"I do," Evan said, closing his notebook, the dozen colorful authenticators committed to memory.

Calm, methodical, efficient. Newbies get nervous, get too excited, end up in trouble. Newbies and murderers.

CHAPTER
FIFTY-SEVEN

Grand Cayman Island in early August. Hot. *Really* hot. Humid. *Wet*, actually. Hot *and* wet. "Good if you're with a lady, bad if you're in the jungle," Evan said to himself, applying Mork from Ork's disjointed but humorous truism to Owen Roberts International Airport's blistering tarmac.

Dancing waves of heat and fogged-over aviators obscured his view of the A-frame shack mansion that passed as a terminal here in offshore investors' hellish heaven. He looked over his shoulder at the Cayman Airways jet, parked alone in the sun, and wondered how long it would take for the air inside the fuselage to superheat from seventy degrees to a hundred and fifty, slow-roasting the baggage handlers inside. He could taste their sweat, and his stomach turned. He choked back the bile, swallowed it; a faint taste of stale airplane peanuts flavored the sour burn. *Welcome to Paradise.*

Evan's underwater weekend in BFE Pennsylvania had passed without incident, and his scuba certification card arrived via FedEx three days later, the same day Kennedy closed the short positions and options strategy that could turn the spreadsheet of his life into reality. A new titanium Ocean Master folding dive knife was safely zipped in his checked luggage. All systems were *Go.*

The Ritz had a car waiting for Evan; actually, it was some sort of skinny butt-ugly Eurocrap minivan. The driver was a short, very dark black guy wearing white Bermuda shorts, a white short-sleeve shirt, and thick white tube socks pulled up nearly to his knees. Evan thought he looked like Angus Young's photographic negative.

Evan's high-priced oceanfront suite was indeed ready for his arrival, the front desk person said importantly, as if she was doing him a generous favor. She was unaware of the ruby red lipstick on her teeth.

"Splendid," Evan replied, wondering how this specimen managed to escape from jolly olde England.

"Has the conference activities desk opened yet?" Evan asked, deciding to have a little fun with her.

"No, sir, I am afraid it has not. The vast majority of conference attendees arrive tomorrow, in fact. Our conference activities centre will open at twelve o'clock at the top of the Grand Staircase, for your convenience, near the registration centre."

"Brilliant!" Evan replied, drawing an odd glance from the verbose and obsequious Brit. "Perhaps, if it is not an imposition, you could share with me the name of your colleague who will staff the activities center, so that I might make a preopening inquiry?"

"Most certainly, sir. Nigel Charles Talbot-Ponsonby is our primary conference activities centre coordinator." She paused to check a printed list under the counter's glass. "This afternoon he is servicing guests in the Blue Tip Clubhouse adjacent to the Nick Bollettieri tennis courts . . . a map for you, sir."

"Spec-tacular! I shall locate *Chuck* forthwith and register my preopening inquiry."

"Please pardon, sir?"

"Nigel Charles Talbot-Ponsonby . . . he does prefer 'Chuck,' I presume?"

Finally the stoic Brit cracked a small smile. "No sir. He prefers 'Nigel.'"

"Oh my! A negligent presumption. Please pardon, I do most earnestly apologize!"

•   •   •

After checking out his splendid suite and tipping the overeager bellman to make him go away, Evan went on his quest for Chuck. Wandering through the lush and meticulously maintained grounds, he spotted the Blue Tip Clubhouse and, inside, stringing a snow shovel–sized Prince tennis racket, Nigel Charles Talbot-Ponsonby.

Chuck was a mid-twenties Hugh Grant look-alike, the quintessential Englishman in crisp tennis whites with thick brown hair held back by Persol Havana sunglasses worn as a headband. From a distance, he looked aristocratic, congenial, and competent. As Evan approached he noticed Chuck's sleek IWC watch and he understood: *This isn't a job for this blue-blood, it's a freakin' field trip to Her Majesty's little island in the tropics.* Evan sensed within himself an unusual mix of envy and pity. This guy didn't earn his rewards; they'd been served to him on a sterling silver platter, purchased eons ago from the vaults on Chancery Lane. Nonetheless, he made a mental note to look up the Talbot-Ponsonby family in the latest edition of *Debrett's Peerage and Baronetage.* One never knows when a titled Englishman might come in handy.

"Nigel?"

Chuck continued to focus for a moment, finishing a recalcitrant string, then straightened up before addressing Evan. When he stood, he removed his sunglasses, nonchalantly smoothed his shiny moppish head of hair with his hand, and replaced his makeshift Persol headband to hold it perfectly in place. By appearance he was so cliché, so stereotype, Evan couldn't help but wonder if he was a next-generation animatronic, perhaps purchased from the exclusive Disney Ritz collection.

"Well . . . yes . . . how may I help you?" Chuck's charming smile and affable, open attitude were surprisingly down-to-earth, instantly putting Evan at ease. *This kid's got real talent,* Evan said to himself. He extended a friendly hand.

"Nigel, my name is Evan Stoess and I'm here for the one-plus-one conference. I'm hoping to do some advanced wall diving, and I understand you're the conference activities coordinator."

"Indeed I am. I'm putting together charters for all experience levels, novice to technical."

"Great. I'm hoping to dive with a prominent colleague of a friend. I've never met him, but I really want to do business with him, and I thought diving would be a casual way to get to know him."

"Certainly. Understood. What's the gentleman's name?"

"Thomas Hayward."

A flash of recognition appeared on Chuck's face, and a big grin. "You, ambitious sir, are in luck. I have chartered a boat for Mr. Hayward and five fellow attendees tomorrow afternoon, East End wall dives, the *best* in Cayman. It's a Cayman Diving Lodge charter and I've requested Mickey, their finest divemaster. He's a Yank like you, and he'll chauffeur the group to pristine sites not on the map. I have room on the boat for two more conference attendees, first-come, first-served."

"Count me in," Evan heard himself say confidently, but his pulse quickened and he suddenly felt queasy. *Tomorrow?* He'd expected a few days to settle down and mentally prepare, both for the reality of voluntarily dropping a hundred feet below the ocean's surface and the execution of his unusual business model.

"Wonderful, Mr. Stoess. Will you need equipment?" Chuck reached for a Ritz stenciled minipencil and golf scorecard on which to jot notes.

"Only regs, BC, and lead. I flew in from another meeting and could only carry my mask-fins-snorkel. Been on the road for a while, couldn't schlep all my gear unfortunately. Yep, I'll miss my own regs, but—"

"No worries, Mr. Stoess," Chuck gently interrupted, "some of your colleagues also require equipment. Although CDL's rental gear is top-notch, I plan to outfit your charter with new gear from our shop which we shall then add to our rental inventory."

"Oh, excellent. Thanks. And how do I pay?"

"I'll bill it to your room, for your convenience."

"Perfect," Evan said, checking his pockets for his card key and the little paper sleeve with his suite number on it. "I'm in an oceanfront residence . . . I don't recall the number."

"Don't worry about it, Mr. Stoess. I shall find it."

Evan stopped searching. "Please, call me Evan. Now, how do I get out to the East End?"

"I've arranged a van, Evan. Meet below the sculpture of the twin angelfish at the Grand Staircase at noon. Or, if you have a rental vehicle and would like to explore the island a bit, simply meet at the Cayman Diving Lodge at one o'clock. You'll find the Lodge on all of the maps."

"Will Mr. Hayward be riding in the van?" Evan asked tentatively.

"His assistant did not say, but I *do* know that at least three members of his party plan to meet below the angelfish at noon."

Evan exhaled between pursed lips. "Thank you, Nigel."

"My pleasure, Evan. I'd say 'good luck tomorrow,' but you don't strike me as a man who relies on luck."

Evan smiled as he turned toward the door. *Indeed, this kid's got talent.*

CHAPTER
FIFTY-EIGHT

After contemplating it for a few restless moments in his ridiculously gargantuan California king-sized bed, Evan decided *not* to ride in the van. It wasn't worth the risk.

Say too much and you tip your hand, people find out who you are. Motive.

Say too little and you're the quiet loner, a memorable mute. Suspicion.

He dialed the Ritz's concierge. A Suzuki Grand Vitara—*huh?*—would be delivered from the resort's favored "for hire" agency in the morning. "Please recall, sir, that in Cayman one drives on the left, not right, side of the road." *Got it, Jeeves.*

Evan reviewed Junior's list of scuba slang one last time, turned off the light, and recalled the pliable youth's parting words of wisdom. *Calm. Methodical. Efficient.* He held firm to those words as he drifted off to sleep, hoping they would stick. They did not.

In his dream the Vandevelde family sat in Le Castiglione on the rue Saint-Honoré, enjoying the magnificent cheeseburgers, a happy rich family, together in body and in spirit. Out of breath, with them but hidden from their sight, Evan pounded on the invisible barrier that kept him outside their warm circle of humanity. They laughed, carefree, and he cried out, but they could not hear him. He pounded and pounded, suffocating in his cruel bubble of isolation, energy draining from him like a character in a video game. He could see his life force dwindling, a little gauge in the top left corner of his nightmare. Green . . . Yellow . . . Red. *Danger*. Exhausted and near empty, he stopped struggling, hyperventilating the mantra, *Belong*. At once a calm, reassuring peace joined him in his invisible cell. Another gauge appeared, center screen, numbers rolling up quickly, dollar signs, his bank account. As the money poured in, his life force increased. Red . . . Yellow . . . Green! Calmly, without moving, he emerged from the bubble and joined the family at the table. His cheeseburger was still warm, their greeting even more so.

CHAPTER

FIFTY-NINE

The Burger King looked out of place. A typical fast-food box sitting on a zillion-dollar piece of Caribbean-front property, with postcard-perfect gin-clear water within cannonball distance of the pickup window, the Burger King was freakishly, almost *disturbingly* out of place. The sight was so shocking, so *wrong*, Evan *had* to pull over and order a soda, for the novelty of the drive-thru sea view of Georgetown's cruise ship–packed harbor and, yes, for the oddly disconcerting certainty that it wasn't a mirage.

The island was only twenty-eight miles long, but Evan had allowed three hours to drive from Seven Mile Beach to its opposite end. Sitting in Burger King's parking lot, sipping a Sprite and watching a shimmering Carnival virus factory carry the obese over the horizon, he was glad he had.

He stared at the horizon as the ship fell over the edge. Closing his eyes, the image of sky-meets-sea remained, a silhouette background for deep thoughts.

Or *Deep Thoughts*.

Like Jack Handy's bizarre musings, Evan's own deep thoughts scrolled across his mind's eidetic movie screen, a long lost Ridgewood recitation from the paleo-objectivist world of Rucellai's term paper costar, Leon Battista Alberti.

Wealth is gained from profits, and these depend on our labor, diligence, and industry. Poverty, being the opposite of wealth, must then be caused by the opposite qualities: negligence, sloth, and inactivity. Poverty keeps virtue hidden and unknown, in the shadows of misery. It is better to die than to suffer and live in poverty.

Evan opened his eyes and started the Suzuki. "Because, hey, *free dummy*," he said to the sea with a smile.

Driving east on Church Street, the scenery transforming from affluent Georgetown suburb into Caribbean slum, Evan's excitement began to bubble, and deep thoughts turned to random thoughts, random dreams, random hopes, a random shopping list that would leave Donald fuckin' Trump green with envy.

> *A 1920s Pierre Chareau dining table and chairs.*
> *A case of Colgin Cellars 2002 Cabernet Sauvignon.*
> *No, scratch that. A case of 1995 Krug Clos d'Ambonnay.*
> *A day on Avenue Montaigne with Nicole, à la Richard Gere in*
> *   Pretty Woman.*
> *Is the Société du Vin really tasting a '45 Petrus? Skeptical. Must*
> *   investigate.*
> *These pretzels are making me thirsty.*
> *Make time in the spring for Ferrari's F1 Clienti program. Order*
> *   Ferrari.*
> *Maybe start a hedge fund? Everybody's doing it.*
> *The wisdom of Adovardo, the naïveté of Lionardo.*
> *Reminder: Buy a case of the Ott and a dozen cans of Funaguchi*
> *   for the Ditch Plains party next week.*
> *Mom, I love you but this trailer's got to go.*
> *Money is the barometer of a society's virtue.*
> *Don't be a hoover, newbie, charlie foxtrot, cattle boats suck.*
> *The cube.*

To calm his nerves, Evan wanted to be exactly a half hour early, no more and certainly no less, so he stopped at the blowholes to *ooh* and *ahh* with the Teva'd tourons. As he planned, Evan was the first diver on the boat. He spoke with Mickey for a few minutes, the short, shirtless and shoe-less divemaster with long curly brown hair and zero body fat. Mickey sug-gested he go ahead and set up his gear; the rest of the group would have more room if he was ready to go. Evan had feared his inexperience would be evident if he had to set up his rental equipment on a bouncing boat, so he seized the opportunity to take his time and not worry.

When the rest of the garrulous group walked onto the pier, with Thomas Hayward in the lead, Evan was stretched out on the bow of the *Nostromo,* the forty-eight-foot Pro 48 dive boat, out of their view. Taking Mickey's cue, he decided to stay put for the time being, allow his fellow divers time to get situated in the space-limited stern before introducing himself.

He could hear and sense Mickey directly behind him in the main cabin, prepping for departure. From both sides, swirling around the cabin with the hot wind, the peripheral noise was more prevalent, enthusiastic rich men engaged in highbrow locker room banter. Two guys vigorously debated the Rule of Thirds. Another announced that he brought his hot assistant to the conference and planned to "close the deal" later that day in his private beach cabana, where the little lass was at that moment slurping potent Bar Jack Rum Runners. He hoped her tits were real. Another guy with a whiny nasal voice, probably a lawyer or accountant, kvetched about his leaky two-thousand-dollar camera housing. Hard Luck didn't say much, but when he did Evan recognized his authoritative voice and the fawning genuflection that followed. Hayward was undoubtedly the alpha male, surrounded by beta sycophants.

The noise suddenly ceased when Mickey presumably joined the group. *"Does anyone need any lead?"* Mickey asked. *"Let's have too much on board rather than too little."*

Evan's stomach lurched and adrenaline poured into his bloodstream. *If Hayward can ditch a weight belt, this could get ugly, or not happen at all.* He sat up on his elbows and turned his head carefully to tune in the re-plies. The group grumbled incoherently in unison, but Evan heard Hay-ward's self-confident boast. *"No wet suit, no lead. Even in salt water I'm negative at two meters.*" Evan exhaled forcefully, draining the adrenaline and calming his pounding heart. He pushed his forefingers into his wet-with-sweat temples to clear his vision, and he lay back down.

"Hey! On the bow! Wake up! Any lead?"

Evan heard the group laugh as they shifted about, settling in, their gear ready for departure. He pushed up to his elbows again. "No, I'm good!" he shouted. He had an extra five-pound square of industrial gray lead in his BC's pocket, but no one needed to know about it.

"Okay!" Mickey replied. "Five minutes!" He left the boat and walked up the rickety wooden pier, entered the Lodge via its screen door, mission unknown. The group resumed its boisterous chatter and two of them appeared on the bow's starboard side—the whiny deal killer and a really tall, thin, pale, bald guy who looked exactly like the lead singer of Midnight Oil. *Beds are burnin'.*

"Mind if we join you?" Eyebrowless Midnight inquired.

"Not at all," Evan replied. "I'm starting to *burn* so I'm heading back anyway."

They made quick introductions as he stood, then Evan exited, stage left.

When he stepped down onto the stern, Hard Luck was in deep conversation with a hirsute man in neon yellow board shorts and an obviously brand-new Stingray brewery T-shirt.

"Maybe we should consider a dividend recap?" Hayward asked. *He* was a sturdier, unambiguous replica of Anderson Cooper, Evan noted, with intense steel blue eyes and powerful tan hands. He wore a limited edition, super-cool Richard Mille RM 032 "Dark Diver" watch, waterproof to a ridiculous two thousand feet. It looked like the watch Darth Vader would wear.

Well, at least it may survive, that's a plus. Evan thought matter-of-factly.

"We could lever up about twenty million, add the cash on hand, and take out fifty, maybe sixty million." Hirsute sounded excited.

"Be careful," Evan interjected, causing both men to turn their heads in surprise. He sat on a long, low Igloo cooler close to them.

"I'm sorry. I couldn't help overhearing. Dividend recaps. Have you read about the KB Toys case?"

Hayward turned toward Evan, showing Hirsute his back and functionally dismissing him.

"No, I haven't. This isn't my thing. A coupla years ago one of my companies bought out a relatively small rival and we're trying to figure out a way to get some cash out of it." He extended a hand. "I'm Thomas Hayward."

Evan shook his hand. "Yes sir, I know who you are and I'm really looking forward to your talk at the conference."

"Excellent. So tell me about this KB case."

Brutally rebuffed, Hirsute stood up and headed for the bow. Evan watched him disappear along the narrow gunwale before answering.

"Bain acquired KB from Big Lots, borrowed seventy million and paid out *it* and nearly *all* of KB's cash as a special dividend. Bain's top dogs pocketed forty million."

"Sounds good so far," Hayward said seriously, focused intently on what was to come.

"*Two years later* KB filed Chapter eleven and creditors sued Bain, claiming the recap contributed to the insolvency, which of course it *did*. Bain got butchered in court, had to disgorge and pay punitives."

"Ouch," Hayward replied, shaking his head, his chin dropping to his chest with exaggerated despair. "I guess that rules out a dividend recap."

"Not necessarily. There are steps you can take, a special committee of independent directors—"

"Nah," Hayward interrupted respectfully. "Chapter eleven is a real downstream possibility for this fly-on-my-ass, so it's not worth the risk."

Evan slapped his hands down on both knees, sat back on the cooler. "Fuck it! We'll be *wall diving* in half an hour, a million miles away from *that* shit."

Hard Luck smiled broadly. "Hell yes! Well said. What do you want to see down there?"

"*Everything*. You?"

"I want to get a few shots of some monster bugs for my six-year-old son. There's some new Pixar flick . . . at the moment he's *obsessed* with lobsters."

Evan recalled an article he'd read in *Scuba Diving* magazine during the research phase of this project. "Last August I did the Key West bug hunt and I know where they hide. On this wall they'll be below the hundred foot limit Mickey has set for us. You mind dropping down the wall to one twenty or one thirty with me?"

"Hell no, I love to break the rules. It's how I got my nickname."

"Nickname?"

"Hard Luck Hayward."

"You don't say."

"Totally undeserved," Hayward said with a wink.

"I'm sure," Evan said sarcastically, standing up as Mickey approached the boat with a teenaged first mate carrying a large bowl of fresh fruit slices. "We'll hang at the back of the group and I'll signal you when I see a good spot for the two of us to drop down and find your monster bugs."

"Understood," Hayward said quietly. "Thank you."

Mickey skillfully maneuvered the boat through the reef-protected shallows and out the South Channel into blue water, at which point his first mate abandoned his lookout spot on the bow and took over the controls, turning the *Nostromo* southwest and opening the throttle.

On the sunny stern, Mickey asked for everyone's attention and launched into his predive briefing.

"Gentlemen, I have a special treat for you today. This wall, off East Point, is not on any of the dive site maps. It is *pristine,* with massive, healthy coral formations, huge schools of creole wrasse and black durgons, more tarpon than Chub Hole, an occasional reef shark, and, cruising just off the wall, large pelagics. The vertical drop-off falls to over *five thousand feet,* so watch your computer or depth gauge. That coral head you see below you looks so close, but it could be at two hundred feet. The water is gin clear; distances are tough to figure. Got it?"

Mickey waited for nods from all the divers and rolled his eyes when Midnight and Hirsute high-fived. Testosterone killed far more divers than sharks.

"Gentlemen, this dive is what I call a *guided tour.* Because of the depth and currents and intricacies of the wall face—cuts and canyons, pinnacles and ledges—I'll dive with you and lead the way. Instead of buddy teams, we'll move along the wall as a group. You're all advanced divers and I know you'll spread out, but make sure you can see the diver ahead of you, down current, at all times, and no one goes below *one hundred feet. No one.* As a little incentive to keep it tight, if you stay with me, I'll point out the best stuff, most of which is in the ninety-to hundred-foot range, including a massive green moray named Pickles. Can I get a *booyah!?*"

The group laughed, and Evan gulped as he sensed their anticipation. *You're all advanced divers.* Mickey continued.

"We will not anchor. The *Nostromo* will drift down the wall above us with the strong east-west current and our able first mate, Jeff Albertson, will pick us up. *When you surface,* signal 'okay' and be prepared for a quick exit so Jeff doesn't lose those of us still at depth. I'll be the last in and the last out of the water. If anybody outbreathes me, I'll buy the Red Stripes when we get back."

"Have you *ever* bought the beers?" Hayward asked with a grin.

"No. And I don't plan to today." Mickey was not amused, and he gave Hard Luck a *you done?* look. Out here, in the open ocean, the normal human hierarchies did not apply.

"Okay. After a giant stride entry, wait for me at twenty feet. If you surface and Jeff's picking up somebody else, inflate your BC, keep your reg in your mouth, and wait. Don't crowd the stern. Your time will come."

Mickey looked to the distant shore, then to sea, gauging landmarks. "Okay, we're almost there. Gear up!"

Evan choked a bit on the acid that has crept up his throat during Mickey's briefing. Hirsute gave him a look.

In space, no one can hear you scream.

Floating weightlessly in a column of water a mile high, Evan modified the *Alien* tagline: *Under water, no one can hear you scream.*

Hovering at twenty feet, the five-pounder in his lower vest pocket and knife in the upper, he could hear only his mechanized respirations and the bubbles that pushed past his ear with every exhale. Another waiting diver was taking his regulator out of his mouth, looking skyward, and blowing big smoke rings of bubbles. He didn't dare try to replicate the trick. Instead, laying flat, arms outstretched in a Superman pose, Evan Stoess was flying.

Looking down to his right, he could clearly see the edge of the wall, starting at about fifty feet, its sheer face punctuated with extraterrestrial explosions of color and form, massive coral heads framed by delicate sea fans, a fragile, enchanting eternity. The wall dropped vertically down, but it wasn't always ninety degrees flat. In addition to the dazzling coral formations attached and emerging, in places the wall angled up and down, steep slopes concealing dark shadows, marine treasures waiting to be discovered. Fissures and escarpments added to the mesmerizing topography. It was indeed an alien world unto its own, unlike anything he could imagine. Photographs in glossy magazines failed to capture its quiet immensity, and Evan knew immediately why people got hooked.

Behind the wall, the undersea shelf of the island stretched back to shore, a mottled garden of coral and rock.

To his left, the open sea, blue infinity.

Directly below, blue faded to gray and then to black. The Cayman Trench, the deepest spot in the Caribbean Sea. *The abyss.*

Mickey signaled that it was time to descend, and he did so, effortlessly, head first. Hard Luck also upended and finned down to the wall, while Evan and the other divers raised their BC hoses over their heads, pushed the button that dumped air from the hose's end, and dropped feet first, gradually adding little bursts of air to their vests to slow their descent, the goal to be neutrally buoyant at Mickey's rally point on the wall's edge.

One by one Evan's fellow divers disappeared into a dark crack in the wall that would carry them down at a sharp seventy-degree angle and deposit them on the vertical face, a hundred feet below their drifting boat, the abyss once again below.

The crack barely wider than his shoulders, Evan fought a torrent of fear-laced claustrophobia when his turn came to enter the breach. He paused, focused on Hirsute's neon trunks as they glided down the narrow crevice, and finally exhaled fully to aid his descent.

One minute later, as if birthed from the womb of a gentle sea dragon, he emerged from the prehistoric passageway, the sight and sunshine nearly blinding him. Brilliant colors and impossible shapes glued to a mountain of bedrock held him in place on the wall, the gravitational pull of *mer firma* protecting him from the infinity in front and the abyss below. The sensation was indescribable, and he just floated there, wide-eyed, stunned, liberated, a fleeting new life in the cradle of *all* life. For an instant, he forgot who and why he was.

Then Mickey grabbed his arm and pulled him away from the seam's narrow exit. The final divers arrived, Mickey signaled for everyone to check their gauges, Evan scanned the faces for Hard Luck, and the *real* dive began.

Evan could now feel the current pulling him along the wall, and it took him a few minutes to maneuver his way back to Hard Luck's side. The divers were spreading out, both horizontally and vertically, a loose chain of overgadgetized human invaders, each with his own agenda, Hayward and Evan the final two links.

As they approached a ledge supporting a mustard yellow barrel sponge large enough to swallow a Volkswagen, Hayward motioned for Evan to position himself for a photo. *For scale,* Evan thought, wishing he could get a copy.

As he pushed against the current's steady tug to stay in position, Evan felt the mild, pleasant euphoria he assumed was nitrogen narcosis. Trying to smile despite the regulator in his mouth, he recalled Junior telling him about the "Martini Law" of scuba diving—every fifty feet of depth is like having one martini, nitrogen's assault on nerve transmission. He glanced at his depth gauge as Hayward set his strobe. One hundred and five feet. Two delicious martinis. No wonder they called the water *gin clear.*

Hard Luck's memory finally preserved, Evan looked down current. About thirty feet ahead, the wall had a slight curve to it and the last potential witness was drifting out of sight, beyond the curve. Evan finned out from the wall's face until he had the upward angle necessary to spot the rising bubbles. Sure enough, he could see a long line of bubble columns to his right. The farthest column, maybe a hundred feet beyond the curve, was much thicker than the others, probably three divers' exhaust, Mickey and his curious hangers-on.

Anxiously, Evan checked the same angle to his left, up current. Nothing. For no reason at all he adjusted his mask, then he checked again. Nothing. Time to earn his reward.

Hayward was about twenty feet from the curve and had bumped up to ninety feet to photograph a majestically swaying purple sea fan bigger than a beach umbrella. Evan looked ahead and down, scanning the wall. At what he guessed was one hundred thirty feet, a small rock ledge protruded from the hollow elbow of the curve. Lobsters would *love* to hide in the overhang's darkness, Evan told himself, clueless in reality. He kicked hard toward Hard Luck Hayward.

Negatively buoyant at six feet, Hayward would sink like a stone at a hundred feet, so his vest's internal air bladders were well-inflated with air from his tank to keep him neutral, Evan noticed while tapping him on his shoulder and pointing down to the ledge. He motioned with his hand that they'd need to get under it and look up into the covered elbow. *The monster bugs will be hiding there*, Evan communicated telepathically. *A good father would want photos.* Hayward didn't hesitate, flashing the "okay" sign and leading the way.

The area under the ledge was larger than Evan expected and, until his eyes adjusted, Hard Luck disappeared into the relative darkness. But Hayward didn't bother to search for bugs. Up current about ten feet, where the overhang was narrower and the light brighter, a motionless school of six silver tarpon clung to the wall. Eight shimmering feet long and three hundred pounds, Hayward was ecstatic, transfixed, and he cautiously moved into position for a photo. When he raised his Aquatica-housed Nikon to his eye to frame the shot, Evan acted.

He removed the titanium Ocean Master knife from his vest pocket, unfolded its three-inch blade, and approached Hayward from behind. Gently resting his left hand on Hard Luck's tank, he pushed the knife into the right rear side of Hayward's BC, puncturing the air bladder inside. Bubbles rushed out, but the distracted photog didn't notice. Evan could feel Hayward's equilibrium begin to shift; he moved the knife to his left hand and, by cupping his right hand under Hard Luck's tank, supported him while he eased the blade at an angle into the left air bladder. He slowly twisted the knife, the BC bled bubbles, and Hayward felt them stall in his armpit. When he turned to investigate, Evan lost his grip and Hard Luck began to sink.

Looking down at his gear, checking his gauges, two and a half martinis narced, Hayward didn't notice. Evan turned with him, remained behind him, quickly folded his knife and returned it to his pocket, and dumped air from his BC's shoulder overpressure valve so he too descended.

His camera in his right hand, Hayward was patting his empty BC with his left when Evan moved to face him. Hard Luck's blue eyes were wide and clear, his pupils dilated. He knew something was wrong, but his training and life experience taught him not to panic.

Evan pointed to the inflator hose on the left side of the sabotaged BC. As Hard Luck turned his head left and reached for it, Evan slipped his five-pound square of lead into the large pocket on the right side of Hayward's worthless vest. The weight transferred; Hard Luck plunged and Evan began to rise.

Thomas Hayward looked up at Evan, his entire being pleading for a solution, pleading for *help*. He pressed and held down the UP button on his BC's inflator hose, but the air just rushed out of the two gaping holes, the bubbles racing up around him. He kicked aggressively for the surface, but he was too deep, too negative, and it was too late. Had he known about and ditched the five pounder speeding his fatal descent, it wouldn't have mattered. Hard Luck Hayward stopped kicking. His situation was hopeless. Without help, he was done.

Evan reached for his own inflator hose, worried that the depth might compromise *his* judgment. As he added air to his vest and drifted up and away, he saw Hayward drop his camera, forever surrendering it to the deep, and extend his right hand up toward him. Hard Luck opened and closed his hand twice, a final, desperate plea. *Come back, buddy. Help me,* his eyes begged. *My boy wanted lobster photos.*

For a moment, Evan felt remorse. Remorse that he hadn't been more aggressive with his options strategy, remorse that he'd left millions on the table. Nonetheless, in the doomed man's eyes, spiraling down into dark oblivion, Evan Stoess saw dollar signs.

CHAPTER

SIXTY

Rising past the ledge, the current pushing him around the wall's natural curve, Evan took one last look toward Hard Luck's final resting place. No bubbles. *No bubbles.* Trying to stop his free fall, Hayward had emptied his tank through the holes in his buoyancy compensation device. Evan presumed he drowned before the pressure crushed his chest like a tin can and ripped his eyes from their sockets.

It is done, Evan said to himself. *Time to get the fuck out of this bottomless fishbowl.* He looked down current but could not see his remaining brethren, his view blocked by a jutting coral escarpment. He pulled the titanium Ocean Master knife from his pocket and relinquished it to the deep. Once again he finned out from the wall and looked up. Just past the obstruction, maybe eighty feet down the wall, Evan saw a thick column of crowded bubbles, several divers close together, probably molesting Pickles the green moray eel, and beyond it, the telltale vertical trails of three single divers, separate from the group, ambivalent to Pickles's toothy charms. Above them all, the *Nostromo* and Jeff Albertson waited in a halo of light.

Evan didn't want to be the first on the boat, and he didn't want to be the last. An unmemorable exit was his goal, as always. He let the current carry him as he checked his pressure gauge. Only eight hundred pounds of air remained in his tank. At three atmospheres, it would be gone in minutes, and he'd either be the first diver back on the boat, or the second to die. Neither option appealed to him. He took a deep breath and held it, drifting without effort in the warm Caribbean bath, and formulated a plan.

To avoid the dreaded pneumothorax he learned about in his training video, he exhaled as he finned toward the surface. At fifty feet he reached the top of the wall. Rising above it, the sea opened up like a giant swimming pool with infinite 360-degree views into bright blue whiteness.

Pushing inland from the wall, leaving the abyss behind, Evan took a deep breath, and held it. He floated down current through the coral garden until he was nearly even with a rising column of bubbles, a diver just below. A squat banyan tree of elkhorn coral marked the spot. Evan held its trunk, hidden behind and under its crusty branches, and waited.

He didn't wait long. Within a minute Eyebrowless Midnight levitated above the precipice, his back to Evan, dutifully scanning the chasm's blue water for elusive patrolling pelagics. When Midnight was thirty feet above him, nearing the surface and the *Nostromo*'s rear platform, Evan gently tapped his UP button.

Jeff Albertson's outstretched hand greeted Evan at the surface. "Fill your BC and hand me your fins," the first mate advised, "then climb the ladder onto the platform."

Evan did as he was told, awkwardly struggling with the cumbersome weight of his equipment, the sea's afternoon chop, and the inimitable, oddly pleasant combination of fatigue and vertigo, the mute serenity of zero gravity left behind. Unsteadily standing upright on the platform, wavering *comme un Templier*, as Nicole might say, Evan offered an audible sigh when Albertson lifted his tank and helped him slide out of his still fully inflated vest. Evan half expected a hearty congratulations, but "have some fruit" was all the smiling Good Son had to say.

CHAPTER

SIXTY-ONE

Forward on *Nostromo*'s starboard side, Midnight was dipping his camera housing in the freshwater rinse tank, his back to the stern. Evan grabbed his towel and some orange wedges and slid along the port gunwale to reclaim his spot on the open, sunny bow. Laying out his towel, he could hear at least two more members of Hard Luck's entourage exit The Deep.

"Awesome!"

"Did you see that giant grouper?"

"I got incredible macros of a cleaning station."

"Coral heads as big as freakin' Smart Cars!"

Apparently the heathens were pleased.

It didn't last.

Evan twisted his torso and peered around the cabin's corner. A line of divers bobbed on the surface behind the boat, each waiting his turn to climb the ladder. Last in line, overseeing the process, he could see Mickey's mane of hair, barely restrained by his mask strap.

"Where's Tom?" He heard someone on the stern ask with no reply, the others preoccupied with organizing and rinsing salt-sensitive equipment. *"I see Mickey back there but I don't see Tom."*

Evan stood and shuffled down the narrow gunwale, stopping at the end of the cabin and observing the action from above.

The inquisitive whistle-blower with narrow shoulders appeared to be in his mid-forties, a plush Ritz towel wrapped around his thick waist. He had a body like a melting candle. He shielded his eyes with his hand, a pasty wet salute, and looked off the back of the boat, toward and beyond where Mickey patiently surveyed the scene. Endomorph was alarmed.

"Seriously, guys. *Where . . . is . . . Tom?*"

This time, Hirsute looked up from his apple wedge.

"What's up, Jacob?"

"I don't see Tom."

Hirsute stood, stepped shoulder-to-shoulder with his Canyon Holdings colleague.

"Eight divers plus Mickey went into the water, right?" Endomorph asked rhetorically. "Four . . . now five of us are on the boat, right?—and there's Lewis and Phil, divers six and seven, in the water . . . and Mickey.

"Where's diver eight? Where's Tom?"

"He's not on the bow," Evan contributed. "Maybe he's in the head, seasick or something."

Both men looked back at him and fake-chuckled nervously. "Yeah, Thomas Hayward *seasick*—that'll be the day," one of them said with nervous sarcasm. "He'd die first."

They remained silent and still as Jeff helped diver six, Lewis, slide out of his gear. When diver seven lingered off the stern, struggling a bit to remove his fins, Hirsute spoke up.

"Uh, Jeff, I think we're missing a diver."

"What?" Jeff was startled by the unanticipated disruption of his routine.

"We count seven divers plus Mickey, should be eight." Hirsute's tone was calm, matter-of-fact. He didn't want to appear the alarmist wuss in front of the dudes, Evan guessed, but he also didn't want to delay action if there was cause for concern.

Jeff did a counterclockwise scan around the stern, glanced at the water, then back at Hirsute and Endo. "Okay, he's probably here somewhere. Check the head and cabin and off both sides." He looked at Evan. "Why don't you check the bow and see if he's snorkeling around the front of the boat."

Evan dutifully did as he was told. On the bow, he leaned over the low railing and looked for a stray snorkeler in *Nostromo*'s shadows. Just as the brochure promised, the water was truly gin clear, the sun reflecting off the backs of three barracuda below.

When Evan returned to his perch on the port gunwale, Mickey was conferring with Jeff as five men looked on.

Midnight stepped out of the covered cabin area and into the light. "He's *definitely* not in there."

Mickey turned his focused gaze to Evan.

"He's not on the bow or snorkeling around the boat, and I couldn't see any bubbles down current," Evan said with a shrug.

Mickey clapped his hands with both anger and resolve. "All of you, sit down here. *Do not move* and *do not speak*. Jeff, radio for help on VHF 16. Hopefully some other boats are in the area, maybe DOE. Then call 9-1-1 and get RCIPS out here. Then call the Lodge and rally the *Pandora* with the extra emergency equipment. When all that's done, call CHS and tell them to have the chamber ready." He reached for his mask and snorkel. "I'm going to check under the boat."

When Mickey dove into the sea, everyone moved with military precision. The group sat silently on the stern benches, pensive and restless, while the first mate made his calls from the cabin. Evan assumed his fellow divers were contemplating the ramifications of the potential loss of their acclaimed leader.

Mickey reemerged and ignored the group, crossing between a gauntlet of confused eyes to speak with Jeff in the cabin, out of earshot.

Jeff started the engine, moved the *Nostromo* inland about a hundred feet over the island's undersea apron, and dropped anchor. Mickey stepped out onto the stern and crossed his arms.

"Help is on the way, an RCIPS maritime unit—Cayman's coast guard— and our other boat, the *Pandora*, as well as some WaveRunners from Morritt's to help with the surface search.

"Who saw him last?"

The group didn't flinch and no wide eyes left Mickey.

"C'mon! *Somebody* saw him. Anyone . . . the last time you saw your friend."

The men looked at each other like nervous students.

Mickey raised his eyebrows and sighed with frustration.

Finally, Endomorph spoke: "The last time I saw Tom was when we came out of that crack or whatever and then waited on the wall for everybody. He was waiting there, taking a picture of black coral . . . last time I saw him."

"Me, too," Hirsute said.

"Yep," Lewis added, "last time I saw him was when we first got on the wall."

The group robotically nodded, including Evan, and said nothing more.

Mickey looked at the sky, emptied puffed cheeks, and returned to Jeff's position in the cabin. *"No one move,"* he ordered.

Five minutes passed without a sound from the seven men. Midnight held his bowed bald head in his hands, perhaps offering up an emergency flare prayer to a god he had the courage neither to accept nor deny. Phil stared at the horizon, Lou at his sunburned feet. Hirsute mindlessly fiddled with a cleat. Another guy studied his watch and then caught Hirsute's eye. He tapped his watch and shook his head.

"Tom is dead," he announced.

The bold pronouncement took hold and unleashed a brief communal upwelling of unguarded sentiment. Evan listened, moved by the friends' spontaneous, uncensored lamentations.

Midnight muttered an anguished sigh and was the first to address the group of shattered mourners. "I wonder who will get the wireless division?"

"I'm willing to take over consumer products," Endomorph offered graciously.

"Did Tom sign the liability release form? I told him not to," the lawyer added helpfully.

"I hope they don't cancel Eric Ripert's dinner tonight. I love Le Bernardin."

"I need sunblock, *bad.*"

"The board did backdate his options, right?"

The cathartic eulogies ended and a serious powwow ensued.

"Yeah, but could his estate exercise the vested options?"

"It actually depends on a variety of case-specific factors."

"Such as?"

"Let's start with the terms of the most recent option plan . . ."

A fascinating topic, Evan paid close attention, taking mental notes.

CHAPTER

SIXTY-TWO

A Royal Cayman Islands Police Service cutter arrived, then the *Pandora*. RCIPS divers wasted no time gearing up and splashing in backwards to search the section of wall the group covered, fearing Hard Luck got hung up and drowned. When the police captain learned Hayward's net worth, he called in a Merlin helicopter from the HMS *Richmond*, a Royal Navy frigate that happened to be in port, to search down current. A mosquito control plane that heard the VHF call for help also joined the search. Hard Luck might have surfaced far from the boat and drifted away.

Evan saw a painfully distressed Jeff Albertson pull Mickey aside. "No way, Mickey. *No fucking way.* I had a fix on all the divers. No downstream divers. Never. *None.*" Mickey protectively patted him on the back. "I know, kid, I know. But we've got to go through the motions. The guy was a CEO or something, had a ton of money."

Finally, after what seemed like an interminable wait in the punishing Caribbean sun, Mickey announced that the *Nostromo* would take the men back to the Cayman Diving Lodge.

During the journey, theories abounded on the specifics of Hard Luck's fate. He got narced, ran out of air, and drowned. He tried to outlast Mickey and failed. He tried to outlast Mickey, *succeeded*, and surfaced alone down current, *Open Water*–style. The helicopter would find him. The helicopter would *not* find him, but he would survive on a tiny deserted island, Tom Hanks–style.

Then suddenly the unnamed Tom-is-dead dude had something to say, an "Aha!" moment that could not wait.

"I *know* what happened to him! Did anyone read 'Lessons for Life' in last month's *Scuba Diving* magazine? The guy whose BC malfunctioned and wouldn't hold air? He sank like a stone but hit bottom at like two hundred feet and was rescued by his buddies. If Tom's rental BC malfunctioned—"

"That's' right!" Midnight exclaimed. "I remember that story. The bladder walls stuck together or something and the air ran right out. That guy was lucky—"

"He wasn't wall diving in the Cayman Trench." Hirsute finished Midnight's thought, and the crowd fell silent.

A bored, stone-faced representative of the Maritime Authority was waiting for "the survivors" at the Lodge, as was the pretentiously dour General Manager of the Ritz, who stoically offered his most sincere grim-faced condolences and promised them "safe passage" back to Seven Mile Beach, as if the lack of five-star amenities at the humble Lodge, or the *uncivilized* East End itself, had somehow killed Hard Luck Hayward. The juxtaposition of the slovenly slack-jawed bureaucrat and the snobby Ritz dandy was almost comical.

Evan politely declined the GM's offer and was headed for his rental car when Lawrence Brine, of the Maritime Authority, stopped him. "I need to interview all of the survivors," he said while simultaneously chomping on an unlit quid pro quo Cohiba Exquisito.

"Certainly," Evan replied, and the group gathered on the screened-in porch to recount the afternoon's events. Midnight and Tom-Is-Dead did most of the talking, shared their bad BC theory while the other survivors nodded, and Brine took a few notes and asked a few uninspired questions. A Lodge employee brought a copy of the fortuitous "Lessons for Life" article to Brine; he glanced at it, folded it with his notes, and looked long and hard at his prehistoric Texas Instruments watch. He pushed back from the wooden table and spoke through his tortured cigar.

"Gentlemen, accidents happen. We had one at Little Tunnels just recently, and even a death at Kittiwake, so we know they happen. This could have been an equipment failure, it could have been an out-of-air situation, but it was indeed *an accident*.

"The sad truth is, we'll probably never know. If the *Richmond*'s helicopter comes up dry, which I sadly believe she will, it is highly unlikely that a body will be recovered. Mister Haywood will be declared dead in seven days. I'll contact your consulate in Kingston—the one here is not staffed at this time—and have them contact the next of kin. And I'll get all the paperwork done, which is no small feat, I tell you.

"Rest assured that my investigation will conclusively conclude that your crew, the Cayman Diving Lodge, and the RCIPS did everything *by the book* and are in no way responsible for this sad, tragic accident.

"Good day, gentlemen. I hope you enjoy the rest of your stay with us."

Evan half expected him to hand out discount coupons for a wondrous stingray encounter or timeshare buffet, but he did not.

On the way back to the Ritz, Evan stopped at the Burger King for a combo meal with an extralarge soda. He was sure Eric Ripert's wildly anticipated dinner would not be cancelled, but, despite the fruit wedges, he was starving. Overlooking Georgetown's harbor, enjoying a fry, he watched the Merlin helicopter return to the HMS *Richmond*.

CHAPTER

SIXTY-THREE

The next morning, still satiated from the previous evening's transcendent cuisine, Evan checked out of his pastel chintz bamboo suite and called Nicole on his way to the airport.

"I'm coming home early. I had a super productive meeting with that guy but the conference is a real snoozer, plus it's hotter than hell. How was your week?"

"*Fluctuat nec mergitur*," Nicole replied with a dramatic sigh.

"Huh?"

"Paris's motto . . . *fluctuat nec mergitur* . . . she is tossed on the waves but does not sink. Pretty much sums up my day."

Evan filed that fascinating morsel for future reference before saying, "So let's *go* to Paris tomorrow."

Silence, then . . .

"Evan, are you serious?"

"As a margin call. On me. All expenses paid."

"But what about your networking conference?"

"Like I said, I've had enough."

"Great! Paris! *Je kiffe grave!*" Nicole exclaimed. "Hopefully we'll be able to get the Coco. And a reservation at Frenchie; I'll call Marie and Greg directly; we'll need gifts for their kids. We can meet Augusta at Verjus beforehand. We must check The Paris Kitchen for Wendy's latest news." Nicole was talking to herself now. "It'll be warm, what to wear? I'll bring my K. Jacques sandals for sure and my crocodile Cabat. We'll buy saffron from Jean Thiercelin. You should wear your Varvatos jeans and Weston wing tips . . ."

"Okay, okay," Evan interrupted, surrendering to her unbridled enthusiasm. "I'll text you from the cab when I get home, Billy Mumphrey. Book the flights, too."

His next call was to Mac Kvamme.

"Mac, I'm flying back today, going to Paris for a few tomorrow. What's the word?"

"Evan? Good God, we're up like a hundred million. Kennedy already closed a couple of your positions, said they hit rock bottom. The guy, Hayward, he's *dead,* Evan. Reports say a scuba diving accident."

"I know, Mac. I was on the dive boat with him."

Evan held his breath while his stunned colleague digested this news.

"You *met* him? You were *with* him when he died?" Mac asked with evident dread, lowering his voice. "Are you *serious*?" He almost hissed.

"Every diver on the boat wanted him dead, Mac. What did the reports say?"

"It was an accident. He drowned in a trench or something and his body wasn't recovered."

"There you have it," Evan replied conclusively. "I helped with the search, actually."

Mac's mood lightened. "A few people here are calling you *Dead Pool* after that Dirty Harry movie. I guess some guys are just lucky."

"I make my own luck, Mac. *I make my own luck.*"

A fresh *New York* magazine sat on the seat of Evan's yellow cab. Approaching the Midtown Tunnel, on page seventy-five he learned that a "Best Bet" was a $3,500 bottle of 1945 Château Haut-Brion, "considered by many connoisseurs to be one of the best bottles of wine ever made" and available at a shop in the Village. Thirty-five hundred dollars. For one bottle of red wine, albeit a fine "first growth" Bordeaux. *Le vin anoblit*, indeed.

He asked his Senegalese driver to detour west to Le Dû's Wines; the address was listed in the magazine. While the taxi waited, Evan went inside and bought a bottle, just to impress the shop's clerk. He figured the wine would be good enough. Nicole would like it. But the look on the clerk's face was priceless.

CHAPTER
SIXTY-FOUR

Evan's taxi double-parked in front of his building in the middle of the afternoon rush, the sun reflecting off of Gehry's glorious Bernini folds. When Mister Senegal popped the trunk, Henry the doorman sprang into action, carrying Evan's Briggs & Riley Torq rollerbag into the lobby.

Inside, Carlos the concierge stood behind the reception desk, sorting packages. He looked up and smiled.

"Hey Evan, welcome home! Your guest is already upstairs waiting for you."

"Shit. I told her I'd *text* her and I forgot."

Carlos's smile turned to good-natured confusion.

"Her?"

Evan stopped walking.

"Yeah. Nicole."

"It's not Miss Vandevelde; it's a gentleman."

"A *gentleman*?" Evan repeated as if Carlos could not discern the difference between the genders. "You sure?"

Carlos laughed. "Quite sure, amigo."

"Was he on the list?" The New York by Gehry tower maintained a list of guests' names and the time or dates they were allowed access to a residence. With the exception of Nicole, Evan's list was blank.

"He had a key and he knew your security code."

"O . . . kay," Evan said, bewildered by this unexpected turn of events, resuming his cross-marble journey to the elevator. "Must be someone," he muttered to himself and then chuckled at his scintillating observation.

Sure enough, Evan's gentleman caller had a key—the apartment door was closed but unlocked. Evan pushed open the door but remained in the hallway, his bag trailing behind him, the bottle of Haut-Brion in his left hand.

His visitor sat facing him in a chair on the opposite side of the open apartment, quite a distance away. Backlit through opaque curtains by a powerful summer sun, the stranger was a blazing silhouette, intact but featureless, reminiscent of a bare-bulbed jailhouse interrogator.

Evan shielded his eyes for a moment until they adjusted to the radiant onslaught, and an overwhelming sense of déjà vu almost drove him to his knees. The lean silhouette sat comfortably, his left leg crossed gracefully. His elbows rested on the armrests, his fingers intertwined just below his chin. Evan stepped inside and the door closed behind him. The silhouette did not as much as twitch, but it did speak.

"How many *executives* do you think you can *kill* before people start asking *questions,* Mr. Stoess?"

The accent was unmistakable. The office Mystery Man. *"Hans."*

Evan's bowels rumbled and he nearly soiled himself.

"Excuse me?" He said, frozen in his foyer.

"How many *executives* do you think you can *kill* before people start asking *questions,* Mr. Stoess?" Hans repeated the question slowly, patiently, still motionless, his words seemingly carried on the piercing splinters of sunlight.

Evan's brain shut down in stages. His vision blurred as his heart clenched like a fist.

"Fifty, maybe sixty million cash . . . should be enough for now," he replied mechanically.

"It's *never* enough, Mr. Stoess," he heard the voice say. Evan felt unsteady on his feet.

"Money, Mr. Stoess. You can never have too much. You *will* never have too much. Of all people, you should understand that reality."

Hans uncrossed his legs and lowered his hands to his lap. He studied Evan.

"Relax, Evan. Take a seat. We have much to discuss."

"I am aware your lovely paramour has purchased two Delta tickets to Paris, first-class, returning four days hence." Hans had shifted his chair to face Evan, returned to his favorite pose. The goatee, the hair, the impeccable bespoke suit—he was *Die Hard*'s Hans Gruber, but for the English accent.

Although Evan had managed to walk across his apartment and sit down, the trancelike fog of stupefying shock would not lift.

"Yeah. Probably." Was all he could muster.

"Adopting Colette's philosophy, *le sage repliement sur soi-même*?"

"Huh?"

"Do you plan to *lay low* in Paris, Mr. Stoess?"

"Uh . . . no . . . yes . . . I guess so, but not really. Just getting away. Celebrating?"

"As my fellow countryman Richard Cobb said, 'Wonderful country, France . . . pity about the French.'"

Evan managed a half smile and fought hard to file that quote to torment Nicole. He squirmed in his seat, looked out the curtain-covered window, took a deep breath. Held it. Hans was perfectly still.

"Relax, Evan.

"Speak."

The invitation evoked an immediate, knee-jerk response.

"Who are you? What do you want?" Speech cleared Evan's head.

"Why, I want what you want, of course."

"Money?"

"Money." Hans delivered the one word with a measured ferocity that caused Evan to tremble to his core.

"Who . . . *who* are you?"

"I have been watching you for a long time, Evan, observing your progress, weighing your abilities against a few other well-chosen, like-minded souls."

"Watching me? Evan asked. *"Well-chosen?"*

"Dr. Mitchell LeMaire did not die of a heart attack, Evan."

The words struck Evan in the chest like a cannonball.

Hans gave him a moment before continuing.

"But let us not focus on the past." He casually took in his surroundings. "You have a charming apartment here among the rabble. Frankly we were surprised when you relocated downtown. You overcame New Yorkers' congenital *campanilismo*." Hans looked directly at Evan and raised one eyebrow. Evan held his own, raised two, inquiring. Hans complied.

"*Campanilismo*. Loyalty to one's own bell tower."

Evan smiled and nodded knowingly. New Yorkers were nothing if not fiercely loyal to their neighborhoods. Hans smiled as well, then unsmiled and crossed his arms.

"Evan, you have done an appreciable job for Contrafund to this point. You have identified, planned, and executed two profitable strategies . . ."

Pardon the pun? Evan thought to himself.

". . . but you have done so in a manner that can not be sustained. You have had some success, but your model is *not* infinitely replicable; in fact—"

"Thank you," Evan said spontaneously, shocked at his own interruption.

Hans looked surprised, pleased actually. He uncrossed his arms.

"For what?"

Evan studied Hans for a moment and contemplated his next move. *Honesty or a platitude?* Hans's three-piece suit was a hand-stitched H. Huntsman. He chose honestly.

"Thank you for not saying 'we.'" Evan looked Hans in the eye before continuing in a steady, calm voice. "The word 'we' is as lime poured over men, which sets and hardens to stone, and crushes all beneath it, and that which is white and that which is black are lost equally in the gray of it. It is the word by which the depraved steal the virtue of the good, by which the weak steal the might of the strong—"

"—by which the fools steal the wisdom of the sages." Hans finished. And they sat in silence. Evan believed he sensed *mutual* admiration.

"You are a student of Ayn Rand, an objectivist?" Hans finally asked.

"A *disciple*," Evan replied. "As are you. Few mere *students* know *Anthem*."

"Indeed."

"It's the only religion that has ever made sense to me," Evan continued.

"Religion?"

"It's a belief system, like any other. Neither you nor I can prove it's right but no one can prove it's wrong. I have *faith*.

"God or no god, I must have faith in its truth, in its power to guide me, in its power to define me, to *transform* me. You probably do too, or you wouldn't believe. That's *religion* in my book."

"Indeed." Hans paused for a moment, staring a spotlight on Evan's soul, and quoted: "And now I see the face of god, and I raise this god over the earth, this god whom men have sought since men came into being, this god who will grant them joy and peace and pride. This god, this one word: *I*."

"*My* will be done," Evan concluded.

"As I was saying, your business model is not infinitely replicable; in fact, I would suggest that you have but one more opportunity to cash out a position before you are compromised."

It required little thought to realize the analysis was correct. Evan nodded and Hans continued.

"I—my entire global organization—will help you leverage that position. You will execute, and then you will retire the model . . . and retire from Contrafund. Will two hundred million U.S. dollars satisfy you?"

Evan choked on his tongue. "Excuse me?"

"When the firm closes the position, you shall earn two hundred million U.S. dollars, free and clear, in a numbered Swiss bank account. Your money will work for you. You need never answer to anyone again."

Evan tried to speak, but he could not, so he closed his mouth wide open. *How could Hans guarantee two hundred million dollars?*

"Do you . . . have a . . . position in mind?" Evan managed to ask with great effort.

"I do. A unique opportunity."

Evan leaned forward, his senses sharp, his focus on Hans intense and singular.

Hans adjusted his tie before he elaborated.

"Last week we were made privy to a confidential communiqué between the offices of four multinational conglomerates that we have been monitoring for some time. Critical assets of these targets, and perhaps two others, plan to surreptitiously meet to view a parcel of land they intend to purchase jointly."

"A parcel of land?" Evan asked curiously.

"Sixty million acres of virgin rainforest, located in Amazonas in both Venezuela and Brazil. Following Johan Eliasch's example, the purchasers intend to preserve permanently the land and allow medical researchers to utilize it in the search for next-generation pharmaceuticals."

"I presume these critical assets lead companies in diverse industries and are never in the same place at the same time, hence the *unique opportunity*?"

"Correct," Hans said. "But that is only half of the story. The assets are purchasing the parcel from Monsieur Karenia Brevis, who will be in attendance at the meeting. Do you recognize the name?"

Evan shook his head, *No.*

"Karenia Brevis is the most influential, and reclusive, member of OPEC's Economic Commission Board and the driver of OPEC's current policy of virtually open quotas. Most of his colleagues, the Arabs in particular, oppose him, but he has maintained a fragile coalition to keep the oil flowing and, therefore, barrel prices low. If he were to perish—"

"Holy shit! Oil prices and futures would *skyrocket*, across the globe, in every market! Auto stocks would tank . . . airlines too . . . trucking . . . even groceries! It's *genius*!"

Hans smiled. "I share your enthusiasm."

Evan leaned back, ran his fingers through his hair. "Now I get the guaranteed two hundred million, but how will I position the firm . . ." He let the last word trail away slowly.

"You are tasked *only* with eliminating the assets, for which you have demonstrated a cool talent. The firm will plan and execute the multiple positions. With the exception of New York, for obvious reasons, all of my offices and all of my subsidiaries and affiliates shall be heavily involved.

And *exposed*. Billions of dollars will be committed to positions that are worthless in the current environment. Do you understand?"

"I can not fail," Evan said, knowing the stakes had been raised from *hero or goat* to *life or death*.

"You can not fail."

Silently they sat, studying each other. Evan had never encountered, never *experienced*, a person who could stay so perfectly *still*. Evan watched Hans's chest and shoulders for that gentle rise and fall that signified life, but he did not appear to *breathe*. The air around him cooled, not an atom vibrated. Evan measured his own heartbeat in his temples. Slow. Purposeful. Around fifty beats per minute, the pulse of a napping Kenyan marathoner. This unnamed man Hans was a black hole for anxiety, fear, and doubt. He sucked them in and spun out *calm*.

"I will not fail," Evan whispered unconsciously, but Hans heard him.

"I have the utmost confidence in you," Hans replied, standing and breaking the spell. Checking his ultrathin Patek Philippe 5959P timepiece, he added, "Enjoy Paris. Further information will be awaiting you upon your return, everything you need to execute."

Evan looked up at him. "That's it?"

"For now, Mr. Stoess." Hans buttoned his suit jacket and adjusted the cuffs of his bespoke Budd shirt.

Evan had no choice but to stand and accept Hans's handshake. Confident and unnaturally cool, of course. In his palm Hans passed something metal to Evan. As Hans crossed the room to exit, Evan opened his hand. A shiny brass key. To his front door.

CHAPTER

SIXTY-FIVE

Evan sat still for several minutes, his heartbeat slowly but steadily rising to its normal resting pace. Without moving his head, his eyes glided in their sockets from right to left, taking in the expanse of his apartment.

He was alone.

From below and surrounding him he could hear the muffled buzz of New York City, a honeycomb of endless activity, drones servicing their queen.

Two hundred million dollars.

He would purchase his spectacular town house cube on South Street, and a cottage in East Hampton—the megarich called them "cottages" regardless of their size. South of the highway, of course, far removed from the Bonackers in the wooded north. Next door to Geoffrey Buchanan, if possible. He would invite the Buchanan family over for a barbecue. He and Geoffrey would sit by the pool, shoot the shit, drink D.O., talk business. Victoria and Nicole—Nicole?—would roll their eyes as the boys opened *another* bottle of the Ott. All together they would lament the decline of the Summer Colony and curse the Philistines at the hedgerow. Eventually, Tyler and Ashley would call him "Uncle Evan" and he would take them to Citarella for treats.

Triumph. Sweet, vindictive triumph.

He had the key, he would open the door, and he would, finally, *belong*.

Her many texts ignored, Nicole phoned Evan at eight o'clock. He answered and she was already talking.

"Are you home? Everything's set. I'm sooo excited. We got the Coco Chanel suite and despite the short notice it all worked out with Augusta and Greg and Marie tomorrow night, Verjus on rue de Richelieu and then a late dinner at Frenchie—it'll feel early to us of course." Nicole took a quick breath. "The next day we're going to explore the nineteenth century shopping arcades, the *passages couverts*—did you see the *Times* article? 'Diminutive cathedrals to commerce and leisure'—I love that! They're in the second. We'll start at the Passage des Panoramas—you've been to Racines with me—then cross over to the Jouffroy—I'll buy you a *flâneur*'s walking stick at M.G.W. Segas, then a quick visit to Passage Choiseul to explore *and* see Offenbach's famous theater, then to Galerie Vivienne where Berlioz used to hang out, and *then*—thank you Wendy—Daniel Rose is making something special for us at Spring. Can you believe it? Can you? It'll be great. What do you think?"

"*Flâneur?*" Evan asked, exhausted from the recital.

"A well-dressed gentleman stroller of the city streets, the consummate man about town, an impartial observer of contemporary urban life."

"An unemployed voyeur?" Evan joked, but not entirely.

"You'd prefer to be a *fauve,* a wild beast like Matisse?"

"*Flâneur* or *fauve* . . . perhaps both," Evan replied, and across the city, he could feel the warmth of Nicole's smile. "What time does our Delta flight leave tomorrow morning?"

"Six o'clock. Hey! How did you know I booked Delta? I always fly Air France, but first-class was sold out."

"I know *everything*, young lady. Remember that."

CHAPTER

SIXTY-SIX

Karenia Brevis. The only child of a wealthy *von* Nazi who escaped to Venezuela in 1945 and adopted the maiden name of his Italian wife. When the Boscán Oil Field was discovered in 1946, Brevis's Gestapo father voraciously acquired rights to it and other reserves in both Venezuela and Brazil, ruthlessly dispatching rivals in the process. Until his death in 1980, the father also bought up Amazon rainforest, confident it concealed *something* of value and, if not, he could harvest its timber and still make a profit.

Educated at Princeton and the London School of Economics, Brevis joined the family business, concentrating on the Orinoco tar sands of eastern Venezuela. He became Venezuela's national representative on OPEC's Economic Commission Board twelve years ago and was the sole proponent of OPEC's generous quotas. How he managed to enforce his will on the swirling cauldron of billionaire megalomaniacs was the subject of much speculation. Some sources pointed to his impressive intellect and infamous reclusiveness—when he spoke, people listened. Other sources said blackmail, secret dossiers on the major oil families inherited from his ruthless father. Regardless of the reason, his influence on world oil markets was *substantial.* As one *Economist* commentator pointed out, "Woe is when Karenia Brevis leaves OPEC."

Evan smiled when he read it. *Woe is me.*

•   •   •

"Woe is me," Evan said with satisfaction as he closed his MacBook Pro computer.

Nicole opened one eye. "I can't believe you brought that thing to Paris."

"I kept my promise—only on the plane. It never left our safe at the Ritz."

"True," she acknowledged, and the eye closed.

The days and nights in Paris had passed quickly, Evan going through the motions, playing his role to perfection. *Camus said, a man defines himself by his make-believe as well as by his sincere impulses.* He was excited and anxious to get home to the "further information" that awaited him. Nicole didn't notice; twelve years at Ridgewood and eighteen in unpleasant hell had taught Evan to be a master thespian, more at ease *in* the charade than out. It was an adaptation that money could not fade, much less erase.

As anticipated, the death of Thomas Hayward crushed the stock price of Canyon Holdings and all of her offspring. High over the Atlantic, an e-mail told Evan that Kennedy was covering all of Contrafund's positions. Evan calculated his take-home pay to be forty-five to fifty million. Spreadsheet had become reality. His jubilation was muted, however, his focus having already shifted to the final position that must be executed.

Hans presumed a successful outcome. If Evan failed, he was quite certain Hans would add him to the list of assets to be eliminated.

CHAPTER

SIXTY-SEVEN

Kevin was behind the concierge desk speaking with a real estate agent when Evan anxiously walked into his lobby. Without a word he handed a thick manila envelope to him, hand-delivered, no return address. From its weight and feel, Evan surmised it contained maybe a dozen or so sheets of paper and something else—a thin book perhaps?

In his apartment, standing at his black granite kitchen counter, he carefully opened the envelope and removed its contents. On top was a small, old novelette, a delicate first edition antique by the looks of it. A typed note was inside. "Enjoy the original *Anthem*, published in the U.K. in 1938, eight years before your colony's intellectuals embraced its genius. You will appreciate page 134."

Evan flipped to the page. Rand's "we" diatribe was longer, more personal, than the version he had memorized. He read aloud: "I have destroyed the monster which hung as a black cloud over the earth and hid the sun from man." He closed the book and set it aside.

Beneath where the book had been, the top page was a travel itinerary prepared by Contrafund's preferred travel agency, with old-school hard copy plane tickets attached. On Sunday, apparently, Evan was flying to Caracas, Venezuela, from JFK on Continental, connecting to Puerto Ayacucho on an airline called Conviasa, return trip on Thursday. Evan had never heard of either Puerto Ayacucho or Conviasa and presumed the former was a third-world mosquito trap in the rainforest and the latter was the state-owned "we" death trap that carried one there. Fascinated, he turned the page. He was confirmed for four nights at the Atures Lodge in a deluxe *churuata* with a view of the Orinoco River. He flipped the page: A glossy photo of a middle-aged white guy he recognized from a recent *Business-Week* cover story, the first of Hans's "critical assets" and the CEO of a Fortune 100 satellite communications company. Four photos followed, the last one of Karenia Brevis. The final page offered three typed sentences:

Additional individuals may be present. Consider them assets.
Further instructions will be provided upon arrival at Atures, as will a package providing everything necessary to capitalize on the opportunity.

Evan read the sentences three times. Four rich do-gooders were quietly buying rainforest from a reclusive oil Nazi, and they might have an entourage suffer collateral damage? A package providing everything necessary to eliminate them? What the fuck? What could the "package" contain? Would he be murdering Mr. Brevis in the study with a candlestick? Could the package contain something as bluntly unpleasant as a gun? Genuinely perplexed, Evan uttered an audible "hmm" and slipped the papers back in the envelope.

CHAPTER

SIXTY-EIGHT

On one sunny spring Friday during his fifteenth year, Evan came home from Ridgewood with a swollen lower lip and a small splatter of blood on the collar of his white button-down shirt, the remnant of a bully's locker room sucker punch.

Caffeinated into a civilized mood by two liters of uncut Mountain Dew, George Stoess did not administer his usual beating. Instead, George declared, "Sheee-it, time for Richie to learn how to shoot."

Evan wondered if George intended him to take a .357 magnum to school and put a bullet in the next snob who took a swing at him. But he didn't ask. He knew in his heart, mind, and soul that *his* revenge would be to get more of what they wanted than they had. In their world a martyr's death was no disgrace, but to *have* more than them was to *be* more than them, a fate *worse* than death, and their dismay would be his vindictive triumph, his victory over them. *Whenever a friend succeeds, a little something in me dies.* At age fourteen Evan hadn't formally learned this yet, but he *knew* it like the salmon know to swim upstream. He was the "friend"; his self-defense was success. It would drive a stake in the black heart of Ridgewood.

George peeled himself out of his fetid recliner and disappeared into the double-wide's "master bedroom." After some closet rummaging accompanied by the familiar grumble of muttered profanity, George emerged with a battered Hush Puppies shoe box. "Grab that two-liter and git the Falls Shitty cans outta the garbage and we'll walk over to Jesse Livermore's cornfield," he said.

Evan dutifully obeyed, and twenty minutes later he was pushing a clip into an old Colt .45 semiautomatic handgun and aiming it at an empty bottle of Mountain Dew. "Two hands," George said, "and brace yourself for the kick." His first shot left him deaf and numb but the Mountain Dew bottle exploded, ripped to shreds. "Nice shot," George exclaimed, "you've got a knack. Maybe Richie ain't worthless." For the next hour they took turns shooting at whatever they could find and pushing squat bullets into three rusty magazines.

Evan didn't much care for the activity, certain the Ridgewood royalty would label it "redneck" and quite sure that shooting clay pigeons with an expensive shotgun was the more dignified way for a man to blow shit up for no good reason. Evan had recently studied a discarded catalog in study hall, and greasy, shirtless George in his torn relic earth shoes wasn't exactly LL Bean material.

When the ammo ran low, George bent over the shoe box in search of a few loose shells. Sweat yellow with thick cornfield dust matted the hair on his scaly back. The sight of it sickened young Evan, and he had to fight back a wave of brackish nausea.

Secretly, slowly, he pointed the gun at the base of George's spine. If he pulled the trigger, he could walk out of juvenile detention on his eighteenth birthday and shit on George's grave. If he pulled the trigger, Kmart would be free, never to return to Ridgewood. Richie would never return to Pleasant Grove.

The heavy gun was steady in his hand.

But if he pulled the trigger, George would be free from his hell on earth, liberated to the void where failure knew no shame, mercifully released from the stench of his daily rot. Death. Why give the animal such a generous gift?

And if Evan pulled the trigger, Ridgewood won. "Did you hear?"

they'd say. "Trailer park trash Kmart shot his scumbag stepdad in a corn-field! *Of course he did, that's what* those people *do.*"

Evan lowered the gun as George stood and swiveled toward him.

"Find anything?" Evan asked.

George grunted. Or was it a belch?

CHAPTER

SIXTY-NINE

"Congratulations, chief."

It was Mac on the 212 landline, and it was too early for a call.

"I hear you're going white-water rafting on the Orinoco."

Evan sat up in bed. "How'd you hear *that*? I was gonna call you later."

"Don't worry. The company sent me an e-mail saying it was rewarding you with a trip. I didn't know you were into the ecotourism-rafting thing."

"I'm not," Evan replied, thinking fast. "It's more about the total escape from everything. Equatorial rainforest . . . total B-F-E . . . no e-mail or cell phones . . . girlfriend's been driving me a bit nuts lately so I want to fall off the grid for a few days." Evan took a quick breath.

"The *company* sent an e-mail? Who, specifically?"

Mac laughed. "You know there's no 'who.' It came from HQ in Zurich."

"Of course," Evan said, masking his frustration.

"The last guy who got an attaboy trip from the company, like five years ago, never came back."

Evan gulped. *"Dead?"*

"What? No, chief. He bought an eighteenth-century piazza near

Bellagio, on Lake Como I believe, and, the last I heard, a vineyard in Veneto somewhere." Mac chuckled, then continued. "*Dead?* Where the hell did *that* come from? This ain't some bad Grisham novel."

"I'll be back, Mac. I'm a radical Manhattanist. New York is in my blood."

"Yeah, I know that about you. So tell me about your trip, in two minutes or less."

"I'm flying down to Puerto Ayacucho, the capital of Venezuela's Amazonas state, on the border with Colombia, and staying at a really nice, superexpensive lodge about twenty miles outside the town. My suite is a fancy freakin' *hut*, an Indian *churuata* made out of palm leaves, wood, and adobe, overlooking the Orinoco River." Talking about it, Evan actually looked forward to the adventure.

"A *hut*? Seriously?"

"Well, it's a hut built for the ecofriendly-yet-gas-guzzlin' Range Rover crowd—air-conditioned, marble bath with whirlpool tub, ceiling fans, restaurant and bar—but no TV or phone, in the middle of nowhere, surrounded by untouched rainforest."

"The first thing I do when I walk into a hotel room is turn on the TV," Mac said.

"Yeah, me too. Why do we do that?" They contemplated it for a beat.

"Well," Evan continued, "I'll call you when I get back." He pushed OFF and laid back in bed. He speed-dialed Nicole.

"What's up? Are you jet-lagged?"

"No way, I'm on cloud nine! Such an awesome trip! Totally *chantmé*! Thank you thank you THANK YOU! What a great time! What a—"

"Easy," Evan interrupted. "I've got a little disappointing news."

"Uh-oh. What?"

"I can't go out east this weekend. I have to fly out on Sunday morning, business. But I'll be back for next weekend and I say we just stay out there through Labor Day."

"Uhh! Again?" Nicole replied, exasperated.

"It's *work*."

"It's *Super Saturday*. I made reservations at Pierre's in Bridge and

Muse in Sag and in East I wanted to buy you those awesome Solid & Striped swim trunks at Scoop. The Water Mill classic! Speaking of which, I need a new bikini from Tomas Maier, not to mention a yoga reservation with Kiley at POE, and . . ." She flamed out and fumed for a moment.

"Work . . . *le petit quelque chose qui fout tout par terre* . . . but whatever. I'll shift the ressies or take Libby as my date. She's a highly mentionable interior designer, you know, and depending on what everyone wants to do, well . . . *so frustrating*. It's *The Season*. You do realize that, right?"

"I know, and I'm sorry, but this is a *big* one. If it goes well, let's just say I'll be shopping for houses on Further or West End."

"*Seriously?*"

"I'm dead serious."

"*What*, exactly, do you *do*?" Nicole asked half jokingly.

"I quote Della Famiglia, of course: 'To those of noble and liberal spirit, no occupations seem less brilliant than those whose purpose is to make money.'"

"Amen," Nicole said. "If it gets a house on Further Lane, *amen* and *hallelujah*."

She and I worship the same god, Evan thought, *the only god who can buy us joy and peace and pride. This god, this one word: I.*

CHAPTER
SEVENTY

The state-owned death trap sputtered, rattled and wheezed over vast, verdant waves of wilderness and a curvy maze of muddy ribbons of river. Built by the French during the Reagan era, the ATR 42's tired twin turboprops balked at their mission, and every jungle updraft threatened to bounce the battered bird from the sky.

Evan cursed the collectivist coffin and white-knuckled the gnarled armrests for the ninety-minute ordeal. He considered checking the armrests for the broken fingernails of past victims but, when his eyes left the horizon, Continental's partially digested beef stroganoff threatened to make an encore appearance.

Venezuelan military aircraft dominated Puerto Ayacucho's airport, a function of the town's proximity to Colombia and the cross-border drug trade. Evan audibly sighed with relief when the ATR 42 rolled to a stop; he immediately dreaded the return trip to Caracas.

A small man with a handwritten STOESS sign waited for Evan inside the terminal. He sported pleated khaki pants, tan sandals, and a crisp kelly green golf shirt with the Atures Lodge logo. His skin was dark brown, and he wore his straight black hair in a bowl cut. His eyes were as black and shiny as polished onyx.

Exiting the airport, Evan became quickly and acutely aware that he had quit his first world for the third world. Stepping into the misty sunshine, he saw an ad hoc parking lot bazaar staffed by nearly naked tribesmen right out of *National Geographic*, selling everything from crude handmade wooden bowls to green parrots to what looked like a small pile of raw, uncut diamonds. Evan's determined tender maneuvered around the barefoot natives' silent, earnest pleas and guided him to an early-nineties Mercedes-Benz 300 diesel sedan.

Rumbling through Puerto Ayacucho, the brown man identified himself as Napoleon, a proud Yanomami named after an American anthropologist who lived in his family's village in the 1960s. Napoleon humorously chastised the mixed-race *criollos* who lived like animals in the town's expansive slums. They could find work, he was sure, if they really wanted it. He was good-natured and chatty, and Evan seized the opportunity.

"Anything exciting going on at the lodge over the next few days?"

"No sir, not at all. Tonight we're nowhere near capacity. Ten of the thirty guest suites—we call them *churuatas*—have been reserved by one group, arriving tomorrow. Our central *churuata*, with the lounge and restaurant, will be closed for several hours tomorrow afternoon and evening for a private event. Guests not attending will be served a complimentary buffet dinner in the garden overlooking the river, however, so you need not worry about going hungry."

"Who reserved the cabins? A celebrity with an entourage? Is Turtle driving?" Evan asked.

Napoleon smiled and caught Evan's eye in the rearview mirror. "My boss won't say. A prominent Venezuelan, I'm guessing, probably a military or government official, based on the catering list I saw earlier today. Native specialties are being brought in from all over Amazonas for tomorrow night, including some traditional Yanomami delicacies."

"Really? And what would those be?"

"Spider croquettes, and roasted paca with stewed sweet manioc, a tuber that must be leached and dried to remove the naturally occurring cyanide."

"*Spider? Cyanide?* Do I even want to know what 'paca' is?"

"A paca is a big ratlike rodent with spotted stripes, but no tail. Delicious."

"Oh good god, I might be sick." Between the big tailless rat reference, diesel fumes, and lingering stroganoff, Evan wasn't joking.

"Please, sir, I beg you, not in the vehicle."

They rode in silence for a moment, leaving the town behind.

"Sounds like quite an event," Evan finally said. "Will security be tight?"

Napoleon smiled broadly again. "You've never been to the lodge, have you, Mr. Stoess?"

"This is my first visit."

"The rainforest and river, which encircles the resort on three sides, are all the security we need. Not to mention the anaconda and piraña. You'll see."

When Napoleon turned off the last paved road and pointed the mustard-colored sedan toward what appeared to be a tunnel cut in a mountain of seething green, Evan understood. For twenty minutes the car bumped through the narrow "tunnel," impenetrable rainforest on both sides, until it emerged at the Atures Lodge on the banks of the Orinoco River.

"Why 'Atures'?" Evan asked.

"The Atures rapids. Puerto Ayacucho was founded because river traders had to stop to get their goods past the rapids. No rapids, no Puerto Ayacucho, no lodge. Today the rapids are great for rafting and fishing. Jeremy Wade stayed with us last month."

The *churuatas* were round structures on stilts, with wide wooden ramps, resembling gangplanks, leading up to their entrances. Their roofs were constructed of, or more likely just covered in, Gilligan's Island–style palm thatch, but they sloped up dramatically to a point, reminding Evan of an upside-down funnel. Evan could see many smaller *churuatas* loosely arranged around a large central one, and as they approached he noticed a line of inviting basket chairs on the main structure's deck, with a view of the fast-moving river.

"Looks great," he said.

"The most luxurious accommodations in Amazonas," Napoleon replied proudly.

Evan assumed it was a low hurdle, but he held his tongue.

CHAPTER
SEVENTY-ONE

Evan's *churuata* sat perched on the edge of the river, the farthest from the central rotunda and its annex lobby. He declined the bellman's services and let himself into the suite. The AC hummed and the room was almost chilly. The décor was a well-conceived combination of Disney Animal Kingdom and luxe Caribbean and, to his surprise, Evan liked it.

He scanned the open, round *churuata* for the "package," or *anything* unusual that might explain how he was going to murder a sequestered group of spider-eating rich guys attending a private meeting in a glorified teepee. Nothing. No television, no phone, no "package."

Evan quickly unpacked and sat on the plush, king-sized bed, his feet flat on the floor and hands on his thighs, a philomath's Anubis. With the exception of the AC's gentle white noise, he decompressed in a mildly disconcerting cocoon of silence. As in New York, outside his walls a world of life buzzed around him. But here in the wild, it served a different master.

Still a bit unnerved by the totality of the circumstances—the rickety flight to the middle of nowhere, the *Heart of Darkness* jungle, the round room, the isolation, eliminating the assets, *the quiet*—Evan talked to hear his voice.

"Okay, what do I do now? Get some dinner I guess, see what happens."

Resolutely he stood, surveyed the room once again, and followed the manicured path to the restaurant.

Evan surprised himself and ordered the paca burger, not that lobster sliders or pulled pork were an option anyway. *Oh, for some Southern Hospitality,* he thought. As he chewed and swallowed, he repeated what he christened his new third-world mantra: *It is not a rat burger, it is* not *a rat burger. . . .*

Satiated with rat burger and manioc, pitch-darkness met him when he stepped out of the grand *churuata*'s halo of light, and vertigo overcame him. He closed his eyes and took a deep breath. A strong breeze pushed a mélange of unique odors into him which he chose only to describe as "jungle." When he opened his eyes he could just make out the small green reception lawn and the marked path through the jungle brush to his fancy native hut.

Halfway down the path and out of sight of the central building, the clouds parted and equatorial moonlight revealed a shirtless Indian about forty feet ahead, holding a black backpack by his side, its shoulder straps dangling to the ground.

Evan flinched but kept walking. The Indian had striped tattoos or paint on his face and chest, and long porcupine quills stuck through the septum of his nose and somehow protruded from the fleshy area of his face, above his chin but below his lower lip. He was wearing baggy Nike swoosh soccer shorts and nothing else. When Evan was ten feet from him, the fascinating native raised his arm straight at shoulder level, a sweeping motion, offering the backpack. Evan slowed but kept walking, took it from him, and in a blink, the man was gone, disappearing into the tangled jungle scrub. Evan resumed his normal pace, the "package" by his side, a seamless exchange.

The simple schoolboy backpack held a small box of wooden matches, one typed page of single-spaced instructions, and a wooden box marked HENNESSY ELLIPSE, its contents an expensive bottle of cognac housed in an elliptical Baccarat crystal decanter. As Evan read the instructions, his pulse quickened and his temples began to throb. The rat burger gnawed at his insides.

.   .   .

The assets would follow a rigid schedule, a reminder of Karenia Brevis's Teutonic DNA. Tomorrow at six o'clock, "1800 hours" in the instructions, they would gather at the big teepee for pre-meeting cocktails as the sun set over the Orinoco. Evan would deliver the boxed bottle of brandy to target Edward Meeker at approximately 1915, before the private seated dinner of bizarre delicacies began at 1930.

His cover story was provided: Meeker lived in Manhattan, his wife was a friend of a Contrafund board member, and the bottle was a happy coincidence birthday surprise from Olivia Meeker to Ed Meeker. After dinner the assets would conclave privately in the rotunda to view a slideshow of the land they planned to purchase. To ensure privacy, the many sliding doors would be closed, and heavy curtains drawn. The large room would be sealed, its valuable occupants safely inside. Evan would do what was necessary to ensure that the package was in the rotunda before dinner commenced at 1930 hours.

The bottom of the cognac box was lined with a thick layer of powder, a next-generation Novichok nerve agent. Fifteen minutes before delivering the surprise to the grateful husband, Evan would hold a burning match under the box until the wood just started to blacken. The heat would begin the activation process and precisely sixty minutes later, at 2000 hours, the odorless Russian nerve gas would vaporize, spread, and kill everyone in the rotunda. Designed to quickly dissipate, the room would be safe to enter within fifteen minutes, and, if investigated, the box would show no signs of its deadly purpose. Evan read the detailed instructions again, made a few cryptic notes on the back of an Atures Lodge envelope, and burned the typed page over the toilet, flushing the ashes.

The plan was inspired genius. A new Russian nerve agent? A reclusive OPEC economist despised by the Arabs? The global intelligentsia would assume that the eleven other OPEC nations had had enough of Brevis and finally found a way to get rid of him. Evan would certainly be questioned, but if the box was clean as promised, and Evan had no doubt it would be, he would walk away. Again.

With two hundred million dollars.

He added a quick note to try to retrieve the bottle of Hennessy Ellipse so it didn't go to waste. He would say that Mrs. Meeker would surely want it back, her thoughtful gift, as a memorial of her lost husband. Then, to celebrate his early retirement, he would drink it.

At 1800 on Monday, Evan Stoess showered, shaved, and donned a new pair of natural linen slacks, a white linen shirt, both by Paul Smith, and brown Warren Edwards crocodile loafers, sans socks. He sat on his bed, eyes closed, until 1900 arrived, at which point he set the bezel on his Rolex and lit the match. The countdown had begun. Sixty minutes.

He gently cradled the box as he sliced through the thick wet air, the grand *churuata* rising before him. The constant breeze evaporated the sweat on his forehead.

Walking up the wide ramp, on schedule at 1910, he looked to the right and was not surprised that the assets were not on the deck watching the sunset. He opened the lobby atrium's door and a man in a grey pin-striped suit greeted him.

"Good evening, sir. I'm sorry, but the rotunda is closed for a private party. A buffet dinner will soon be available in the garden, down the ramp and to the left."

Evan cheerfully beamed his favorite "harmless" smile and looked down at the box in his arms.

"Oh, I know, and I'm sorry to intrude, but I have a very special surprise delivery for Mr. Meeker, one of the party guests, from his wife, Olivia. It's his birthday, I guess, and she's sad she can't be with him."

The look on the gatekeeper's face could only be described as complete, abject shock. He literally took a step back, as if *struck* by the words.

"And . . . and how do you happen to be *here*, with this *gift*?"

Evan introduced himself and launched into his spiel, his boss's wife's friendship with Mrs. Meeker, the amazing coincidence, the confidential request—the party was a secret for some reason—and here he was with the gift, Mr. Meeker's favorite bottle of brandy, in a fancy crystal bottle, no less. As he opened the box to reveal the non-bomb inside, he finished with a flourish.

"Are the guys here for some male-bonding or something? Going fishing or zip-lining or rafting tomorrow? Maybe I can join them?"

The gatekeeper had regained his composure. "No, they're here on business." He paused, studied Evan and the box. "Follow me."

They crossed the small atrium and its humble reception counter and approached the double-door entrance to the rotunda. Two stone-faced military-looking guys in dark blue jeans, white golf shirts and blue blazers flanked the doors. From their look and steely countenance, and given the unique natural resource they surely guarded, Evan guessed they could kill him with their thumbs, with no need for the weaponry the blazers conspicuously failed to conceal. The gatekeeper nodded at the men as he opened a door for Evan.

The broad open space had been rearranged since Evan dined in it the previous evening, the far windows covered and a large screen set up on a bamboo frame.

"Have you met Mr. Meeker?" The gatekeeper asked.

"I have not," Evan answered honestly.

"I'll take you to him and make the introduction."

They walked toward the river side of the room. Evan saw two men sitting in big basket chairs, smoking massive cigars. He recognized the man on the left from the photos—Edward Meeker. He looked at the second man and stopped dead in his tracks. His face went numb and his heart fell into his stomach. He almost dropped the box.

"Good idea," the gatekeeper commented. "Wait here for a moment and let me speak to Mister Meeker."

Paralyzed, Evan was incapable of a response. The gatekeeper humbly approached Ed Meeker and said several words to him, gesturing toward Evan. Both men nodded in agreement and as the gatekeeper passed Evan to return to his post, he said, "Mister Meeker is on the left."

Evan took a dozen delirious steps forward and spoke not to Meeker, but to his attentive companion. Evan was trembling, petrified by what he saw.

"What are you doing here?"

"Do I know you?" Geoffrey Buchanan asked kindly, a faint glint of recognition in his eyes.

"Good god, what are you doing here?"

"Do I know you?" Geoffrey asked again, glancing curiously at Meeker, then back at Evan and the box he cradled in his arms like an infant.

"Please . . ." Evan implored, pleading with him as a child might. "How can you be here?"

Meeker noticed the inscription on the box and, when Geoffrey looked his way again, he offered his confused friend a small "go ahead" nod.

"Well, I'm here to explore the rain forest," Geoffrey began. "This jungle has some of the world's most isolated and fertile micro-systems—"

"Geoffrey here plans to discover the cure for cancer," Meeker intervened.

"Indeed, I do. There, I've answered your question. Who, might I ask, are you?"

"I am Evan Stoess."

Now it was Geoffrey's turn to sit in stunned silence. His hand twitched and cigar ashes fell on the big basket chair's armrest.

Meeker reached over and brushed them off.

"Geoffrey, do you know him? I presume that bottle of Ellipse he's carrying is for me, the gift the maître d' mentioned."

Geoffrey looked Evan in the eye for a long moment and his face softened. He turned to Meeker.

"Ed, believe it or not, Evan is my son."

CHAPTER
SEVENTY-TWO

"It's true, Ed. Evan is my son. I saw him on TV years ago but this is the first time in person. In this context . . . *here* . . . I didn't recognize him."

Meeker's jaw dropped and he leaned forward.

"*Seriously*? Have you two never *met*? How is that *possible*?"

Geoffrey turned to Evan but spoke to both men.

"Well, I'm not sure where to begin. At the beginning, I guess." Geoffrey took a deep breath.

"How long has it been? I guess about thirty or so years ago, when I was just a teenager, I spent a weekend on the Jersey shore with a classmate and his family. Evan's mother sold Sno-Cones on the boardwalk. She and I spent one night together. *One night.* I never saw her again and found out months later she was pregnant. I was in high school, Ed. My parents and their lawyers took control of the situation and I was not allowed to see the baby or his mother. They told me not to worry, my father had arranged for twelve years of tuition at a top private school in New Jersey. 'At least he'll get a decent education,' Pop said. I was in *high school*. Later I found out she named the boy 'Evan' and he had her husband's last name, 'Stoess.' They lived in a small town somewhere in Jersey. Then life went on."

Geoffrey glanced over at Meeker, who was stunned silent by the revelation, then turned back to Evan.

"Evan, what in God's name are you doing here?"

Two hundred million dollars was his only recognizable thought, and Evan stared down unfathomable terror and despair.

On countless occasions he rehearsed for this moment, dreamed about it. Meeting Geoffrey Buchanan, face to face. He lived for it. Meeting his father. Literally, *he lived for it.* Telling him he wanted to be his father's son, *deserved* to be his son. He deserved to *belong* to Geoffrey's world, on the inside, far from Pleasant Grove and Ridgewood and the alien life he had endured. He had earned it, goddammit, earned this tragically misplaced moment. Bled for it. Killed for it. He had *earned* it, he had paid the price to belong. Paid the ultimate price. But now here he stood, in the jungle, an errand boy, sent by grocery clerks, to collect a bill.

"I have a birthday present for Mr. Meeker, from Mrs. Meeker," Evan replied without emotion. "She thought he would enjoy it tonight after his business dinner."

"Indeed, I will," Meeker said, accepting the box from Evan with a look of confused amazement. He carefully placed the box on a rattan end table next to his chair.

"How, exactly, did this work out?" Meeker asked.

Evan could not answer. Meeker looked at Geoffrey, then back at Evan.

"Would you like to sit down, talk to your . . . uh . . . Geoffrey?"

Before Evan could respond, as his numb nightmare slowly transitioned to panic, Meeker stood, took Evan's arm, and guided him into his now empty basket chair.

Evan plopped down into it like a ventriloquist's dummy.

"He has a right to be upset," Meeker said to Geoffrey while shooting him a look of troubled concern. "I'll leave you two alone."

It was now 1920. Evan glanced sideways at the Hennessey, then slowly turned towards Geoffrey.

"Evan. What are you doing here?"

"I have a birthday present for Mr. Meeker, from Mrs. Meeker," Evan recited from memory.

"Yes," Geoffrey replied patiently. "You said that. But what are you doing here?"

Evan processed the query slowly, methodically. He was now off-script, and he was terrified.

"I'm here, in Amazonas, for the same reason you are: money."

"Money?" Geoffrey tilted his head, curious.

"You're here to make millions. So am I."

"Evan, I'm not sure *what* you've heard from *whom*, but I'm here to *lose* millions. We all are." Geoffrey waved his hand toward the men talking in the rear of the room. "I'm buying this land with my own money. I'm betting the cure for cancer is in this forest. *The cure for cancer.* My company can't make that bet, but I can."

"Lose millions," Evan repeated, robotically.

Geoffrey studied his son. "My net worth, my *ultimate* worth, is measured in far more than dollars, Evan. Everyone's is."

The Hennessey box cast a long shadow. Evan's eyes moved from Geoffrey to the box then back to Geoffrey. *Collateral damage. Additional individuals may be present.*

"I'm so sorry it turned out this way, Evan. Not getting to know you. You not getting to know me." Geoffrey sighed. Evan didn't speak.

"And I truly regret your childhood. Such deprivation. Especially Ridgewood. I bet those many years were no picnic for a kid in your . . . *situation.*

"You were surrounded by privilege, smothered by it, I imagine. It *had* to be awful.

"But you *survived*, Evan. And you did it, on your own, I'm sure. Ridgewood. College. Wall Street.

"I saw you on television a while back, and I've seen you in the papers a few times since. I couldn't believe it was you. Such confidence, such tenacity. And then . . . well . . ."

Geoffrey paused for a moment, remembering the unexpected pain he felt for a child he'd never known.

"You're right, I *did* do it on my own," Evan finally said. "And Ridgewood did *not* beat me. Soon I'll have more than any of them. They'll be smothered by *my* success." Evan gripped the rattan armrests with both hands. Geoffrey took a moment before responding, carefully enunciating each word.

"Some people believe the only cure for envy, the only remedy, is to become the envied. But that is *wrong*, Evan. Dead wrong. If you envy, you will *always* envy. Someone will *always* have more than you. More money. More talent. A hotter wife. Cuter kids. More *time* on this Earth. Try to buy youth, Evan. You'll realize soon enough it cannot be bought. Envy is not a symptom of not having enough. It is a fatal disease caused by not appreciating what you have."

Geoffrey took a breath, then shifted in his seat. Evan said nothing. "Would you like to meet—"

"No!" Evan blurted. "I have to go. I don't want to interrupt," he said, standing. "I'll be in contact back in New York."

"Wait . . . Evan—" Geoffrey pleaded, but Evan had walked away.

Steps from his cabin, tears streaming down his face, Evan cried deep sobs that shook his shoulders and cramped his soul. Birds took flight around him; a frightened howler monkey replied in kind. Pushing open the door and stepping inside, Evan wept.

He looked at his watch: 1945. Fifteen minutes. Two hundred million dollars. *Calatrava's cube. The cottage. The cash.* He could have anything he wanted, everything he needed. He'd have real money; he'd be *safe*. Finally free of Kmart and Richie, he could buy the life he deserved. He could buy Nicole. Finally, he could buy joy and peace and pride.

But the price was Geoffrey Buchanan.

He pictured the magic moment three years ago, Geoffrey and Victoria floating out to their shiny new Bentley with little Ashley and Tyler in tow.

Could he possibly *buy* that life? Could Evan Stoess—*I*—become *that life*?

He looked up at the stars, then down at his open, empty hands. *Eat what you kill.*

Can I do it? Can I kill Geoffrey Buchanan? Can I kill my father? Can I?

A false idol in his heart, envy, monstrously brought to life by his idle hands.

Evan turned and ran full speed back to the giant teepee.

The gatekeeper met him at the door. Evan was flush and dripping sweat. "Mr. Stoess, are you all right? Can I help you?"

Evan looked at his watch: 1950. Ten minutes.

"Oh my god, my boss will *kill* me. I forgot to attach Mrs. Meeker's card to the gift. She hand-made it, she's an artist, it's very special, I *have* to have the box back."

"No worries, I'll get it. It's no big deal."

"No, I'll do it," Evan said, pushing his way past him and moving quickly toward the rotunda's closed doors.

The gatekeeper considered stopping him. One word and the anxious young man would be on the ground with a commando's boot on his neck. But the buffet dinner was about to start and he didn't want to cause a scene, so he flashed an "okay" sign to the alert sentinels.

When Evan entered the rotunda it was dark, the slide presentation in progress. The light from the opened doors caused most of the men to turn and look. Geoffrey saw Evan make a beeline for the box, and he quickly moved to intercept him.

Evan had the package and was on the way out, clutching it to his chest with both arms, when Geoffrey stepped into his path.

"Evan, what are you doing? Let's talk after the meeting. Tomorrow we have a helicopter taking our group to tour the rainforest, so let's talk tonight after the meeting. I want you to use your gifts, Evan, use your talents for something far more important than making money. I can help you."

Evan looked at him, looked *into* him, and felt a feeling he had never experienced, warm and trusting and clean. His heart skipped a beat, reset and recalibrated.

"Thank you, Geoffrey."

"Thank you? For what?"

"For saving my life."

Evan stepped around him and headed for the door. The gatekeeper opened it for him.

1955. Plenty of time.

"You made the right decision," Evan said to the man as he passed.

He crossed the atrium and stepped out into the night. With feral strength he hugged the box to his chest and walked down an unmarked path that twisted into the jungle, toward the uncoiled Orinoco, away from the lodge, away from the assets, away from Geoffrey Buchanan. He walked into the darkness.

1957.

Evan held the box tightly to his chest and sat down on the trunk of a fallen tree.

Hans said, *"It's never enough, Mr. Stoess."*

And Evan knew he was right. Two hundred million dollars.

It would never be enough. The life he had, the life he believed he deserved and money would deliver, all landfill for his empty soul. It would never be enough. *I* was not a god he could trust; *I* was not a god he could have faith in. *I* was always the first to disappoint, the first to criticize, the first to fail. His god *I* would never grant him peace and joy and pride. A ruthless and merciless master, *I* would never be satisfied. *I* could never deliver—and no amount of money could purchase—the one thing that Evan wanted, but would never have.

A new *I.*

"I am Evan Stoess." He whispered.

He stood and continued down the path, the jungle's hot breath drying his tears.

2000.

With all his might, Evan squeezed the box to his chest, freighttraining the one-word wish through his being: *Belong.*

He inhaled deeply, expecting to die, but Ridgewood would not let him go that easily, and a memory flashed.

Not what we call death, but what beyond death is not death, we fear, we fear.

Evan knew not what was beyond T. S. Eliot's *death*, but he knew he could never fear *it* more than he feared the life he deserved.

His muscles seized, the box splintered, the shattered bottle cut into his chest, his palms, his forearms, the flesh torn and ripped. Blood mixed with brandy, but he did not feel the sting.

He took a shallow breath.

The tropical breeze blew oxygen up his nose, down his throat.

The searing pain in his chest and arms and palms now drove him to his knees. He dropped the splintered box and shattered bottle.

• • •

Geoffrey Buchanan stood on the grand *churuata*'s deck, scanning the darkness for his son. The meeting went on behind him.

He heard a primal scream, like nothing he'd heard before or ever wanted to hear again. His son's agony shivered his core. Excruciating pain, beyond comprehension and far beyond the mere physical. A broken body screams for mercy. A tortured soul screams far louder for salvation.

"Evan. What have you done?"

EPILOGUE

O Lord, the God who avenges,
O God who avenges, shine forth.

—THE OLD TESTAMENT, PSALM 94:1

The freshly painted ship labored against the Orinoco's impatient ocean-bound current.

On the bow just past midnight, a stocky young man in a crisp white jumpsuit swept the starboard shallows with a powerful spotlight.

"Boto on the right, thirty meters!" He shouted, turning toward the craft's glowing bridge.

"Swing to starboard! Swing to starboard!"

"Is he dead, Doc?" the white-haired captain asked with a thick Liverpool accent.

"He lost a lot of blood and nearly drowned, but he's alive. He'll make it."

The stocky young man, his uniform now covered in crimson river muck, was standing next to the captain. He wiped his hands and crossed himself. "*Es un milagro*. It's a miracle."

"Let's get him down to the infirmary," the captain said. "Let Doc patch him up."

"Who is he? And what in God's name was he doing out here?" Captain William Smith asked Doc the next morning.

Doc fished something shiny out of his pocket. "I found this money clip in his pants, but no ID. Judging by the looks of him, he's a tourist. Probably fell overboard, maybe got hit by a propeller."

Smith nodded but didn't seem convinced.

Evan listened. He could open his eyes, but he chose not to. He could feel the IV at his elbow and the bandages on his head, chest, and arms. The men in the room apparently meant him no harm, and that was a peaceful relief.

"But I'll tell you one thing," Doc continued, "he's a *rich* tourist. The money clip? I looked it up on the Internet. Oriens & Grey. This stone is a rare white jade from China. Six thousand dollars. His crocodile shoes? Warren Edwards is on Park Avenue in New York City. Three thousand. And his—"

"Okay, I get it, I get it," Smith said with a wave of his hand, cutting off his friend.

Doc smiled and looked at his patient. "Stay with him for a few minutes, Skip, while I run down to the stockroom for sterilizer."

"Sure, take your time. I'll watch over him."

Alone in the room with the kind captain, Evan opened his eyes.

"Where am I?" His voice was crusty and pale.

"Easy son. Take your time."

"Where am I?"

Captain Smith thought for a moment before replying. "You're on the BBC research vessel *Redemption*, on the Vichada River heading west into the Colombian Llanos."

"How . . . ?"

"Late last night, before we left the Orinoco and headed up the Vichada, one of our mates was on the spotlight watching for boto—endangered pink river dolphins.

"He thought you were a boto. You were hung up in some vines, stopped you from going under. We fished you out and Doc patched you up. You're extremely lucky to be alive, young man." Smith rested his hand on Evan's bare shoulder.

"Now, you mind telling me who you are and what you were doing in the Orinoco River in the middle of the night, ripped to pieces?"

Evan closed his eyes.

A heartbeat later, Doc nonchalantly entered the room with two bottles of Hibiclens sterilizer. He stopped dead in his tracks when he saw Smith's face.

"He woke up, Doc. He asked where he was and how we had him, but that's all I got from him."

Doc placed the bottles on a stainless-steel counter and regained his composure.

"He's in shock, Skip, and still recovering from the trauma. Give him a couple days, he'll come around."

A few hours later, Evan sensed a presence standing over him. It wasn't Doc or the captain. He opened his eyes.

The young man had jet-black hair and wide, gentle dark eyes. He was gazing at Evan with a look of utter amazement.

"I'm supposed to let you rest, but I'm the one who spotted you. *Yo soy Amadeo.* I'm Amadeo. I can't believe you're alive."

Evan nodded. *Thank you, Amadeo.*

"It's truly a miracle," the first mate said eagerly, crossing himself. "God saved you. *Usted es un milagro. You* are a miracle. God has great plans for you, my brother, great plans for the gift He has given you, this saved life."

Evan frowned and looked away. *God? But there is no god? Could it be possible? Could a god—the God—have saved me?* Then Amadeo spoke.

"Here . . . I want you to have this Bible. Please, read it. Find God's plan for you." Amadeo placed the shiny new tome by Evan's right hand, which recoiled instinctively.

With the speed of a cobra, Amadeo snatched Evan's hand and demanded his eye.

"As I stand here before you, the man who pulled you from the waters and saved you from death, I tell you: God has a plan for you. Find it. *Embrace it.*"

He held Evan's hand, slowly loosening his grip, and looked down at Evan. He put his hand on Evan's heart.

"*Dios te bendiga, mi amigo.* God bless you, my friend."

Amadeo backed up slowly, still facing Evan, then turned and exited

Redemption's infirmary. Alone in the room again, the ship at anchor, he could hear only the beat of his heart.

Oddly overcome by what had transpired, Evan opened a Bible for the first time in his life. *"In the beginning . . ."*

The next morning, after a hearty English breakfast, Captain Smith and Doc were once again by Evan's side.

"Son, is your name Evan Andrew Stoess?" Smith asked. "We got a missing persons report from the authorities in Puerto Ayacucho. We pulled you out of the water not far downstream from the Atures Lodge. Are you Evan?"

"No, my name is James Gatz. I was alone on my boat, heading downriver, when—"

Smith turned to Doc. "Damn. I thought for sure we'd found him. What the hell's going on out here? A missing person, a helicopter crash—"

"Helicopter crash?" Evan lurched forward, ripping the IV out of his arm. "What helicopter crash? Was it men from Atures Lodge?"

"Easy son, easy," Smith said, steadying Evan with a hand on his chest. "The morning after we found you, a helicopter left the Lodge and exploded over the rainforest. There were several casualties, including a top OPEC minister."

"Exploded? Casualties?" Evan pushed forward into Smith's hand.

"Yes, it exploded, for no apparent reason. The names of the victims haven't been released, other than the oil man. But there are no survivors."

Evan collapsed. His breath—his life?—flowed out of him.

"Good to see you up, James," Smith said the next morning. "You seem better, more relaxed."

"Indeed I am, Captain." *I have found. I have embraced.*

"And I see you've been reading the Bible. A gift from Amadeo, I presume? He's our resident missionary, a true believer."

"Thanks, Captain. Yes, the Bible is from Amadeo."

"Powerful book. It'll change your life. You've read it before?"

"No. But I'm in the market."

"For what? A new life?"

"Yes, a new life. And a new God."

"A new God?"

Evan closed his eyes, clutched the Bible to his bandaged chest, and took a deep breath.

It is mine to avenge; I will repay. In due time their foot will slip; their day of disaster is near and their doom rushes upon them.

O God who avenges, shine forth.

ACKNOWLEDGMENTS

Starting a first novel is a lonely leap of faith and, without the encourage-ment and support of family and friends, few first novels would ever get finished. *Eat What You Kill* certainly never would have.

First and foremost, I give thanks for my patient, amazing, talented wife, Christi Scofield. When I would come home from several hours of writing and excitedly read to her a particularly great paragraph (or sen-tence . . . or a few words), she would very rarely ask "Is that it?" Instead, she'd say "I love it!" and then "What happens next?" Her faith in my abilities and her shared enthusiasm for a well-placed adverb were my daily fuel. I am her biggest fan.

It is neither a cliché nor an obvious understatement to proclaim that you would not be holding this book today were it not for my Mom and Dad, Tiffany and Wolfe Scofield. Without their unconditional support and assurance, I never would have written a word. They gave me the courage—and ability—to pick up a pen. They gave me *life*, not once, but twice.

I cannot pretend to have the words to adequately acknowledge Christi, Mom, and Dad. I would need to write a second book to do it justice.

Many novels are written, but few are published. I am truly blessed to be working with the accomplished professionals at St. Martin's. Steve Cohen was the first person to believe in my book and I can not thank him enough for dropping it on the desk of my editor, Charles Spicer, who embraced EWYK from the first moment. In addition to making it a better book, every time I talk to Charlie, I feel like a better writer. He has a magical and much appreciated ability to instill confidence, even in neurotic writers like myself. Special thanks to April Osborn and the entire St. Martin's team.

Novels don't go far at great publishing houses without strong literary agents behind them. Many thanks to my *agent extraordinaire*, Krista Goering. She knew from day one that EWYK would find a home.

I imagine every novelist has Hollywood dreams. Thanks to Stephen Cavaliero, Jon Katz, Ed Pressman, and the dedicated team at Pressman Film, mine may very well become a reality.

"He's an aspiring author." I'm sure when my future in-laws heard these words, they cringed. But they never let on, and I deeply appreciate them for their patient endurance. Carol and Bill, *thank you*.

Before I wrote the first word, a generous group of supporters helped make the decision to put pen to paper a fiscal possibility. I offer my heartfelt gratitude to Brian Cook, Angie and Bob DeWeese, Afshin Ghazi, Betsy and Greg Howard, Paulita Keith, and Chuck Thieman.

I am blessed with knowledgeable and enthusiastic friends who assisted with dialogue, geography, and industry insight. Many thanks to MaryAnn Doyle, Duane Eatherly, Mike Hughes, and Alberto Rojas.

Early readers gave me sound feedback and tremendous confidence. Thank you, Brady Hayden, Michael Palka, Aaron Rothschild, Richard Steel, Michael Strong, and Webster Younce.

Writers need a sanctuary, and Randy Lynch provided mine. Thanks, Randy. I will always have Lockwood.

Finally, special thanks to Tim Keller for fortifying guidance early in the process, and to Susan MacNeil for identifying and rebuilding the broken pieces.